She sank several _____ against the well-packed powder and echoing into the night. The wind howled, and she closed her eyes, giving herself a minute to catch her breath before moving on with her task.

"Rough day?"

The deep voice behind her made her pulse kick start at the same time it calmed her frayed nerves. She turned, and warmth settled over her chilled heart. "What are you doing sneaking up on an unsuspecting woman on Christmas Eve?" She couldn't hide the amusement that leaked into her words. Dylan Gilbert's booming laugh took over the stillness of the night and finally worked to bring a smile to her lips. Maybe she could smile again after all.

Dylan emerged from the shadows and into the shaft of light illuminating the front porch. "I haven't snuck up on anyone in my life."

Meg twisted her lips to the side and glanced from his broad shoulders to his handsome face…even if a thick beard covered it. The one time he'd shaven it off made Meg nostalgic for the man she'd always know. The man who'd somehow morphed into her best friend, even if her older brother claimed that title with Dylan first.

Praise for Danielle M. Haas

"Danielle Haas is the master of sweet romance."

~Liv A.

~*~

"This book has it all: forbidden romance, internal struggles, character growth, along with a family dynamic that keeps you engaged with every single character. *A PLACE IN THIS WORLD* will become one of your favorite, go-to books to enjoy again and again!"

~Samantha Keith, Author

~*~

"*A PLACE IN THIS WORLD* continues the Sheffields' story with Meg wondering where she fits in. Her fiancé-turned-criminal is nowhere to be found. When her brother's best friend gives her a shoulder to lean on, she knows she's found her place in this world."

~Celeste Cook

~*~

"The second book in the Sheffield Series is even more heartwarming than the first. Family dynamics and the heartbreak of Alzheimer's are touched on beautifully in this book, which focuses on two souls trying to find their footing in their families. Danielle Haas delivers a touching story about love."

~Becky Lower, Author

~*~

"Danielle Haas is a must-read author. She weaves a spellbinding story and keeps you hooked until the last page."

~Brenda Hill

A Place in This World

by

Danielle M. Haas

The Sheffields, Book 2

A Place in This World

Cover Art by *Tina Lynn Stout*

The Wild Rose Press, Inc.
PO Box 708
Adams Basin, NY 14410-0708
Visit us at www.thewildrosepress.com

Publishing History
First Sweetheart Rose Edition, 2020
Trade Paperback ISBN 978-1-5092-3323-6
Digital ISBN 978-1-5092-3324-3

The Sheffields, Book 2
Published in the United States of America

Dedication

To my little sister, Caitlin.
You are my best friend, my sounding board,
and the best Tee-Tee my kids could ever ask for.
Thanks for letting me borrow your thick, blonde braid
and fierce loyalty for inspiration for Meg.
You make my life better by just being in it.
I love you!

Chapter One

Meg stepped onto the worn wooden steps of her mom's front porch of the old house that stood just outside the Smithview city limits and embraced the frigid bite of an Ohio night air as it hit her face. The icy blast cooled the flames of turmoil burning inside her, but her burdens still sat heavy on her shoulders. Snow fell on her upturned face, and the heat from her flushed cheeks faded. She shoved bare hands into the pockets of her heavy winter coat, and she twirled the grainy sugar cubes for the horses between her fingers. Her aching soul yearned for a sense of peace and only one place offered her comfort—the stable.

The star-filled sky couldn't compete with the multi-colored twinkling lights blazing atop the barn on the opposite side of the yard. Usually the strobing decorations made her smile, but not tonight. Nothing would make her smile this year.

Christmas was supposed to be a time of friends and family coming together to celebrate love, hope, and faith. Normally, Meg spent a few hours on Christmas Eve with her mom to make sure the preparations were ready for the arrival of her sister's family, and then head home to catch a few hours of Christmas cheer with her fiancé before tucking in themselves for the night.

This year, the only role her ex-fiancé, Blake, played in her Christmas plans was runaway criminal who'd almost ruined her brother's life. Her stomach churned, and anger heated her blood. Their relationship hit a rough patch over the last year, but she never guessed Blake would go so far. Now a month had passed with no word.

She slid her left hand from her pocket and glanced down at the glittering diamond that still dominated her finger. Meg fisted her hand until her fingernails dug into the tender flesh of her palm. The ring represented a lie, and the urge to rip it off and throw it in the snow washed over her.

But for some stupid reason, she couldn't take it off. She couldn't face the reality she'd wasted the last five years of her life on a man who threw away everything and left her to pick up the pieces. She sank several inches, her boots crunching against the well-packed powder and echoing into the night. The wind howled, and she closed her eyes, giving herself a minute to catch her breath before moving on with her task.

"Rough day?"

The deep voice behind her made her pulse kick start at the same time it calmed her frayed nerves. She turned, and warmth settled over her chilled heart. "What are you doing sneaking up on an unsuspecting woman on Christmas Eve?" She couldn't hide the amusement that leaked into her words. Dylan Gilbert's booming laugh took over the stillness of the night and finally worked to bring a smile to her lips. Maybe she could smile again after all.

Dylan emerged from the shadows and into the shaft of light illuminating the front porch. "I haven't snuck up on anyone in my life."

Meg twisted her lips to the side and glanced from

his broad shoulders to his handsome face…even if a thick beard covered it. The one time he'd shaven it off made Meg nostalgic for the man she'd always know. The man who'd somehow morphed into her best friend, even if her older brother claimed that title with Dylan first.

"I guess that would be one of the disadvantages of being like eight feet tall." Meg shrugged.

Dylan chuckled. "Eight feet…six foot seven… same thing." Rubbing a hand through his beard, he smiled, and his eyes crinkled at the corners.

She itched to yank on the hair covering his chin. She grinned into his kind, green eyes. She liked the way the snow clung to his beard—the white flakes melting into the red whiskers. "Really, though, what are you doing here?"

"I have gifts for everyone, and I don't know if I'll have time to bring them tomorrow."

As she studied him, she tilted her head and narrowed her eyes. Blue jeans molded against his legs and hid all but the snow-covered tips of his work boots.

He burrowed his hands into his heavy black coat.

"I don't see any presents."

"I saw you standing out here in the cold like a lunatic and left them in the truck."

Meg lifted her gaze to the fat flakes fluttering down from the black sky. "I'm taking treats to the horses and just needed a minute."

"Makes sense."

Dylan's soft voice soothed her soul. He always understood her and never asked too many questions. Not like he'd needed to. Everyone in Smithview knew about Blake and the fire he started at Dylan's farm, and then set up Jonah to take the fall. If one more person asked how she was doing with a fake smile and fabricated sympathy, she'd be forced to do something she'd no doubt regret.

But that was her small town—a close-knit community where everyone's business was on display. And if they didn't know, all they had to do was ask their neighbor. Meg again started toward the barn with her shoulders hunched to fight off the constant breeze whipping across the flat land.

Without a word, Dylan stepped into stride beside her, and his hulking form blocked the light of the moon.

"Where's Nora?" Dylan asked.

Meg tilted her head toward the old farmhouse behind her. Her gray and white, spotted Australian Shepard usually trailed her every move, but the high snow would freeze her furry friend's paws. "I left her inside with Mom by the fire. She'd be irritated by the cold and just bark at the horses if she were out here. Easier to let her be lazy."

"And warm." Dylan shivered. "Inside by the fire sounds pretty nice right about now."

Meg laughed, and her breath spiraled through the air. "I can't argue. Let's hurry."

Dylan beat Meg to the barn and opened the heavy door.

The door creaked on the old hinges, and a soft whiney sounded from inside. Meg stepped out of the snow and onto the dirty concrete floor of the aisle. A wall of warmth greeted her along with the smells of hay and horse. She removed her right hand from her pocket and handed Dylan a few sugar cubes. "You take the stalls on the right, and I'll take the stalls on the left."

Soft muzzles poked over the stall gates.

Meg strolled along the wide aisle, scratching each horse's nose and feeding them their holiday treats.

At the last stall, a large white head thrust through the opening of the half door and bobbed up and down.

"Hey, Snowball, how are you?" Meg cooed and patted the horse's nose. She gave her horse a sugar cube, then flattened her forehead against the wide width of her nose. The rough hair tickled her skin, and the horse's musty scent clung to the inside of her frozen nostrils. She needed to be here—needed the comfort of her horse right now. The weight in her shoulders melted away, even as her throat tightened around the tears fighting to break loose.

Get it together, girl.

She sniffed, her face never leaving Snowball's warm coat.

Dylan scratched Snowball behind her ear. "Do you want to ride her? I know how much you love taking her out."

Meg inhaled the familiar scent of her beloved horse. "I wish I could, but I don't have time tonight. I need to head home soon. Just being near her is enough for right now. I'll take her for a ride tomorrow."

"Do you want me to go inside? Give you some privacy."

"Honestly, no." Tears coursed over her cheeks and fell on the horse's velvety nose.

"Any word from Blake?"

Dylan's voice stayed calm and quiet, soothing both Meg and the horse. "I'm not sure I want to hear from him. What's left to say?"

"An apology, for one. A man doesn't just leave the

woman he loves, even if he was running away from a giant mess he made." Dylan cleared his throat. "You're better off without him."

She turned her head and rested her cheek on Snowball's nose. Dylan's words warmed a part of her heart Blake left frozen. "The guy's a jerk, but I'm struggling to let go. I had my future all planned out, and now…" She shrugged and sniffed back the rest of the moisture rimming her eyes. She couldn't put the extent of her emotions into words. How could she explain her need to grieve a man she didn't love anymore?

Dylan put an arm around her shoulders and gathered her close. "Now, it's not. But sometimes an unplanned future can be exciting. You can do whatever you want, Meg, and be whoever you want to be. And now you can do it without a man like Blake holding you back." He placed a kiss on the top of her head. "Hurry and finish. I can't feel my toes."

A shiver of anxiety raced down her spine. The idea of a future with limitless possibilities was exciting, but it also scared her. She liked having a plan, and Blake ripped her plan to shreds. Meg glanced up at the guy who'd always been her brother's best friend, the guy who'd become one of her favorite people in the world, and then buried her head into his chest.

Dylan wrapped his other arm around her and gathered her in a hug.

Her heart pounded in her chest, and she relaxed in his arms. *These arms would always keep me safe.* She straightened her spine and stepped away. Where had that thought come from?

She showed Dylan her back so he couldn't see the emotion pulling down her mouth and marched up the aisle to the barn door, ignoring the rapid beat of her heart. "Come on, big guy. Let's head inside. Hopefully, someone got you new boots for Christmas so you can stop being such a princess." His larger-than-life laughter echoed behind her. She hurried to her mom's house and waited on the front porch.

Dylan ran to his truck. He clambered beside her with his arms full of gifts. Hurrying inside, he kicked off his boots and moved farther into the house.

She stepped inside, closed the door, and bent to yank off her shoes. Straightening, she spied Dylan already in the living room. A tiny box sat on the bench beside the door with her name written on the top in his messy handwriting. She darted her gaze around the room. Should she open the gift in front of him? Her family always opened presents on Christmas morning, but Dylan wouldn't be around tomorrow.

Unable to wait, she opened the lid, and a smile sprang to her lips. Inside the box, a beautiful, delicate silver chain held an intricate horse charm. As she entered the living room, she hooked the necklace behind her neck. She stroked the charm as she watched Dylan lean down and hug her mom. He fit so well here. Her chest tightened and warmth filled her body. Dylan wasn't just her brother's best friend—he was family.

****

Meg stood and stretched her arms over her head. The tart smell of apples mixed with cinnamon and made her sleepy. Maybe the two pieces of pie caused her fatigue and not the soul-soothing scent. Rubbing a hand over her full stomach, she straightened her spine and prepared herself for the same argument she had with her mother every year. She'd spent the entire evening preparing for Christmas morning, but now she needed to go home and sleep.

"Are you sure you don't want to spend the night? You can stay in your old room. It seems a little silly for you to drive home tonight just to come back again in the morning." Annie sat at the head of the kitchen farmhouse table and pushed the last bites of pie around her plate with a fork.

Meg cleared the dinner dishes from the table, letting her mom's words slide off her back as easily as the snow slid down the window. She cast her mom a quick glance and ignored the disappointment clouding her blue eyes. "You make this same argument every year."

"Yes, but this year you're going home to an empty house. Wouldn't you rather stay with me?" Annie carried her plate to the sink and stood next to Meg. She brushed a piece of hair from Meg's forehead.

Gripping the sink, she jerked away her head and lowered her gaze to the mahogany floor. "It's been a long day, and I just want to be in my own bed tonight." She spoke the truth, but she bit back the part about wanting to be away from her mom's prying gaze. Annie Sheffield was like a dog with a bone, and she wouldn't be appeased until they'd talked through every angle of Blake's disappearance. Meg didn't want to talk to anyone about Blake.

Especially her mom.

"But it's Christmas Eve. You shouldn't be alone. Not to mention how dangerous the roads might be with all the snow." Annie cupped Meg's shoulders and smiled.

The slight whine in her mom's voice grated against

Meg's nerves, and she fought every instinct not to roll her eyes. Meg faced Mom and pressed the small of her back against the counter. Spilled water from the sink seeped into the back of her long sleeve T-shirt. "I like being alone. Besides, Emma and the kids will arrive soon, and I don't think I can handle them all right now."

Tears hovered along Annie's lashes, and she blinked, her lips trembling as she pressed them together. "I'm sorry we're so bothersome. I'll make sure to let your sister know we need to give you some space while she's here."

A flash of guilt shot through her. Meg dropped her head and pinched the bridge of her nose. "You're not a bother. I'm tired and obviously a little cranky, and the kids don't need to be around a bad attitude when they get here. I don't want to ruin their Christmas."

Annie tucked a thumb under Meg's chin, lifting it so their gazes met. "You won't ruin anything for anyone. I promise."

"Fine." Meg folded her arms over her chest. "I'll stay if we can talk about my plans for the inn. I've wanted to show you my ideas for months, and every time I bring up my thoughts you brush them aside. We have so much room for growth, not to mention the added income an indoor riding arena would generate." Dylan was right, her future held limitless possibilities. She wanted to build something she loved—something she could be proud of. All she needed was her mom's cooperation.

Annie dropped her hands and sighed. "Christmas Eve is not the time to discuss your ridiculous plan for an indoor riding arena I don't need at my inn."

Meg bit the inside of her cheek. Being the youngest Sheffield child meant no one ever took her ideas seriously, especially her mom. She'd worked hard to outline a new business venture that would capitalize on the clientele her mom already had and make them both a lot more money. But whenever she brought up the issue, she'd endure her mom's scoffing and introducing a new topic.

"I just want to go home, put on my pajamas, snuggle in bed with Nora, and get lost in a book. I don't want to have to explain why." Meg fought hard to keep the quiver from her voice. She wouldn't let her mom know how much her dismissal stung.

Annie nodded. "Okay."

"Okay?" Meg reared back and raised her brows. Her mom wasn't one to give up so easily. If she was, she wouldn't have transformed their family home into a successful inn after her father died when she was a girl. "Seriously?"

"I get it." Annie shrugged. "I understand needing time and space to lick your wounds in order to heal. Getting over a broken heart takes time."

"You think I'm licking my wounds?" Amusement and irritation battled inside over her mom's description.

"Well, aren't you?"

Meg chewed her bottom lip. "Maybe I'm mourning a broken future." She hadn't admitted to anyone she hadn't been in love with Blake for a while but had been too chicken to end their relationship. Or maybe she'd been too proud to admit failure, and she'd clung to the possibility they could rekindle what they'd shared when they'd first met.

Annie stepped back and studied her face. "No, I

guess you aren't. I've seen anger and confusion and sadness since everything happened but not a broken-hearted girl who's devastated her fiancé left town. How did I miss your true emotions?"

Meg turned back toward the sink and grabbed a washcloth. Stepping toward the granite-topped island behind her mom, she wiped away the crumbs from the cookies they'd baked earlier. Tomorrow was soon enough to frost the sugar cut-outs.

"Meg, honey, will you please look at me?"

The tenderness in Mom's voice caused pressure to build in her chest. "What?" She twisted around. She didn't want to talk about her failed relationship—didn't want the stupid tears to erupt again.

"A better man is waiting. A man who you will love with your whole heart." Dipping her chin, Annie frowned and furrowed her brow. "Blake was an idiot for not realizing the gem he'd found. If he ever comes back, I'll put my foot so far up his bottom he won't sit for a week."

Meg laughed so hard her stomach muscles cramped, and she needed to stop. "Thanks. What time should I be here in the morning?"

"As early as you can." Annie glanced at the clock on the wall. "Emma should be here with Luke and the kids in a couple of hours. She hopes the kids will be fast asleep, and they can put them right in their assigned beds. I'm sure Sophie will be eager to open her presents first thing in the morning."

Meg snorted. "You think? Sophie will be up at the crack of dawn, which is one of the reasons I want to be in my own house tonight. I don't need the munchkin waking me before I'm ready." She inhaled one more

11

scent of vanilla and cinnamon before heading toward the front door.

Annie laughed and followed Meg. "I can't say I blame you. Drive safe and call me when you get home."

"Seriously?" She rolled her eyes. "I live like ten minutes away."

"Yes, seriously."

"You're ridiculous." She pulled on her coat and boots then gave Mom a kiss on the cheek. "But I love you anyway."

"I love you, too."

Meg hurried to her truck with Nora by her side. She stopped and glanced at the sky one more time. The stars were so beautiful tonight. She let her gaze drift to the barn, and an image of Dylan popped into her head. She smiled. He always had a way of making her heart a little bit lighter, no matter how miserable things were in her life.

Strange how he was the only person she could talk to. Even when Blake was around, she took her problems to Dylan. But not this time. Blake screwed over them both. Dylan couldn't be expected to pick up the mess Blake left for him to clean up, as well as help her over the hurdle of frustration in front of her. Healing might take some time, but she'd get there.

Maybe her mom was right. Maybe someone else waited on the other side. But until she found Mr. Right, she needed to figure out how to make her mom finally listen. She had a future she wanted to build, and the inn was the perfect place to build it.

Chapter Two

Dylan opened one eye and then the other. He glanced at the alarm clock on his night stand and groaned. He still had twenty minutes left to sleep. Shutting his eyes, he dragged his blanket over his head and snuggled into the warmth of his bed. He wanted those extra minutes of rest, even if he wouldn't get back to sleep. The day's to-do list circled in his brain, just as it had for the past few weeks. He could never get the amount of sleep his body craved with so much weighing on his mind.

Oh hell, I might as well get up.

Heaving a heavy sigh, he tossed off his blanket and stretched both arms above his head. The movement tugged the hard muscles in his side. He sat and settled bare feet on the hardwood floor. The cold shot up his legs, and he shivered. He really needed to get a rug. Snaking a hand over his beard, he tried to rub away his fatigue.

The gentle motion didn't work.

He stood and threw on his clothes before heading downstairs for a cup of coffee. The house was dark. Lisa wasn't awake yet. Big surprise there. Nothing short of an earthquake would make his sister rise at this early hour, least of all farm chores. Only a few days then she'd be out of his hair, and he'd have back his house.

When the coffee finished brewing, he filled a mug and stepped outside. He blinked to adjust to the darkness. The sun wouldn't rise for a couple more hours. He'd woken before the sun on Christmas many times, but never to do the chores alone. Memories of the past barreled into him, and he rubbed his chest in an effort to ease the pain that seized his heart. Even a year ago, things were different. His father manned the farm while his mom cooked a big breakfast. Dylan was just the hired help.

But not this year. This year, the responsibility was all his. He glanced around the farm his family owned for generations, and the weight of the world settled on his shoulders. How would he manage all the work? He shook his head and took a sip of coffee. The hot, bitter liquid coated his tongue and slid down his throat. He had no answers right now—only chores. He squared his shoulders and averted his gaze as he passed the singed pile of rubble still heaped yards away from the house. He didn't have time to dwell on anything but what work he needed to finish this morning.

Hours passed, and Dylan lost himself in his work. When he was done, he walked to the house and entered through the back door. He threw his muddy boots in the corner and left his overalls in a heap on the floor. He'd pick them up later. Right now, he needed food.

Lisa sat slumped in a chair at the kitchen table with her long, messy hair hanging over her shoulder. She curved a slender hand around her steaming mug of coffee, while her other hand held a thick blanket snugly around her huddled frame.

Her red-rimmed eyes told him more than he needed to know about the amount of sleep she'd gotten the night before. He snorted, and disgust swirled in his gut. Leave it to Lisa to go out with old friends until all hours of the night without a second thought to the morning chores needing done. Work on the farm was of no concern to her, and honestly, never had been. Even as a young girl, she lifted her nose at the hard work that was needed to keep their farm afloat. The work always sat squarely on his shoulders, and not Lisa's. Her being in town for a few days wouldn't change her attitude— nothing would. He grabbed a fresh cup of coffee and spared her a glance. "You just wake up?"

"What's that supposed to mean?" She lifted eyes to meet his and pressed together her lips.

Dylan put down his mug with a sigh. "It's a pretty straight forward question. I just wondered if you'd been up long." He glanced at the clock on the wall, and a ping of resentment shot through him. It read nine a.m.

She raised her head, her chin jutted and eyes narrowed. "Yes, I just woke up. I mean, it's still early. I would still be in bed if today wasn't Christmas. I thought you might want some company for breakfast before we head into town to see Mom and Dad."

Dylan softened. He couldn't stay mad. She was who she was and would never change. She didn't have the same ties to the land he did, even if he needed her help right now. "How about I make eggs and bacon after I shower?"

Lisa smiled. "Why don't you head upstairs and get ready while I cook breakfast?"

He lifted an eyebrow. "Really?"

Laughing, Lisa stood. "Yes, really. Consider my fabulous cooking your Christmas present."

"So, you didn't actually buy me a Christmas

present?"

"Of course not, silly. Do I ever?" She slipped her brown hair over her shoulder and grabbed a pan from the cabinet.

A teasing glimmer battled through her bloodshot eyes, and he chuckled on his way to the bathroom. At least she owned who she was, but he wished she would be a little more considerate and a lot more helpful. Especially now, when he wasn't sure if he could keep everything together. His life shattered into a million pieces this past year. As hard as he tried, he didn't know if he could put those pieces back together again— at least not by himself.

Cold water splashed down on him. He showered too quickly to worry about warming the icy spray. His stomach rumbled in protest to coffee being the only thing it was fed. Thank God Lisa cooked breakfast, though he didn't exactly trust her in the kitchen. Hell, he didn't exactly trust her anywhere.

He threw on his clothes and rushed down the stairs. The smell of bacon wafted into his nose before he saw it and the table set for two. A pitcher of orange juice sat in the center of the table, and he helped himself to a glass as he took a seat and watched her flip the eggs.

Lisa carried a large platter of bacon to the table and placed it under his nose. "Merry Christmas, big brother. Enjoy."

He heaped mounds of food onto his plate. "The food smells amazing."

"You don't have to sound so surprised." Lisa took her seat across from him. "I've been on my own for years now. You shouldn't be shocked I can put together a simple breakfast."

Swallowing, he pushed down a bite of food, as well as his opinion of her living on her own. After leaving home, she'd jumped from relationship to relationship and man to man. She always found some fool capable of taking care of all her endless problems. Once those problems weren't handled to her liking, off she left to find someone new.

He shoveled eggs in his mouth. She'd be upset if he told her his opinion of her lifestyle—safer just to eat. "Did you get a chance to see Mom and Dad yesterday when you arrived in town?" The words came out in between bites.

"No. I met friends uptown when I got in." She lifted a slim shoulder and picked at the small pile of eggs on her plate.

Her answer didn't surprise him. She'd avoided seeing their parents for the past six months. She'd been nowhere to be found when he helped their mom pack all their parents' belongings and moved them out of their home. She was off living her own life as he and their mom made the painstaking decision life on the farm was no longer safe for their dad. She hadn't watched their mother cry silent tears as she placed careful thought and consideration into what would fit into the modest apartment she now shared with her husband and what would need to be given away. He squeezed his fork and the cold metal dug into his skin.

But now she was here, and she couldn't put off seeing the person their dad was becoming. Alzheimer's stole a little bit more of his mind every day. Dylan understood her reluctance to watch the man they loved and admired slipping into the darkness of his own mind. He didn't want to see it either, but he'd never had a choice. "Will you be ready to head out as soon we're done eating?"

She picked up the material at the shoulder of her sweatshirt. "Do I look like I'm ready?"

"Will you hurry and get dressed so we can leave soon? Mom needs us this morning. I don't want her worrying over how Dad will handle being away from the farm on Christmas."

"Fine. I didn't need to finish my food anyway." Lisa threw her fork on her plate and stomped from the room.

Her heavy footsteps echoed around the room and matched the beating against his temples. My God, she was infuriating. He cleaned the kitchen, gathered the presents to take to his parents' place, and returned a call to his best friend before Lisa again made her way downstairs.

Lisa shoved her feet into her boots. "Who were you talking to? Mom?"

"Jonah."

"I'd heard Jonah moved back to town. How's he doing?" Lisa glanced up as she finished lacing her boots and put on her coat.

"Really well, actually. He just got his contractor's license, and he's back together with Jillian."

Lisa laughed. "Didn't take long for them to reconnect. I guess no one was surprised."

"Not at all. I think Jonah and Jillian were the only ones who didn't see it coming." Dylan paused while he put on his own coat. He hadn't told Lisa about Jonah's role in one of their barns being burnt to the ground, and Lisa never asked. "Jonah wants me to come to the inn later for dinner."

Widening her eyes, she jutted her bottom lip. "Are you going? It's Christmas."

Dylan fought not to raise his eyes to the ceiling. "Yes, it's Christmas, but I think you'll see plenty of me by then."

"But what am I supposed to do?" Fisting her hands on her hips, Lisa shook her head.

"You haven't been home to see Mom and Dad in close to eight months, and you're throwing a fit because I won't be there to hold your hand in front of Dad for a couple hours? Are you serious?" Blood pounded in his ears. How could she be so selfish? He pushed his fingers into his eyes to stop the headache threatening to ruin his day.

"I don't need you to hold my hand," she snapped. "I'm scared. I don't know what to say to him. I don't know what to say to Mom to make her feel better about what she's dealing with. I'm not good with complicated relationships." Lisa stared at the floor and picked at the hem of her coat.

The ice of resentment cracked inside him. "Do you think I know what to say? How to act? I have no idea if I'm doing or saying the right thing. I do what feels right." He dropped his hands on her shoulders. "Sometimes, just showing up is the only thing you can do."

She wiped away tears with the tips of her fingers. "You're right. I know I need to be here more. I'll try harder."

Dylan wrapped her in a quick hug. "You being here will mean a lot to Mom, and it will help me if I don't have to worry about her constantly. Now come on. You've put off seeing Dad long enough. Let's go."

They rode together in silence, his truck bouncing along the country roads as he made his way toward town. He pulled his truck into the parking lot. Rows of brick buildings stood two stories high. Low shrubs covered in snow lined the sidewalk. He stole a glance at her. Her pinched-together face showed her struggle to regain her composure, and his heart split in two. Sorrow and fear spilled from her eyes, but a smile spread on her lips. Her obvious effort was enough. He hoped it would be enough for Mom as well. Leaving the parked truck behind, Dylan led his sister toward the apartment their parents now called home.

His mom rushed out of the door with a wide grin and her brown hair pulled away from her round face. She gathered him and Lisa into her arms. "Merry Christmas!" She wrapped one arm tight around Lisa's shoulders and the other around Dylan's waist.

The sheen in his mom's eyes reflected that of Lisa's. He leaned down and gave her a kiss on the top of her head, then stepped inside. "Merry Christmas to you, too. How was your morning with Dad? Is he in a good mood today?"

Mary and Lisa followed Dylan into the apartment. "Today has been a good day, thank heavens. He's excited to see you guys."

Dylan glanced around the tiny living room, and joy tugged at his heart at what his mom had done to add some Christmas cheer. A small tree sat in the corner, dressed in most of the same ornaments he had loved since he was a kid, although it wasn't big enough to fit them all. The little figurines his mom treasured decorated several spots throughout the room, and four red stockings hung from hooks on the fireplace.

Lisa stepped inside before closing the door behind her.

Dylan hoped, for his mom's sake, she focused on how much love and warmth his mom created and not on the size of the apartment. He approached his dad, who sat in his favorite recliner in the corner. White hair nestled on top of his head—thinning at the top of his scalp. Whiskers poked through his chin. Seeing him with his feet in the air, remote in hand, and a cup of coffee on the side table painted a picture of the man Dylan grew up with.

His dad stood to give him a hug.

Dylan released a long breath.

"It's about time you two got here. Your mother's driving me crazy. She looks out the window every two minutes, apparently thinking staring into the snow would get you here faster." Walter slapped Dylan on the back then focused on Lisa. "And what do you think you're doing over there? Come over and give your old man a hug."

Lisa ran and threw her arms around his neck. "Oh, Daddy. I'm so happy to see you. You look great."

"Of course, I look great. Why wouldn't I?"

Lisa shifted her gaze to Dylan and drew together her brows.

He gave a slight shake of his head. Now wasn't the time to explain about his mood changes. Now was time to be thankful they could enjoy this moment together, and hopefully make some good memories for at least one more Christmas.

"Good point." Lisa grinned and cupped Walter's cheek in her hand. "You always look good."

Mary chuckled. "No need to inflate his ego any

21

more than it already is. Now, everyone take a seat in the kitchen. Brunch is all set up and ready to go. Besides, I know you all want to open presents, and we won't get to the gifts before we eat." Without waiting for a response, Mary disappeared into the kitchen .

"Some things never change." Dylan muttered under his breath and rubbed his still-full stomach.

"And thank God for that." Lisa raced past him into the eat-in kitchen. "I get to open gifts first once we finish."

Dylan rolled his eyes. "You know we aren't children anymore, don't you?"

"Don't start in on your sister, Dylan." Mary hurried toward the table with a platter of steaming biscuits in her hands.

Lisa locked her gaze with his and raised her brows, a smirk plastered on her mouth.

All he could do was laugh—laugh, and enjoy the simple moments he used to take for granted. These moments might not happen as frequently as they once had, and they no doubt would be fewer in the future, but in this instance, he had everything he ever wanted. He pushed back the pain in his heart that reminded him what he wanted would continue to be ripped away.

Chapter Three

The drifting snow scattered along the road in front of Meg's truck. Her wipers whipped across her windshield to keep the large flakes from obscuring her view. She shot Nora a quick smile and patted the silky fur on top of her head as she made the familiar turns through town and out to the main highway. A small dusting of snow clung to the bare branches of the trees lining the road. She loved this time of year. The air had a bite, and the smallest amount of snow made everyone smile as it fell in soft blankets all around.

Soon, the cold and the snow would become monotonous, and the beautiful dusting that once seemed magical would turn into gray sludge. For now, the light snow just added to the festive atmosphere of Christmas.

Meg pulled into her mom's driveway and wound around to her usual parking spot by the horse barn. Even though the late morning sun shone, her mom turned on the Christmas lights adorning the barn and the large, white Victorian house. The yard looked like a postcard. She slid out of her truck, and snow crunched under her boots as she stomped toward the house, presents in tow.

Nora ran in circles and caught the falling snow in her mouth.

She stopped in front of the wide porch steps and stared at the house she called home. Her mother's resilience in transforming their family home into a successful inn after her father died never ceased to amaze her. She hated living in an inn—always hated sneaking around her own home to find a little peace and quiet. More often than not, she found solace in Mom's garden. She spent hours helping her mom transform the soil between their fingers into rows upon rows of beautiful flowers.

To this day, she'd much rather spend time working at the nursery, or with her horses, than with people. People usually annoyed her.

Nora jumped in the air, and then landed in a pile of snow.

A black nose poked through the white mound like a piece of coal that must have fallen from Santa's sleigh. Meg covered her mouth with a hand and laughed. "Come on, Nora. Let's get inside."

A fresh mixture of cinnamon and vanilla greeted her at the door—Mom must have baked more cookies with Sophie. Meg plopped on the hardwood floor. She grunted and wiggled her feet, freeing herself from the death grip of her shoes. They dropped to the floor with a *thud* next to the small puddle she'd created by the Welcome mat.

Nora barked and took off down the hall toward the kitchen.

The sound of her dog's nails scratching the floor rang in Meg's ears, and she winced. She followed Nora and found her mom, sister, and brother-in-law in the kitchen.

Emma stood in the corner, bouncing a screaming baby Anderson, rubbing a hand over his tiny back and cooing in his ear.

Luke's black-framed glasses slid down his nose, and his finger-length, sandy blond hair stood on ends as he prepared a bottle for his son.

"Didn't anyone tell the little man there's no screaming on Christmas?" Meg joked and dropped her bag of goodies on the floor next to the kitchen table.

"Well, maybe if you showed a little sooner, he wouldn't be so crabby." Emma tore her gaze from the red-faced baby and brushed her dirty blonde hair from her eyes.

Luke hurried over, popped the bottle in Anderson's mouth, and escaped into another room.

"I can tell you're a little flustered, Emma, so I won't take too much offense." Meg crossed to her sister and placed a quick kiss on the top of her head. Emma had the same petite build as their mother—and the same feistiness that kept Meg on her toes. She smiled at her nephew. He was content with the bottle in his mouth. She'd hold him later.

"You'd be a little flustered, too, if you had a three-year-old on your leg for four hours, begging to open presents and asking when her Meg-Meg would get here."

Annie chuckled and removed a sheet of cookies from the oven. "The morning has been interesting. You should have stayed last night and made things easier."

Irritation settled in her gut. "Don't start." Her mom didn't have a filter. She bit the inside of her cheek. The soft *buzz* of her phone saved her from saying something she'd regret. She retrieved the device from her pocket, and a number she didn't recognize dominated the screen. Turning her back toward her nosy family, she pressed the accept button on the screen and lifted the phone to her ear. "Hello?"

Silence filled the line.

Irritation pulsed through her. She checked the screen. The call was still connected. "Is someone there?"

More silence.

She grumbled a groan of frustration. "Fine. Merry Christmas to you, too."

"Don't hang up."

She hovered a finger over the red button when the words hit her ear. She froze her hand in midair and stared wide-eyed at her mom and sister. "Blake? Is that you? Where are you?"

Another beat of silence passed. "I just wanted to hear your voice today."

His soft tone made her tighten her grip on the phone. "Seriously? You've been gone for a month after setting Dylan's barn on fire, and you just want to hear my voice? I'm supposed to what? Cry with happiness you remembered me and beg you to come home?"

"I know I've made mistakes. I want to come back to town to own them. I promise I will, but I need to know where things stand with us."

Meg paced in the kitchen, avoiding the curious glances of her family. "You've got to be kidding me." Hysteria raised the volume of her voice, making Anderson's shrill cries start again. "You can't possibly think you and I still have a future."

"I guess it's a little too much to ask you to stand by your man. I should have known better."

Hatred spewed from his hard words, giving her a glimpse of the man she'd seen way too much of over the last year. Meg snorted and hoped the emotion boiling in her gut didn't leak into her voice. "I guess you should have." She ended the call and tossed her phone on the smooth countertop beside her.

Anderson's cries filled the otherwise-silent kitchen.

Meg hung her head, pinching the bridge of her nose to keep away the tears. Today was Christmas, and she wouldn't waste one more tear on Blake.

****

Wrinkled paper scattered all over the cozy living room. A fire crackled in the fire and chased away the nip still lingering in the afternoon air. Meg's nerves rattled around her body like the toy Anderson shook. She hadn't envisioned her Christmas this way. She'd wanted a nice, quiet day with family. Now, her family tiptoed around her like they were afraid she'd snap if they said the wrong thing.

Thank God for Sophie. The three-year-old only cared about opening presents. Once she ripped open her packages, all the focus was on her, and she loved it. Meg sat on the couch with Nora and watched her attack each and every gift with the enthusiasm only a small child could muster. Focusing on Sophie almost calmed her down and put her in the Christmas spirit.

Almost.

"Presents all gone?" Sophie widened her bright blue eyes, and her long, blonde hair tussled in wild wisps around her face.

Sophie darted her gaze around the room like an addict searching for her next fix, and Meg fought not to laugh. She remembered Christmases as a child and always wanting more presents.

"I'm sure Uncle Jonah will have some gifts for you. He'll be here before dinner with Jillian and Sam."

Emma grabbed wads of discarded wrapping paper from the floor. "Maybe you should thank everyone for the presents they gave you."

"Thank you." Sophie's bottom lip trembled.

"Why don't we open one of your new toys and play until he gets here?" Meg grabbed a box from the floor and held it in the air.

"Yay! Dolls!"

Meg sat on the floor and lost herself in a land of baby dolls and puzzles. Sophie's sweet giggles surrounded her, and Blake vanished from her mind. She gathered Sophie close and inhaled the sweet smell of little girl and Christmas cookies. She glanced out the window and darkness swarmed the glass. Early evening had crept in.

Ding-dong

Sophie jumped up with a wide smile. "Uncle Jonah?"

"I doubt it. I don't think he'd ring the bell." Meg furrowed her brow and leaned to the side to get a glimpse of the front door.

"Then who?"

Dylan popped his head around the corner. "Do I hear my favorite little girl? Come here, Soph." He crouched on his heels and opened wide his arms.

Sophie threw herself into his embrace. "Merry Christmas."

"Same to you, sweetheart." His gaze traveled down to Meg. "And to you. Having fun playing with dolls?"

"Playing with dolls is my favorite pastime, especially when I play with Sophie." She stood, crossing her arms in front of her. "I thought you couldn't stop by tonight."

"I didn't plan on it, but Jonah called earlier and asked me to come when I was done at my parents' house." Dylan rubbed the back of his neck. "He said he has something to tell me, but I'm pretty sure I know what his news is. He sounded too proud of himself."

She slumped forward her shoulders and bit back a sigh. She didn't want to deal with Jonah's announcement tonight. "We'll find out soon. They should be here any minute."

"I want him now." Sophie wiggled out of Dylan's arms and stood by the window. "I'll wait right here."

"She's waited all day." Emma hugged Dylan, and then sat Anderson in his swing before sitting beside Luke on the floral couch.

Annie entered the living with a platter of Christmas cookies and grinned. "It's so nice to see you, Dylan. Are you staying for dinner?"

"Jonah wanted me to stop by, but I wouldn't say no to dinner. Especially if you cooked." His lips quirked in a half smile.

"Eeeek! They're here!" Sophie jumped down from the window and ran to the door.

Sophie's shriek made the hair on the back of Meg's neck stand straight.

Emma laughed and scooped her daughter in her arms. "I know you're excited. But if you stand right by the door, it will smack you in the head when they come in. Let's sit here nicely, and pretend for a minute you have a shred of patience in your tiny body."

Sophie rolled her eyes and slumped against Emma's shoulder.

To keep from laughing, Meg bit into her lip. How could so much sass come out of such a little girl? Meg locked her gaze with Dylan, who fought his own laughter, and then grabbed Sophie from her sister. She held her tight until the door burst open.

"We're here." Sam ran into the living room. Thick, black hair waved around his ears, and he shot everyone a wide smile. "Finally."

Sophie wriggled from Meg's grasp and wrapped her arms around Sam. "Merry Christmas, Sam. I have a gift for you," she said. "Do you have a gift for me, too?"

"Sophie, that's not very polite." Emma fisted her hands on her hips and narrowed her gaze.

"Oh, leave the girl be, Emma." Jonah winked at Sophie before turning to the tree and placing a large pile of gifts underneath it. After he tossed their coats on a chair, he wrapped an arm around Jillian. "It's Christmas, the one time of the year when it's okay to assume you're getting presents. Well, the second I guess. We can't forget about birthday presents."

Jillian cleared her throat, and a smile tugged at her lips. Her long, blonde hair swirled around her back, and she clasped her hands in front of her.

Jonah squeezed her shoulder and shifted his gaze to everyone in the room. His dark blue eyes sparkled as he grinned.

To keep from rolling her eyes, Meg kept her gaze glued to the carpet. This production was ridiculous. Jonah's announcement wouldn't be a surprise to anyone. She glanced at Dylan and lifted an eyebrow. She would mess with them a little bit. "What's going on with you two? You're acting weird." Meg raised her brows and fought to keep from smiling.

"She's right." Emma folded her arms over her

chest and screwed her lips to the side.

Mischief shone from her sapphire eyes. God love her. She might be the peacemaker of the three, but Emma wasn't above giving Jonah a hard time.

"You both look goofy," Emma said.

"You guys are so sweet." Jonah shook his head. "Can't you give me a minute before you jump all over me?"

"Obviously not." Meg snorted. The vein in Jonah's neck bulged, and she sealed together her lips before any more words tumbled from her mouth.

Jillian giggled and held up her left hand.

Annie and Emma erupted from their seats and grabbed her hand.

"Let me see the ring," Emma said. "It's gorgeous. Who knew Jonah had such good taste?"

"I helped him pick it out." Sam's grin spread wide. "He even asked for my permission to marry my mom. He couldn't have asked her without me."

Dylan chuckled and slapped Jonah on the back. "I'm sure you're right, Sam. Congrats, buddy. I couldn't be happier for you."

"When's the wedding? Have you picked a date yet? The inn is always lovely in the spring." Annie wiped tears from her cheeks and clasped her hands under her chin, her smile wide.

Jonah laughed and raised his palms in the air. "Calm down, Mom. We haven't had time to make any plans. You'll be the first to know when we do."

Meg stood rooted to the spot, and her legs turned to lead. Jealousy, hot and raw, shot through her. She wasn't prepared for a joyful announcement about someone else's engagement, even if she wanted her brother to be happy. She glanced at her left hand and stared at her engagement ring. The diamond sparkled from the lights in the tree and mocked her. The urge to rip off the jewelry and throw it across the room consumed her. She just couldn't do it yet. Heat surged through her body, and the intensity caused her stomach to churn. She was going to get sick.

"Waahh! Waahh!"

The shouts of excitement stopped as Anderson cried.

Meg held up a hand to Emma, stopping her. "I got him." She scooped Anderson into her arms. "Congratulations, guys. Your engagement is great news." She pasted on a smile then headed into the kitchen to mix up a bottle. She glanced at Anderson's bright red face. "Thanks, little guy. You saved my butt."

She settled into a chair at the table and stuck the bottle in his mouth. Tension melted from her shoulders. He stared up at her as he ate, his tiny fingers wrapping around hers. The simple joy of a child in her arms is what she wanted. She wanted a family.

"You look good holding a baby."

She glanced up and stared into Dylan's green eyes.

He leaned against the doorframe with his arms folded across his broad chest.

She lifted a shoulder and locked her gaze on Anderson once again. "What can I say? I'm a natural."

Sitting across from her, he leaned against the chair and stretched his legs. "You bolted out of there pretty fast. Are you okay?"

"I'm fine. I'm happy for them." Her clipped tone mocked her words.

"I have no doubt you're happy, but that doesn't mean it's easy to see. Especially with what you're going through with Blake."

She heaved out a deep breath and tore her gaze from Anderson. She didn't want to talk about her broken engagement right now—not even with Dylan. "Blake and I have been over for a long time. Him skipping town after burning down your barn just put the final nail in the coffin of our relationship."

He nodded. "Okay. I'm glad you've figured out what you want."

Meg choked out a laugh that morphed into a sob. She bit into her bottom lip to muffle the sound.

Anderson shifted in her lap.

"Yeah, it only took me five years to figure it out. What a waste of time."

Dylan leaned over the table and placed a hand on her arm. "No such thing as a waste of time. Just a hard way to learn a life lesson."

She snorted, but his words were oddly soothing. "Thank you, oh wise one."

"No problem." He stood and skirted around the table, stopping to stand behind her. He placed both hands on her shoulders. "I'm here if you need to talk. Oh, and the necklace looks good on you."

She glanced over her shoulder, but he had already disappeared. Shifting her focus back on the now sleeping Anderson, she slid the bottle from his loose lips, then placed him on her shoulder. She traced lazy circles on his back, rested her head against his, and sighed.

She needed to return to the rest of her family. Clambering to her feet, she carried Anderson into the living room. As she gushed about how excited she was, she could ignore the ache in her heart. She could push aside her feelings and do what was best for her family. Hell, she'd done it her whole life.

After placing Anderson in Emma's arms, she gathered Jonah and Jillian into a big hug. She forced a wide smile on her lips. "Welcome to the family, Jillian. I'm so excited for you guys."

Chapter Four

The sun peeked over the horizon. Pink and gold hues swirled through the still-dark sky, capturing the night and promising a new day. Dylan stuck the prongs of his pitchfork into the hay he'd moved and leaned on the handle. Early morning was his favorite time of day—the time when the world around him woke and was alive with possibilities.

Even if he was tired as hell. Why had he stayed up so late? He wiped sweat from his brow with the back of a gloved hand, and his mind wandered to the night before. The excitement of Jonah's engagement, and spending time with Emma's kids, kept him out much later than intended.

Then there was Meg. His heart ached when he talked with her in the kitchen. Even if she was better off without Blake. Maybe since she was available…

No, he couldn't go there. She was a good friend and Jonah's little sister. He'd do what he'd done for years—push down his feelings.

Betsy, his ancient golden retriever, barked at the chirping birds and brought him back to the moment. Bitter cold bit into his flesh as he stood staring at the sunrise. He needed to get back to work. Warmth invaded his body and sweat poured from him while he shoveled the hay for his cows. He welcomed the sharp tug of his muscles that kept his mind on the task at hand.

He struggled all night with thoughts of Meg ending her relationship, thoughts of Jonah and his engagement to Jillian, and thoughts of the constant loneliness surrounding him since moving into the big farm house without his family.

Once his work was finished, he studied the explosion of burnt wood that stained his land. Nothing inside was salvageable, and he couldn't just let the heap of useless material lay here. Unused land was a waste of space, and a waste of anything wasn't something he could afford right now. He needed to figure out what to do with the mess and hopefully earn some extra money while he was at it. Between running the farm by himself and getting his dad proper care, he was drowning. He didn't have much time to come up with a miracle that provided the help he needed in the spring and his mom the help she needed now.

Minutes ticked by as he studied the barn. He shifted toward the house and spotted Lisa strolling along the pebbled driveway. He glanced at his watch. What was she doing? She was never dressed for the day at this hour. "Going somewhere?" He shifted, placing all his weight on his left leg.

She stood next to him and kept her gaze fixed on the destruction. "I'm going into town. I have a favor to ask first."

Dylan shot up an eyebrow, and he cocked his head to the side. A favor from Lisa should be interesting. "What exactly do you need from me?"

"I hoped once you're done around here, you could sit with Dad for a while so I can take Mom for lunch."

"Really?"

"Yes, really." She met his gaze. "She's stuck in the apartment with Dad all day, every day. She won't leave him alone, which I honestly don't understand. But I would like to do something nice, even if it's just to get her out for an hour or two."

"You don't understand why Mom won't leave Dad by himself, because you haven't seen him when he has one of his episodes." Dylan's voice dipped low in disbelief. Leave it to Lisa to plan something nice, and then ruin it with a stupid comment.

"Well, he seemed fine yesterday." Lisa rolled her eyes and held up a hand. "I don't want to argue. I just want to know if you'll help me get Mom out of the house."

He lifted a shoulder. "Yeah, I'll hang with Dad. I'm pretty much done. Let me put away some stuff, and then I'll run in and grab a shower. Mom will be happy to get out with you for a little bit."

He hurried to put everything in its place and rushed into the house to get ready. He would make himself something to eat when he got to his parents' place then he could talk to his dad about the farm. Lisa was right; some days his dad's mind was as sharp as it had ever been—as if no war waged over his memories. Hopefully, today would be one of those days, and they could kick around some ideas for the upcoming season. Maybe the old man would have the answer he searched for to keep the farm they both loved running.

When he arrived at the tiny apartment, he watched his mom flutter around like a nervous butterfly.

She stopped to grab his arm. "Are you sure you'll be okay?"

He rested a hand on hers and smiled. "We'll be

fine, Mom. You'll be gone for a couple of hours. I've got this."

Mary released a pent-up breath and shook her head. "I know, but I worry about him when I'm not here."

"You've left him with me before. This time is no different. I can handle him."

Mary bounced her gaze from Dylan to Walter and sank her teeth into her bottom lip. "I've never been gone for a couple of hours before. Maybe Lisa and I should order in."

Dylan placed his hands on her shoulders and forced her to look at him.

She twisted her hands and widened her eyes.

His stomach dropped. "Listen to me. You spend all of your time taking care of Dad. Let me do this for one afternoon while you spend time with Lisa. Enjoy yourself. Everything will be fine."

"But…"

Lisa stepped forward, grabbed her arm, and dragged her toward the door. "But nothing. Dylan has everything under control, and I'm starving. Let's go."

Mary cast one last glance over her shoulder before stepping out the door.

His dad slept in his chair, his mouth slightly open and arms folded across his chest. A stab of disappointment cut into Dylan's chest. So much for talking over plans for the farm. He made himself a sandwich, then returned to the living room to settle in for the afternoon.

Two hours had passed. Dylan tossed aside the second magazine he'd read cover to cover.

His dad thrashed back and forth in his chair and muttered under his breath.

Dylan stood and hurried to the chair. He laid a hand on his dad's wrinkled brow to soothe him back to slumber.

Walter opened his eyes and furrowed his brow. "Get your hands off me."

"You're okay, Dad. Just go back to sleep."

"Who the hell are you, and why are you in my house?" Walter batted away Dylan's hand and stood.

A vise squeezed Dylan's heart, and tears burned behind his eyes. His dad hadn't recognized him before, but being forgotten by the man who meant the most never got any easier. He threw both hands in the air in surrender. "It's just me, Dylan."

Walter charged, his arms flailing wildly.

Dylan grabbed his arm.

But Walter smashed his fist into Dylan's jaw.

Dylan stumbled backward. "Dad, stop! It's me, Dylan. I'm hanging out for a little bit while Mom's at lunch with Lisa." He spoke in a calm and steady voice, even as anger boiled in the pit of his stomach. His dad couldn't recall who Dylan was before, but he never got physical. He grabbed Walter's wrists and pinned them to his sides.

Walter squirmed. "Get off of me. Help! Help! Somebody help me!" He shouted to the empty room, and his face burned red.

The door swung open, and his mom ran into the room with Lisa at her heels.

Mary hurried to Walter, smoothed her palms on his face, and stared into his eyes. "Walter, honey, everything is fine. I'm here. Please, calm down."

She ran her hands up and down his face like a mother comforting a child, and Dylan glanced away.

"Get him out of here. I don't know who he is, and I really don't care. Just get him out of my house."

Dylan pushed past Lisa and stormed out of the apartment. He collapsed on the front stoop and hung his head in his hands, his shoulders slumped forward. The cool air washed over him but did nothing to fan the flames of turmoil erupting inside. The taste of bile crept up the back of his throat. His head spun. He needed to get back inside to help his mom, but he couldn't tear himself off the stoop. He might do more harm than good, at least until she calmed down Walter.

The door creaked open, and shouting poured through the narrow space.

Lisa closed the door and took a seat next to him, blocking out the chaos from inside. She leaned over and wrapped him in a hug. "Seeing Dad so confused might be the scariest thing I've ever seen in my life." She laid her head on his shoulder.

Dylan took a deep, shaky breath. "Me, too."

"Have you ever witnessed him get violent before?"

"I've seen him upset, but I've never seen him get physical." He sat straight and faced her. "He hit me."

"What?" She straightened, and her body went rigid.

"Right in the face. He swung his arms and yelled to get out. He's never hit me before." He rubbed at his cheekbone where the blow landed.

She tented her brows. "Has he ever hit Mom?"

His stomach twisted. "Do you think she'd tell me?" Mary's whole life was about protecting her husband, and Dylan would insist on doing something to shield her if Walter ever harmed her.

Lisa grabbed his hand and squeezed. "Dylan, something has to change. I know I don't live close so what I say might not matter, but Mom being the only one caring for Dad isn't working."

His heart pounded. This arrangement had to work, at least for a little bit longer. "What do you mean? Everything's fine. We've done what we needed to help Dad."

She threw her hands in the air. "At what cost? Mom's a wreck. You see her all the time, so you might not notice a change. But I have. She's exhausted, she's worried sick, and she looks like she's aged ten years in the last eight months. She can't keep up the amount of energy required to take care of Dad."

"Did she tell you she can't take care of Dad?" His voice sounded raw to his own ears. He managed all their problems over the last year. Why hadn't she confided in him?

"She didn't have to. I know her, and I know she needs more help."

Dylan stood. How did Lisa think she could handle this situation? She couldn't even fix any of her own problems. "So you know her better than I do, huh? You've been around to know what she needs and how she feels about everything?"

Crimson flushed her cheeks, and she clenched her jaw tight. "Yes, you've done more than me. You're a better person than I am. I get it. But you're too close and can't see what I see. She's killing herself! This arrangement won't work for much longer, and we need a plan before things get worse."

He paced back and forth, his footsteps leaving prints in the trampled snow. "What do you think we should do? What's your big plan to fix everyone's problems?"

"We either hire help to come to the house, or we find him a nursing home. Somewhere with people who can deal with him without someone getting hurt."

Dylan snorted. "You don't think I've looked into getting help? It costs money—money we don't have. Mom and Dad have too many assets to qualify for Medicaid."

"So, we sell the farm." Lisa shrugged.

The lack of emotion in her voice boiled his blood. Glaring, he dropped his jaw then shook his head. "You've got to be kidding me. Sell the farm we've had in our family for generations? The farm Dad and I put our blood, sweat, and tears in? No, selling the farm is not an option."

Lisa narrowed her gaze. "You don't want to hear this, but it might be the only thing that makes sense. Mom told me you'll have problems paying for help once spring hits. Instead of wasting your time and money, we should sell the farm now. Mom and Dad will have plenty of money to get them the help they need, and you and I will have enough to help with whatever we want."

Dylan ran a hand through his hair and laughed. "I can't believe you. This solution is all about you getting your share of the farm—getting money you didn't earn to live the life you want." He pointed a finger at her chest. "You are the most selfish person I've ever met. How do you always put yourself ahead of everyone else? Your behavior is disgusting."

Betrayal burned through his veins. Stomping to his truck without sparing her one more second, he grabbed his phone. He sent a text to Jonah and Conner. Hopefully, they could meet him uptown at the bar.

Chapter Five

Meg sat with her feet tucked beneath her on the living room floor and studied the cards lined in front of her. Somehow, Sophie found more matches in their fifth game of Memory, and Meg couldn't figure out how she kept winning. "Are you cheating?" She dipped her chin in Sophie's direction and firmed her lips into a straight line.

A wide grin took over Sophie's face, and she shook her head, sending her blonde curls swinging in all directions.

Emma laughed and shifted on the sofa with Anderson nuzzled in her arms. "You should know Sophie can't be trusted. Why do you think I suggested you play with her while I feed the baby?"

Meg leaned forward and studied the now-serious set of Sophie's pink lips and the innocence in her blue eyes. Her crossed arms wrinkled the pink-and-purple princess dress Jonah bought her for Christmas. If she was lying, the government should use her to gain secrets from their enemies. No one could resist her face. "Are you sure?"

Sophie kept her gaze locked on Meg and lifted her shoulders. "I'm smart."

"Yeah, right." Meg threw down the single card in her hand. "You've got Sheffield blood in you. Of course you cheated."

A giggle erupted from Sophie's mouth, and she flung herself into Meg's arms. "You're funny, Meg-Meg. Sleep with me tonight?"

The sweet way in which Sophie pronounced her words made Meg's heart melt like a gooey marshmallow. She glanced at Emma, who only shrugged and kept her gaze fixed on Anderson. "I don't have any more clothes with me, baby girl."

Sophie placed her hands on either side of Meg's face. "Go get some."

A bark of laughter huffed from Meg's mouth. She couldn't argue with the girl's logic. "Okay. I'll run home and grab what I need, and then I'll come right back."

Sophie nodded, kissed Meg's forehead, and jumped up. "I'm gonna find Sam."

She ran out of the room with her little legs pumping like a speeding cartoon character. Meg shook her head and scrambled to her feet. "I can't say no to her."

Emma snorted. "Not many people can."

Jonah stepped into the room, holding his phone. "Where's Sam?" He glanced around the living room.

"He's in our room playing video games with Luke," Emma said. "Sophie followed him a few minutes ago, probably to coax him into playing with her instead."

"Okay, thanks. I need to take him to the bookstore for a little bit with Jillian. I just got a text from Dylan asking me to meet him at The Village Idiot. He seems kind of upset."

"Would Sam rather stay here than go to Kiddy Korner?" Emma asked, referring to the bookstore Jillian owned on the town square. "I haven't heard a sound from him in a while. It's no trouble to keep him here until you get back."

"I'm sure if video games are involved, he'd rather stay here. Thanks, Emma. I'll let him know I'm stepping out for a little bit." He gave a brief nod before turning the corner and heading upstairs.

"I'm taking off, too. I won't be gone long. Do you need anything?"

"No, thanks," Emma said.

Meg studied her sister. A peaceful smile settled on her lips as she stared down at her son. No, Emma didn't need anything. She had it all.

A dull ache squeezed Meg's heart. Her happily ever after ended before it began. She twisted the stupid engagement ring she still hadn't taken off. She needed to let go of Blake and everything she'd hoped to share with him before she could be ready for a different future. Slipping the diamond from her finger, she shoved the ring into the pocket of her jeans. The empty spot on her finger pulsed but not with need or loneliness.

It pulsed with freedom.

****

The wind slammed against Meg as she searched for her keys in her bag. She should have grabbed them before she climbed from the truck. Now her frozen fingers fumbled around the dark pit at her side. Frustration rippled through her. She didn't have a lot of the stuff most women kept in their purses. Finding her keys shouldn't be this difficult.

Finally latching on to the jagged edges of metal, she yanked free the keys and jammed the house key into the lock. She turned it, and the usually stubborn lock slid soundlessly into place.

Almost as if it hadn't moved at all.

Her hairs under the soft, wool hat stood on end. She'd lived in the century-old house a block from the town square for years. Every day she cussed and kicked about the rusty old lock never letting her inside as she wiggled the key to find the exact mechanism to push— unless the door was unlocked. She was in a hurry to leave yesterday morning, and Lord knows she had a lot on her mind.

To clear the lingering bits of unease from her mind, she shook her head. If the door was left unlocked, it was her own fault. A new gust of cold air blew over her, pushing bits of snow onto her exposed skin, and she opened the door and hurried inside the dark house.

Creaks and groans of the settling home greeted her, but something still seemed different. Meg opened the closet door and grabbed an umbrella. Better safe than sorry. Making sure to stay on the tips of her toes, she held the pointed end of the umbrella in front of her and made her way through the living room to check for anything that would make her sixth sense scream for her to leave. One shaft of sunlight beamed in through the window at the top of the front door. Curtains blocked out any other natural light that could dance inside and chase away the shadows in the room.

Meg searched in every nook and cranny, and behind the television and recliner. No monsters reared their ugly heads or armed men jumped out to take her hostage. The tension squeezing her neck muscles loosened. She took a step toward her room, and the scent of expensive cologne and cigarette smoke wafted up her nose.

She froze and swiveled her neck from side to side, darting her eyes in every direction. Blake had been here. All she needed was one whiff of the designer cologne he always doused himself in mixed with the cloud of smoke that clung to his clothes to know.

He still possessed a key. How could she be so stupid? After he took off, she never guessed he'd have the nerve to come back to Smithview at all, let alone to come into her house when she wasn't there.

Tossing the umbrella to the ground, she continued to her bedroom and flipped on the light to the chase away the darkness from her closed curtains. She took in every inch of the space, making sure nothing was taken or messed with. The smell grew stronger, and a shudder of revulsion trickled down her spine. The apprehension from earlier faded away, and fury swept in to take its place.

The unmade bed told her nothing, as she never righted her covers after she woke. What was the point? She'd just be there hours later, messing them up again. But now, they seemed tainted. She yanked on the bedspread and threw it on the floor. Next, she tackled the sheets and pillow cases, until nothing more clung to the mattress she once shared with Blake.

Meg was half-tempted to set the bed on fire to be rid of any remnants of him, but she didn't have the money to buy a new one. Instead, she scooped the soiled linens in her arms and carried them to the laundry room at the back of the house.

Now she needed to get what she'd come for. Pushing the tips of her fingers into her eye sockets, she took a breath and tried like hell to calm her quivering nerves—it didn't work.

A drink would calm her frazzled nerves. Maybe she'd stop by The Village Idiot and grab a quick beer before heading back to the inn.

On a shaking breath, she made her way back into her bedroom. A fierce howl of wind rumbled against the house, and her curtains billowed. Meg gasped and stared open-mouthed at the fluttering curtains on either side of the open window. She ran toward it, thrust her head out the window, and her gaze locked on the fresh footprints imbedded in the snow-covered ground.

She stumbled backward until her knees butted up against the edge of her bed, and she sank down on the soft mattress. Her heart thundered, and her mind raced. Not only had Blake been in her house, he was inside her bedroom while she was there.

She needed to call the police. Blake had been careful not to show a trace of where he was or what he was doing while out of town. No doubt his parents were helping. With the authorities on the hunt, he couldn't even get a job. But now, he contacted her and broke into her house in the span of two days. Maybe the cops could finally track him down and make him pay for what he'd done.

She grabbed the phone with trembling fingers, and indecision tore through her. What could she really tell the police? She smelled her ex-fiancé's cologne in her house, and she's pretty sure she hadn't forgotten to lock her house the day before?

No, a call wasn't necessary. Her frayed nerves screamed for release. She'd head to The Village Idiot to have a drink with Jonah and Dylan and stop by the police station on the way to fill them in on what happened. Overreacting or not, she needed to know the police took her concerns seriously, and maybe they could confirm she wasn't just paranoid.

But a nagging clench of muscles in her gut told her not only wasn't she paranoid, but this invasion of her personal space wasn't the last time Blake would force himself back into her life. She slid her engagement ring from her pocket. She stared at the diamond one more time before she threw it out the window and into the snow. She slammed closed the window, locking out the cold and wind and the stupid dream she was glad never came true.

****

Twenty minutes later, Meg stepped into the mostly deserted bar, and warmth hugged her close and greeted her like an old friend. She glanced around the dimly lit room for a second before she spotted her brother sitting with Dylan and their friend, Conner, each nursing his own beer. She strode over and took a seat next to her brother.

Jonah lifted his eyebrows and parted his lips. "What are you doing here?"

Meg bit back the real reason she'd stopped. Talking about Blake would only leave a bad taste in Jonah's mouth. Not like she blamed him. Blake barely knew Jonah, but their lack-of-relationship hadn't stopped Blake from setting up Jonah for arson before Blake left town.

So instead of the truth, she shrugged. "You mentioned Dylan seemed upset. I thought I'd stop by and make sure everything was all right before I headed to my sleepover with Sophie."

Dylan sat between Jonah and Conner. He hunched

over his beer and peeled away at the label on his beer bottle. He shifted his gaze to peer in her direction. His eyebrows immediately shot up, and he nodded toward her hand. "You're not wearing your ring."

Meg covered her left hand, absent-mindedly rubbing the bare finger where a diamond ring was for so long. "I threw it in the snow."

All three men stared in silence—eyes unblinking, mouths open, their opinion of her rash decision kept strictly to themselves.

"Stop it," she said. "I'm here to drink, not have the three of you act like I'm some poor little bird you're afraid to scare off."

"Sorry," they mumbled in unison.

"Hey, Sally," Jonah called to the bartender. "Bring Meg a beer, will ya? Just put it on my tab."

Sally fetched a beer and placed it in front of Meg. She lifted her blood-red lips in a smirk. "Did you really throw your ring into the snow?"

The words huffed out of her mouth on a wave of condescension. Meg stared hard at Sally and clenched together her teeth. "Yep."

Sally snorted. "You're an idiot. It's bad enough you couldn't keep your man happy, but you were stupid enough to just throw away the ring? Where did you toss it? Maybe I'll do a little digging and come out a winner."

Meg stared at the bartender as she walked away, even the not-so-subtle sway of her hips mocking her. She flung an arm in Sally's direction. "Are you freaking kidding me?" Meg asked to no one in particular.

"Don't let her rile you, Meg. Sally gets bored when she doesn't have a man chasing her around the place.

She's just livening up things," Jonah said. "Unfortunately, poor Dylan doesn't fit the bill, or she'd be content with all his good old-fashioned charm. Poor guy can't catch a break."

Glancing at Dylan, she crinkled her nose and curled her lip as a wave of disgust swirled in the pit of her stomach. Dylan could do so much better than Sally. Sally was a user, and Dylan had a heart of gold that deserved to be cherished. "You have a thing for Sally?" Dylan's narrowed gaze and clenched jaw conveyed enough heated anger to thaw all the snow in Smithview.

Conner laughed and slapped Dylan on the back. "Leave the poor guy alone. He's miserable enough without thinking about what an ugly son of a gun he is."

"You guys are ridiculous." Defensiveness stiffened Meg's tone. "If Sally doesn't fall for Dylan's charm, then she's an idiot. No one in town has Dylan's good looks and kind heart."

"Must be why the guy hasn't had a serious girlfriend in close to six years." Jonah joked. "But Conner's right. I'll lay off, bud, you've had a rough day."

"What happened?" Her earlier experience fled her brain, and she concentrated on Dylan.

Dylan didn't answer.

Conner chimed in. "Lisa wants him to sell the farm."

"What? Why would she want you to sell the farm?" Meg asked.

Dylan sighed and returned his attention to his beer bottle. "My dad's getting worse and needs more care than what my mom can give him. I've looked, and it's not cheap. Lisa thinks we should sell the farm for the needed money."

"And so she can get a nice hefty chunk of change without having to work at the farm or help take care of your dad?" Meg snorted and rolled her eyes. "Am I right?"

Dylan only shrugged before taking another sip of beer.

Meg shook her head and the tip of her braid skittered across her back. Unspoken words burned the back of her throat, but she swallowed them. "You don't have to protect her, Dylan. We've all known Lisa for a long time, and we know how she is. I can't believe what she suggested. Getting rid of the farm would break your parents' hearts…and yours. You aren't considering it, are you?"

Dylan was silent for a minute. "I don't want to. I would die if we had to sell the farm. But selling might be our only option. I can't run the farm alone, and I don't know if we can afford to hire someone to help with the planting. I need to figure out something. A solution I'm not seeing must exist or another way to fix everything."

Meg's heart shattered. The farm meant everything to Dylan. "You guys have a lot of land you don't really use. Why don't I come out and see if walking the property gets any wheels spinning? I have a ton of ideas my mom keeps shooting down. She claims we don't have the land, but she just doubts I know what I'm talking about. Maybe some of the ideas could work for you."

Dylan lifted one side of his mouth in a half-hearted smile. "Sounds like a better plan than I have at this point. Are you sure you don't mind?"

"I'd do anything for you, Dylan. You're like a brother to me."

Dylan's smile didn't falter, but something flashed in his eyes.

Was it pain over the idea of losing the farm? Or something else? Pushing the question out of her mind, she picked up her beer and took a long drink. The amber liquid slid down her throat and fought against the buzzing in her brain. Tension seeped from strained muscles, and thoughts of Blake floated from her mind.

If only all problems could disappear with a quick drink.

Chapter Six

Music blasted through the door and smacked Dylan in the face. He pushed through the crowd of people loitering in the doorway of the bar. Vibrations pulsed through his feet from the pounding bass as he searched the crowd for a familiar face. Hot damn, the place was packed. He didn't expect anything different on New Year's Eve. Anyone who wanted out of the house for the night ended up here.

For once in his life, being part of a large crowd gave him comfort. The crowd drowned out the constant roar of his thoughts. A beer waited and promised to numb his pain for a few hours. His dad was on a downward spiral since after Christmas. His mom needed help, and he still didn't have a plan. Hopefully, Meg had a trick up her sleeve.

He darted his eyes in every direction. Conner was here with his wife, but where were they sitting? His shoulders brushed against person after person as he shoved his way through the crowd and to the bar. Before he searched for his friends, he might as well get a drink.

From the corner of his eye, he spotted an empty seat at the bar next to a stunning blonde with long, lean legs. He dropped his jaw. What was Meg doing here? She stared straight ahead and pressed her lips firmly together. Both hands rested on the bar and rubbed the beer-spattered wood.

Damn, she was cute.

He shook his head and gave himself a mental slap in the face. Thinking about how good she looked in a tight sweater with her long blonde hair trailing down her back was a bad idea. "Hey there, stranger. I wasn't expecting to see you here tonight. Anyone sitting here?" He nodded toward the empty bar stool next to her.

She glanced up and released a heavy breath through her nose. "Oh my God, you have no idea how glad I am to see you right now. Please, sit your butt down and do not get up for the rest of the night."

Dylan laughed and gestured toward the stool with an extended palm.

Meg lifted her eyes to the ceiling. "Someone was there, until she stranded me after dragging me out of the house. All I wanted tonight was to curl up in bed with Nora and read a good book until I fell asleep. Preferably before midnight so I didn't have to think about how pathetic ringing in the New Year with my dog is. Instead, Allie barges over and insists I accompany her because, God forbid, she comes by herself. As soon as we sit, she spots some guy she's crushing on and abandons me. If being dumped by my friend doesn't suck enough, this place is ridiculously crowded, and I can't even get a drink."

"Aren't you a delight this evening." Dylan shouted over the blaring music. He claimed the empty seat and signaled for a drink. Sally sauntered over with her dark hair bouncing and a sultry smile on her heavily made-up face.

Meg stiffened her spine, and the muscles in her

shoulders tightened.

"Four beers, please. If you see one of us getting low, feel free to keep them coming." Dylan handed the bartender fifty dollars.

Sally quickly brought over their order.

Dylan passed Meg an ice cold beer.

"Un-freaking-believable." Meg muttered under her breath. "I thought she didn't notice you."

Dylan stilled, his senses tingling. Could she be jealous? No, she was just in a sour mood. "She usually doesn't. Tonight, however, she wants big, fat tips. Sally might not be the smartest girl in town, but she knows she'll collect those tips more from men than women. Don't take it personally." He picked up his bottle and clinked it to Meg's. "Happy New Year."

One corner of her mouth quirked up. "Thanks. Happy New Year."

"What did you do with poor Nora? Is she stuck at home by herself?"

Meg dipped her chin and lifted her brow. "You know me better than that. I took her to Jillian's. Sam's begging for a dog, and they asked to take her for a night or two to see how it'd go."

"She said she didn't want Sam to get a dog." Dylan furrowed his brow.

"She didn't. But since Jonah is moving in, she's a little more open to the idea of adopting one."

"Makes sense." He took a pull of his drink and travelled his gaze up and down her body, taking in the sight of her. The bitter ale trickled smoothly down his throat, and he tightened his hand on the bottle. Her blonde hair was tossed over her shoulder, exposing the length of her neck. He itched to touch her soft skin.

And God help him, her skirt rode high on her slim thigh. He set down his bottle and cleared his throat. "Besides getting dragged here and then dumped by your friend, how have you been? I haven't seen you much since the last time we were here."

Meg gazed into her beer. "I'm okay. I want to stay busy so I don't dwell on things, but it's harder in the winter months. Most of my riding students stop lessons in the winter because they don't want to ride in the outdoor arena. The nursery is slow, especially since the Christmas crowd is gone. I keep pestering my mom about building an indoor arena to keep more students coming this time of the year, but she insists we don't have the space. We both know space isn't an issue, but I can't convince her. So, I wander around searching for something to do with my time."

"I feel your pain." Dylan commiserated. "I have a world of trouble to figure out and no way to do it. My mind spins in the same circles. I'm wasting more time than anything, and the more time passes by the more my troubles grow."

Meg placed a hand over his and squeezed. "We'll figure out something. I promise."

He glanced at their joined hands, and heat rose to his cheeks. He didn't want to break the contact but was afraid of what he would do if he didn't. Her smooth, pale skin begged to be caressed—to be kissed. His fingertips tingled, and he moistened his lips. She was more intoxicating than the bottles of beer in front of him. He rubbed at the base of his neck. "Sucks about your mom, though. Have you talked to Jonah about any of this?"

Meg yanked back her hand and balled both hands

into fists, slapping the top of the bar. "No, and why should I? I'm the one who has been here all these years helping Mom. I didn't go off and follow my dreams, leaving our mom behind to fend for herself. I stayed in this godforsaken town while he and Emma left to live their lives and do whatever they wanted. I'm the one who helped build her businesses and who was here to make the tough choices and hold her hand when she needed someone. Why shouldn't she trust my judgment? Why should I have to talk to my big brother so he can make sure his baby sister's ideas are good?"

At her brisk tone, Dylan widened his eyes. He'd always assumed she stayed in Smithview because she wanted to, not because of obligation. "I didn't mean any insult. I know you have good ideas. I just meant sometimes having someone on your side to fight for you is nice."

She ran a hand through her hair and paused at the scalp to scrunch the long strands. "I'm sorry. I didn't mean to jump down your throat. I guess it's a touchy subject."

A comfortable silence fell between them, and he glanced around. Every seat was taken, and people stood along the walls and around tables, waiting for a place to sit. Music blared from the jukebox in the corner, and the sound of pool balls bouncing off one another broke through the shouts of the crowd. Scenes from Times Square lit up a large television behind the bar.

A tall, dark-haired waitress weaved through the crowd and delivered party hats and noise makers.

Meg grabbed two of each as they floated by and promptly placed one hat on her head and the other on Dylan's. "All right, enough of this gloomy talk. We've both had a rough couple of months, and tonight is supposed to be fun." She raised her bottle and pointed it at him. "From here on out, we drink and have a good time. Deal?"

He grabbed the noisemaker and blasted a shrill noise. "Deal."

Meg laughed and held up her hands to her ears.

The next few hours, Dylan never moved from his stool, partly because he didn't want to lose his spot and partly because he didn't want to stop spending time with Meg. His prime location at the bar allowed him to talk with friends who saddled up to grab a drink, but his gaze didn't venture far from Meg. He loved watching her—how she interacted with friends, how she laughed with her entire body when she found something really funny, or how she smiled with a wicked gleam in her eye when something happened only the two of them found amusing. She never ceased to amaze him nor did she bore him. Her mind was a wonderful maze, and he stayed on his toes to keep up.

"I'll be right back. Don't let anyone take my seat." Meg shouted above the increasing noise. "I want to use the bathroom before midnight."

Dylan glanced at his watch. "You better hurry. You don't have much time."

Meg nodded and hurried off.

He sat alone for a brief minute. Spending time with Meg was what he needed. She made him forget his troubles and brought him out of his shell...and her laugh. Damn, he could listen to her laugh for the rest of his life.

"Ten, nine, eight..."

He searched for Meg, but she was nowhere in

sight. She must have gotten caught in a line. He braced himself to start another new year alone.

As the shouts got louder and the numbers lower, an arm wrapped around his neck. He twisted. Meg stood behind him with a wide grin, counting down with the rest of the crowd.

"Three, two, one." He grinned and shouted with his gaze locked on Meg.

A small smile curved on her lips, and her brows drew together as she stared into his eyes.

He'd never seen bluer eyes in his life. They were the color of a clear day in the summer sky. His heart constricted in his chest, and he glanced at her parted lips.

Meg leaned forward and kissed him.

The shock of her warm lips on his turned his mind blank. He wrapped his arms around her waist and lifted her against him. Finally, Meg was in his arms. Desire built in his chest and coiled deep into his heart. He moved his mouth against her, savoring her taste and inhaling her scent.

She moaned against his mouth.

Lust shot through his body.

Her arms circled his neck, and her mouth opened.

He welcomed the warmth of her tongue. He tasted the beer on her breath as it swirled inside him. She clung as if he were the answers to all her prayers. His body engulfed hers, and she molded against him. Dylan's heart pounded wildly in his chest.

Pulling away, she gasped. Her gaze flew up to meet his, and she touched her swollen lips.

The pounding in his chest slowed, and he held his breath.

Meg rounded her eyes, then backed out of his grasp.

He reached for her. *Please, don't overthink this.* Even if the kiss meant the world to him, he didn't want Meg to find out how deep his feelings ran. "Meg."

She swiveled and fled. As she shouldered her way through the crowd her hair fanned behind her, and she fled through the door.

"Shoot." Closing his eyes, he rubbed his temples. He'd taken the friendly kiss too far and needed to explain. Grabbing the purse and jacket she'd left behind, he shoved through the sickeningly excited crowd and followed her out the door.

Meg stood on the sidewalk with the lights from the nearby lamp streaming down on her—eyes closed and arms wrapped around her middle.

Relief loosened the tension in his gut. He jogged to her and placed her jacket over her shoulders.

Meg covered his hands with hers and stared with wide eyes.

Her gaze held his, her eyes moving as if searching for answers. "I'm so sorry, Meg," he whispered.

"Are you really?" she asked.

Dylan shifted his feet, and fear spiked in his gut. A war between confessing everything and keeping his mouth shut battled.

"Please look at me, Dylan."

Her hair thrashed around her face, and the snow fell lightly around her body. He couldn't help himself. He cupped her cold cheek in a hand. "Meg."

Narrowing her gaze, she placed her hands over his. "Are you really sorry you kissed me?"

Emotion clogged his throat and made speaking

impossible, so instead he leaned down and rested his forehead against hers. Unable to resist, he brushed his lips across hers—his hands still framing her small face. Before he lost control again, he lifted his lips to her forehead, then broke away. Without another word, he left her standing in the snow. As darkness enveloped him, heaviness settled into his chest. What had he done?

Chapter Seven

Snow fell and dusted Meg's heated face with tiny white flakes. She stared into the empty night until the cold stole the feeling from her fingers and numbness crept into her nose. Shock engulfed her the moment her lips first touched Dylan's. She needed to snap out of her stupor and go home. Go home to an empty house without even her dog to keep her company.

Whatever…being alone never bothered her. She didn't want to talk to anyone right now anyway. She wanted to wrap her mind around what happened with Dylan. With hands buried in her pockets, she squared her shoulders against the wind and headed home.

Memories of her last moments with Dylan played on repeat in her head, and she tossed and turned in her bed. The change happened so suddenly. What caused him to take their simple kiss to a whole other level?

Not that she was upset about how he'd wrapped his arms around her and moved his mouth against hers. Was she?

He was one of her best friends, and her engagement had barely ended. Maybe their kiss didn't mean anything. Maybe he was just as shaken as she was. If he wasn't, why had he left her alone without a second glance after he'd shaken the ground beneath her feet? Why were men so frustrating?

Her mind spun with every crunch of her boots

against the fresh snow lining the sidewalk. Entering her empty house, she kicked off her shoes and switch into pajamas. She burrowed under her soft, down blanket.

Questions bounced back and forth in her mind until she couldn't take it any longer. Meg pushed back the covers and paced. The soft carpet cushioned her bare feet, but she grabbed a robe to fight off the chill seeping through the old window. The longer she paced, the more questions popped into her mind. She grabbed her phone from her nightstand and called Emma.

"Hello? Meg? Is everything all right?"

Emma's voice was heavy with sleep, but Meg couldn't bring herself to feel bad for waking her. "I kissed Dylan."

"What?" Emma hissed through the phone.

Meg glanced at her alarm clock. Twelve fifty a.m. Guilt nagged at the back of her brain. "Were you asleep?"

"Of course, I was asleep. Give me a second."

Rustling bedsheets and soft mumbles came through the speaker.

"Now, start over. You kissed Dylan? Our Dylan?"

"Yes, our Dylan. What other Dylan do we know?" Meg snapped.

"I didn't know you guys hung out tonight. I thought you stayed in."

Meg sighed. "Allie dragged me to The Village Idiot. Long story short, she dumped me when we got there. Dylan showed up, and we hung out the rest of the night. When the clock hit midnight, I leaned forward to give him a little kiss. Then something just kind of happened." Memories of her heated cheeks and the bursts of excitement when Dylan's lips brushed against hers invaded her mind. She twirled a piece of hair between her fingers and continued to pace.

"What do you mean something kind of happened? I bet you freaked him out," Emma said.

"He was definitely freaked out, and so was I. But not for the reason you think, at least I don't think so."

"Wait, what? You're not making any sense."

"None of this makes sense." Meg took a deep breath and replayed the events of the past hour.

"Well, when he pulled you close and really laid one on you, did you like it?"

Meg closed her eyes and rested a hand on her chest. She pictured Dylan's face, and the beat of her heart raced under her hand. Heat consumed her body, and desire pulsed deep within her as memories of his hands on her skin ran through her mind. She opened her eyes and cleared her throat. "Honestly, the kiss was the most intense, amazing, wonderful kiss I've ever had in my life."

"Holy moly," Emma said. "You and Dylan, who would have imagined?"

"Me and Dylan is not a thing." Frustration rose Meg's voice. "For all I know, he got caught up in the moment, and things just got a little out of hand. He might be kicking himself for kissing his best friend's little sister and wondering how to get out of this situation without hurting my feelings."

"Would your feelings be hurt if the kiss didn't mean anything to him?"

Meg sat on the edge of her bed. "I don't know. If you told me a few hours ago I'd kiss Dylan, I'd say you're crazy. If you told me his kiss would rock my world and have me thinking about Dylan completely differently, I'd laugh in your face." She pinched the bridge of her nose. "I'm so confused."

"Sounds like you need to talk to Dylan. He's pretty much a part of the family, and you guys can't just let your kiss go without discussing it. You don't want to ruin your friendship."

Meg heaved a deep sigh, and resignation settled in. "You're right. I need to sleep, then get ahold of him tomorrow. Thanks, Emma. Goodnight, and happy New Year."

"Same to you. Keep me posted. I love you."

Meg disconnected the call and crawled back under her covers. Emma was right…her friendship with Dylan was too important to sweep what happened under the rug. She needed to talk to him as soon as possible. As she drifted off to sleep, she tried to turn off her brain and not obsess about the implications of what happened tonight.

Instead, she closed her eyes and pictured his face and the fire that sparked in his green eyes as he stared down into hers just before he kissed her. She finally fell asleep with a smile on her face and the taste of his lips still on her tongue.

Thunk!

A sudden noise invaded her dreams, and Meg bolted upright. She wiped the sleep from her eyes and glanced over to check the time. Wow, thank God she'd asked her mom to take care of the horses. She hadn't slept this late in years. The sound that ripped her out of her sleep disappeared, and she laid her head back on her pillow.

Forceful footsteps stomped across the floor.

Alarm sparked through her. She reached for Nora,

only to find her spot at the foot of the bed empty. Nora was still at Jillian's.

"Meg! Where are you? I know you're here."

Fury filled Blake's voice as he stormed through the house. What in the world was he doing here? How dare he barge into her home! She wrapped herself in her robe and grabbed the phone from the nightstand. This time, she would call the police, and they could finally drag him to jail.

The heavy *thud* of footsteps continued, and Meg ran from her room just as Blake stepped out of the kitchen. Grease spiked his sandy blond hair as though it hadn't been washed in weeks, and dark circles hung low under his blood-shot brown eyes. "What do you think you're doing?" she demanded. "You can't just come into my house any time you want."

"I don't think you need to worry about what I'm doing." He stepped toward her. "You're the one running around town and hanging all over anyone who'll have you."

Indignation surged through her. "Excuse me? What are you talking about?"

"You know exactly what I'm talking about." He pointed a finger at her chest. "Everyone in town is talking about what you did last night. The way you and Dylan Gilbert were all over each other. Are you serious? I haven't even been gone long."

Her nostrils flared, and she planted her feet firmly beneath her. As anger poured through her veins, heat flushed through her body. "How dare you break into my home and talk to me like this? What I do with my time is no longer your concern. Or did you forget the reason we aren't together is because you set up my brother for arson, and then ran away when the truth was discovered? What happened to owning up to your mistakes? Worry about your own problems. What I do is none of your business."

Blake sneered and lifted his chin. "You're right. What you do isn't my business. How long were you sleeping with him before we ended things?"

His insult slammed into her chest. "I would never cheat on you. Even if you did deserve it. And do not talk about Dylan like that. He's ten times the man you will ever be." Steam all but billowed from Blake's ears, and Meg shook her head. He wasn't worth her time or energy. She lifted the phone and swiped a finger across the locked screen. She'd let the police deal with him. The time was finally here for Blake to pay for what he'd done.

Blake raised his hand and slapped her hard across the face.

The phone fell to the ground, and Meg covered her throbbing mouth with a hand. Shock rooted her to the ground. Pain seared its heat across her face.

Blake shook and curled his lip.

Meg balled her fists at her side and straightened her spine. She could defend herself. Having an older brother who spent twelve years in the Marines taught her a thing or two about fighting. She pulled back her fist and slammed it into his face.

Shock glazed Blake's eyes. Not giving him a chance to react, she swung back her leg and kicked him in the groin.

Groaning, he dropped to his knees.

She curled her fingers into a tight fist and connected it with his nose. A sickening crunch sounded.

Pain shot through her wrist.

He fell to the floor.

Her chest heaved in and out. Five years she'd given him, and for what? For him to treat her like dirt, disappear without a trace, then break into her home and hit her? A warlike cry erupted from her mouth, and her blood boiled. She threw herself on top of him.

Blake covered his face and thrashed around, trying to knock her off.

Strong arms locked around her stomach and lifted her into the air.

"Let me go!" She kicked her legs and threw around her weight.

"Meg, it's me. It's Dylan. Calm down."

She lunged forward, straining against his arms to get at Blake again.

"Get her off me. She's crazy," Blake yelled from his curled-up position on the floor.

"I'm crazy?" she shouted, swinging her arms. "I defend myself after you hit me, and I'm the crazy one?"

Dylan grabbed her shoulders and turned her to face him.

The iron-like scent of blood wafted up her nose. All the color drained from his face.

A low growl snarled from Dylan's clenched mouth. He stepped around her and landed one punch squarely on Blake's jaw.

Blake's head lolled back onto the floor, and his eyes closed.

Relief stole Meg's temper. She sank to her knees, and tears burned behind her eyes. "I'm sorry, Dylan. I'm sorry you saw that."

"Are you okay?"

"I'm fine, it's no big deal."

"Meg, it's me." He placed a hand on her shoulder. "You don't have to be tough."

The gentleness of his voice broke her. He was right, for this one moment she could let down her guard and stop pretending everything was okay. She didn't have to be the one who kept everything together or the one who was always there to lend a hand. She could just be Meg, a woman in pain who needed someone to hold her. She glanced at him through her tears. "Please, just get me out of here."

He bent down, scooped her into his arms, and carried her to his truck. He climbed in beside her and pulled out his phone. "Give me a second. I have to make a call before we leave."

She nodded and leaned her injured cheek against the cool window with her eyes closed. Dylan's hardened whisper broke through the silence.

"Hey, Conner, I need you to do me a big favor. Call the police. Blake's at Meg's house. I'm sure the cops have a lot to talk to him about. Then I need you to change her locks. Bring the keys to my place, and I'll make sure she gets them."

How had she forgotten to change the locks after Blake left town? Add one more bad decision made in her relationship.

"I'll explain later. Just make sure it's done."

The truck lurched forward. She didn't know where he was taking her, and she didn't care. Her head jostled as he drove along, and her lip throbbed. When the truck slowed to a stop, she peered out the window. The peeled, white paint of Dylan's farm house filled her view. She lifted her head from the smooth glass.

He placed a hand on her arm. "Don't move."

Meg had no energy left. She leaned back against the seat, her gaze following him as he got out of the truck and hurried to her door.

He gathered her in his arms.

Grateful he was in charge, she laid her head on his chest. The scent of hay and a little bit of sweat filled her nostrils and calmed her nerves.

Betsy's barks greeted them inside. Dylan shushed the dog, laid Meg on the couch, then stood beside her.

Needing the contact, Meg grabbed his arm and pulled him close again.

He knelt in front of her and brushed hair away from her eyes.

Betsy whined beside them and placed her head on Meg's lap.

"I need to get a wet washcloth to clean your lip."

Meg groaned. "Do you have to? It's gonna hurt." Anger still dilated Dylan's pupils, but a patient smile played on his lips.

"Yes, I have to. I'll be right back. Betsy, stay with Meg."

Meg sat up on the couch and huddled in the corner with knees to her chest. She walked up her fingers to touch her lip, and she winced. Betsy's soft head and sad eyes stayed glued to her side.

Dylan sat beside her.

She reached for the washcloth in his hand. "I can do it, Dylan"

"Just relax. I've got this."

The cold, wet cloth touched her lip, and pain shot down to her toes. To keep from crying, she bit the inside of her mouth.

"I'm almost done. I need to clean off a little more dried blood."

She didn't say a word as he tended her. The pain faded, and a different heat crept inside her. Each gentle caress brought an urge to touch him. She twitched her fingers at her side and her knuckles ached. Her gaze never left his face.

He put down the washcloth and placed a thumb on the corner of her mouth.

Pain ran along her skin. She inhaled sharply and swiped her tongue over her dry lips. "Ouch."

Dylan dropped his hand to his side. "Sorry, I didn't mean to hurt you."

"No, it was me. You didn't hurt me at all." Her body yearned for his touch again. She dropped her gaze to her hands. "Will you sit with me? I'm not ready to talk about what happened, except to say thank you."

"Of course." He put an arm around her and held her close.

She snuggled the top of her head under his chin, and his heart pounded rapidly against her ear. Was his heart beating so quickly from his earlier rage, or because they were sitting so close together? They might not have talked about their kiss last night, but her reaction to his tenderness today gave her all the answers she needed. Relaxing, she concentrated on the steady rhythm of his heartbeat and the warm feelings building inside and not the turmoil Blake's reappearance jumpstarted in her gut.

Chapter Eight

Meg's head rested on Dylan's shoulder. He'd tucked his arm beneath her, and her weight cut off the blood circulation to his limb. She'd fallen asleep shortly after he agreed to hold her. Soon, the needle-like pinpricks of numbness would stab his flesh. He ran fingers through her thick golden hair but kept his gaze fixed on her slumbering face. He didn't see her like this often, without tension and worry etched on the smooth planes of her skin.

As he watched her sleep, the pulsing rage slipped from his body. A mixture of longing and guilt settled in his gut. When he returned from the Marines after serving his four years, he promised Jonah he would watch after her. Jonah had stayed on, and Dylan took his responsibility of looking after Jonah's mother and sister seriously.

She had still been a girl then. Without a father or brother to look after her, it had fallen on Dylan to make sure she was okay. But as she grew older and they became closer friends, his tender feelings of friendship slowly turned into something new—something forbidden. Feelings of longing and—God forbid—lust, for the woman who now lay in his arms. Laid there so vulnerable and so beaten down by what life had thrown at her. Not just with Blake, but everything she heaped on her fragile shoulders to help her family. He was all too aware of what being the only one around to help cost.

Insistent banging thudded against the front door.

Betsy growled at his feet.

Heavy footsteps pounded down the hallway.

He placed a firm hand on the dog to quiet her. At the sound, Meg trembled, and he hurried to find out what was going on before all the commotion woke her. He wrapped a blanket around her, gave Betsy the signal to stay, and hurried toward the door.

"Dylan, Meg! Where the hell are you?"

Jonah. He huffed out a puff of breath. "Keep your voice down, man. What's wrong with you? Barging in here and yelling."

"What's wrong with me?" Lines creased Jonah's forehead, and he ran his hands through his hair. "Why did I get a call from Conner telling me you almost killed Blake then asked him to take care of Meg's locks? What did he do to my sister? And why did she call you? Where is she?" Jonah sidled around him.

Dylan placed a hand on his shoulder and locked gazes. "Meg's here, but she's sleeping. Leave her alone, man. She needs rest. Come into the kitchen, and I'll explain." Without waiting for Jonah's response, he walked to the kitchen. The heat of Jonah's scowl singed his back as he followed. Dylan grabbed two beers from the fridge and took a seat at the table.

Jonah eyed him and settled in across from him. He took a long pull from the bottle, and then placed it back on the table. "What's going on?"

Dylan heaved a heavy sigh. "I stopped by Meg's earlier. When I got there, I heard shouting so I let myself in. I walked into a…" While he searched for the right words, he rubbed his mouth. "A disagreement. The way he insulted her made me mad, so I hit him. Consider me slamming my fist into his jaw finally get a little justice for what he did to my barn." He shrugged, leaned back in his chair, and lifted the bottle to his lips.

"You didn't like how he talked to her, so you hit him? Are you kidding me? Conner said Blake was still unconscious when he got there. He almost called 911. And because of a disagreement?" Jonah rubbed the back of his neck and pinched together his face.

"What can I say? The guy is as big of a pansy as he is a jerk."

"I want to knock out the guy as much as you do, but something else is going on. You could have just called the police, and they would have hauled him to jail." Jonah folded his arms across his chest. "I don't buy it. I want to talk to Meg." He pushed back his chair and stood.

Dylan reached across the table, grabbed his arm, and yanked him back down. "She needs to rest."

"What the heck, man?" Jonah gripped the table with both hands and shook his head. "Why won't you tell me what happened? You know I can't stand Blake. And I know you wouldn't have knocked him out if he hadn't done something pretty bad to my sister. Who do you think you are? You have no right to keep this from me."

Dylan sat still in his seat and peeled back the label of his bottle. The truth churned in his stomach. If any chance existed of getting him out of the house and leaving Meg alone, he had to tell Jonah. "I'm in love with her."

"What?" Jonah exploded from his seat with hands

balled into fists at his side. "You've got to be kidding me. She's hardly more than a kid, and you're my best friend." He paced back and forth, running his hands through his hair.

Dylan waited a beat and gave Jonah a little time to digest the bomb he'd just dropped. "Listen, man. I never meant to fall in love with Meg. My feelings just kind of happened. She and I have spent a lot of time together over the years, and she's amazing."

Jonah pressed together his lips and narrowed his eyes into slits. "You don't think I know she's amazing?"

Dylan winced. This conversation wasn't going well. "You haven't been around for a while, dude. She does a lot for your mom. More than she'd ever tell you or Emma, and I admire the hell out of her. I won't tell you what happened this morning because I respect her enough not to tell her story. I told you my part, and she will tell you hers if she wants. But no matter what, I'd do anything to protect her. For a long time, just being a good friend was enough. But things have changed. I respect her enough to let her make her own decisions. Hopefully, if nothing else, I will at least win her trust."

"Her trust?" Jonah sneered. "That's all you want from my baby sister?"

Dylan flinched. He wanted a lot more, but he wouldn't talk to Jonah about his intentions. "Honestly, I'll take whatever I can get."

Jonah's eyes widened, and his mouth hung open. "I can't listen to you talk about Meg like this." He stormed out the backdoor and slammed it hard behind him.

"Well damn," Dylan said aloud to the empty room. "That didn't go the way I'd hoped." He finished his beer and strolled into the living room. A tiny movement on the couch caught his attention. Leaning over, he let his gaze roam over Meg. Her eyes remained closed and her breathing even, and Betsy now curled in a ball at her feet. She was still asleep, thank God. The last thing she needed was to be disturbed by his argument with Jonah. He tugged the blanket under her chin, and then sank into the old, ratty recliner beside the couch. A magazine on the end table grabbed his attention, and he settled in to wait for her to wake.

After he finished flipping through the pages, he put down his magazine. He glanced over and caught Meg's wide blue eyes locked on him. A pink tinge painted her cheeks.

She tucked her bottom lip between her teeth.

"Are you okay?" Alarm ripped through him. "Your face has a weird look. Are you in pain?" Her pink cheeks deepened to crimson.

As she pushed her hair from her face, her hand trembled. "I'm good. What time is it?"

"It's close to five o'clock." Dylan studied her, not completely trusting her words.

She bolted upright, and the blanket fell to the floor. "What? How can it be so late? I've slept most of the day."

"You must have needed it. Are you hungry?"

Meg laid a hand on her stomach and winced. "Starving, actually. I haven't eaten all day."

"Good. I ordered pizza a few minutes ago. It should be here shortly."

"Pizza sounds amazing." She leaned forward to pick up the blanket and placed it on the couch beside her. "Do you mind if I take a shower? I feel kind of gross."

Dylan swallowed hard. His palms dampened, and his heart thumped against his ribcage. "Not at all Everything you need is in the bathroom in my room."

Meg jumped up. "Great, thanks. I won't be long."

Dylan let out a long, shaky breath. She wasn't the only one who needed a shower. He would need a cold one to put out the fire raging inside him. Flipping on the TV, he tried to lose himself in whatever trash happened to be on.

The doorbell rang.

He got to his feet to pay the delivery man. Grabbing the pizza, he closed the door and turned.

Meg stood on the stairs wearing nothing but a towel.

He staggered back and clenched the pizza box to keep it from falling. She'd brushed back her wet hair from her face, making her wide, blue eyes stand out as she twirled a finger around the top of her towel. Long, lean legs poked out from beneath the towel, one foot rubbing across the top of the other.

"Sorry, I called, but you never answered. Do you have anything I could put on? I don't want to wear my dirty clothes."

"Uh, yeah. No problem." Dylan snapped shut his mouth and hurried up the stairs, taking the pizza. Keeping his gaze on the floor, he squeezed by her on the stairs, then headed to his room. Betsy bounded behind him, no doubt following the smell of marinara sauce and pepperoni. He set down the pizza box and bounced his gaze between his dresser and the doorway.

Meg followed and leaned against the doorframe, watching him rummage through his dresser drawers.

Betsy sat beside her and thumped her thick tail against the floor.

He straightened with a large T-shirt in one hand and a pair of shorts in the other. "Do you want to try on a pair of gym shorts? They'll be huge on you, but you could roll them at the waist a few times."

Shifting her gaze from the clothes to his face, she tucked in the corners of her mouth. She stepped in the room and grabbed the shirt. "I'll put this on. The shirt will fit like a nightgown, so I don't think I'll even bother with the shorts. They'd just be an annoyance."

He swallowed, and his Adam's apple strained against his throat. She would be in his house with no pants? How the hell was he supposed to keep his hands off her?

She walked back into the bathroom to put on the shirt and glanced over her shoulder. "Why don't we just eat in here? You already have the pizza."

He tented his brows. "You want to eat in here? In my bedroom?"

"Why not?" she asked. "Go grab us some drinks, and I'll be ready to eat when you get back."

He lured Betsy downstairs with the promise of a pepperoni and grabbed two sodas and some napkins. He walked back in his room, and his breath caught in his throat.

Meg sat cross-legged on his bed. Her feet were bare, and the shirt she wore sat high on her thighs.

She'd gathered wet stands of hair into a messy bun on the top of her head. No make-up marred her face or hid her red-rimmed eyes, and her fat lip had started scabbing over. She had never looked more beautiful. "Is cola okay?" He took a seat opposite her on the bed.

"Yep, perfect."

Dylan picked up a slice of pizza and took a huge bite. The marinara sauce hit his tongue, and his stomach grumbled. He hadn't eaten all day, and the gooey cheese tasted better than a juicy steak.

Halfway through her first slice, Meg placed her pizza on a napkin. "Thank you, again. I don't know what would have happened this morning if you hadn't shown up."

Dylan shrugged. "You had things under control when I got there."

"I went a little crazy."

"He deserved a lot worse than what you gave him." Dylan stared down at his pizza, and the grease battled against the anger evoked by discussing Blake. "Has he ever hit you before, or was this time the first?"

Meg shook her head. "We fought a lot the last year, and his temper came out, but Nora was always there. Blake's not stupid. Nora would take off his hand if he ever tried something in front of her."

He lifted the corners of his mouth. "Even I wouldn't want to go up against your dog. I still can't believe Blake would risk getting caught by breaking into your house and starting a fight. What was the point?"

Meg dropped her gaze and peeled a pepperoni from her pizza. "He came over because he found out we kissed. I guess my moving on hurt his ego enough to show his face."

Irritation tightened Dylan's chest, and his stomach churned. "He hit you because of me? I'm so sorry, Meg. I didn't think about what people in town would say about our kiss. Truthfully, I didn't think at all when we kissed."

She shook her head and a hard glint sparked in her eyes. "Don't apologize, and don't you dare blame yourself for what Blake did. Blake hit me because he's a jerk, and he freaked out when I grabbed my phone. He panicked over the police being called. Add to that, he didn't like what I said about you."

Her words soothed him, and the acid in his stomach faded. "What did you say about me?"

She shrugged and tilted up her lips. "I told him you were ten times the man he would ever be."

Dylan chuckled. "If you're making a joke about how big I am, I just might be offended."

Meg laughed and slapped his arm. "Stop it."

Dylan grabbed her hand before she could pull away. He clasped her palm between both of his and studied her face. "Are you bothered people in town are talking about our kiss?"

"You know me better than that, Dylan. I've never cared about what people in this town say about me."

"No, you haven't. But this situation is different."

She sank against a pillow. "Yes, I guess it is. People talking still doesn't bother me, though. The only thing about last night that bothers me is not knowing how you feel. Before the craziness happened earlier, I ran the events over and over in my mind. I was afraid you were upset I kissed you, especially when you just walked away afterward."

He glanced at the hand he still held. He traced circles against her palm. "I won't lie, Meg, I was pretty shaken. Not by you initiating a kiss, but by how I responded. You meant to give me a simple New Year's kiss, and I completely lost control. I'm sorry if my reaction scared you."

Meg pulled her hand from his and placed it on his cheek. "The only thing that scared me was how kissing you made me feel. You've stirred up these feelings, and I can't ignore them. I don't know if I would want to, even if I could."

Excitement mounted in the pit of his stomach. He'd yearned for Meg for so long. Never had he imaged she'd return those feelings. Dylan intertwined their fingers again and placed a kiss on her palm. "We have a lot to talk about then, don't we?"

Meg smiled. "Yes, we do."

After hours of sitting in bed, talking about everything under the sun, Dylan glanced at the alarm clock on his nightstand. "I need to go to bed. I have to get up early tomorrow, and I didn't get much sleep last night." He gave Meg a sly smile. "I don't think I'll get much tonight either."

"Is it okay if I stay tonight? It's kind of late for you to drive me home, and I really don't want to be alone tonight." She nibbled her bottom lip.

"Of course, you're always welcome here. Take the bed. I'll grab a pillow and head down to the couch." Dylan cleared the empty pizza box from the bed and reached for his pillow.

Meg grabbed it away and laughed. "Don't be ridiculous. Do you even fit on the couch?"

He shrugged. "Part of me does."

Meg climbed off the bed and held the pillow against her chest. "I'll sleep on the couch. I don't want to steal your bed."

Dylan set the empty pizza box on his dresser and framed Meg's face with his hands. "I want you in here.

I'll be fine. Get some sleep, and I'll take you home in the morning." He pressed a kiss to her forehead, grabbed a pillow, and headed downstairs. It didn't matter if he slept in the big bed or crammed his body onto the couch, he wouldn't get any sleep tonight—not with Meg in his home and his future alive with possibilities he'd never dreamed could come true.

Chapter Nine

The alarm screeched into the silent morning and roused Meg from a deep sleep. Slapping a hand against the blaring clock, she shut off the annoying noise and turned her face into the pillow. The woodsy scent of Dylan's cologne wafted into her nose. A grin erupted, and butterflies danced in her stomach. How had so much changed in two days? Panic seized her heart when she'd overheard Dylan talking to Jonah yesterday. How had she been so oblivious? After their kiss, her feelings toward Dylan were more complicated than she realized, but love? She wasn't sure if she was ready to deal with such a strong emotion.

Things looked different this morning. After talking for hours, both baring their souls, she couldn't turn her back on the feelings bubbling inside her. She wanted to see where a relationship with Dylan could lead, and she had little doubt she'd end at the place she'd searched for her whole life.

Hurried footsteps pounded up the stairs.

Meg shifted to face the door. The heavy pounding shifted into creaks, and Dylan filled the doorway. Her heart flipped at his tousled hair and sleepy eyes. She glanced at the clock and groaned. "Do you always get up this early?"

Dylan chuckled and crossed the room to his dresser. "Usually. You can stay in my bed for as long as you like. I, on the other hand, have a handful of animals waiting for their breakfast and a couple cows who need milking."

Meg sat upright on the bed and let the soft down comforter pool around her hips. "Do you have to go outside right this second? Or can the animals wait a minute or two?" She tilted her head to the side and let her hair trail over her shoulder. Playing the temptress was never her strong suit, but she batted her lashes and hoped she didn't have gunk glued to the corners of her eyes.

Dylan lunged, a deep growl erupting from his throat, and he pulled her around to place her on his lap.

She squealed and wiggled against his arms. Her gaze locked on his, and the laughter stopped. His green eyes were alive with fire. Grabbing his hands from around her waist, she locked her fingers with his.

Again, she considered his face. His green eyes crinkled slightly at the corners, as if he were always smiling through his eyes. Now those eyes were sober, watching her as she studied him. She itched to touch his beard and lazily run her fingers along the strong jawline hidden under his red whiskers. She cocked her head to the side. His beard was a darker shade of red than his hair. How had she never noticed?

Never again would she look past this man who never showed her anything but kindness and compassion and been her shoulder to lean on. "Have I ever told you how much I love your beard?"

A strangled noise crept from his throat. "I don't think anyone has ever complimented my beard."

"Well, I do." She leaned forward to touch his cheek with hers, savoring the way the rough hair brushed against her smooth skin.

Dylan sucked in his breath.

She lifted her head and shifted so her face hovered just above his. "Are you okay?"

Dylan maintained eye contact. "Uh-huh."

She laughed against his neck and retraced her lips down the same path along his neck. She circled his Adam's apple, slowing kissing up his neck, on his jaw, and then to his lips. Pressing her mouth to his, she savored the taste of him—the feel of him.

He pulled away and swiped the curtain of hair from her face.

"Dylan?" Meg asked, unsure of where his mind had gone.

His smile grew wide. "I think I need a cold shower."

"What? You want to stop?" She let her jaw drop, and a stab of disappointment embedded itself in her stomach.

He glanced at the clock and shook his head. "Honey, trust me, I'm gonna need a lot more than ten minutes to do all the things I want." He gave her another kiss before jumping up and heading into the bathroom.

Emotion danced in her throat, and she sank into his bed and closed her eyes. If he hadn't stopped, she wasn't sure she had the strength to. Her pulse raced, and she wiped her sweaty palms on the blanket. His last words rang in her head. If what she just experienced was a small sample of what they might someday share together, she couldn't imagine what he'd do if he let himself go. A shiver ran up her spine.

Five minutes passed before Meg's heart slowed,

and another five for her to roll out of bed.

Dylan emerged from the bathroom with his towel slung low around his hips.

Water glimmered off his hard, chiseled muscles. She caught her bottom lip between her teeth, and let her gaze roam up and down his length.

"Knock it off, or I won't control myself." Dylan kissed her cheek, then grabbed his clothes from his dresser and retreated into the bathroom. Seconds later, he emerged prepared for the winter weather.

A bite of disappointment nipped her at seeing him covered from neck to toes. A wash of adrenaline zipped through her at the image of Dylan clad only in a towel. She pressed her hands to her tummy and fought the flutter of a thousand butterflies. "Fine. If you're playing the gentleman, go ahead and hand me a pair of your sweatpants."

Dylan drew together his brows. "Why do you want my sweatpants?"

"So I can help with your chores. It's the least I can do."

"The weather is freezing outside, Meg. Why don't you crawl back in bed and sleep until I'm done? Then we can grab some breakfast before I take you home."

"Nope. I'm not going back into bed without you." She folded her arms across her chest.

Dylan sighed. "Here you go." He handed her clothes. "You don't have to help, though."

"I know, but I really don't mind. Besides, I can take a better look at your property and see if I come up with any ideas to bring in more money." She grabbed the clothes and walked into the bathroom to change, emerging with her hands in the air. "What do you think?" The waistband of his gray sweatpants hung loose around her hips, even though she'd rolled them five times to keep them up. She hauled his sweatshirt over her head and the Ohio State hoodie gobbled her up.

"If nothing else, you'll be warm." Dylan studied her and chuckled.

"That's what matters." She lifted her chin and added a little bit of swagger to her walk as she left the room.

Once outside, he divided the chores and got to work. Meg knew her way around a barn, so Dylan didn't have to waste much time with instructions. Luckily, Blake hadn't destroyed the barn that housed the animals and most of the Gilberts' equipment. She toiled over the chores in silence, until all her tasks were complete. Meg put away the tools she'd used and made her way to the burnt-down barn her ex destroyed.

Dylan sidled up beside her and took her dirty hand in his.

"What will you do with this wreck?" she asked.

"I don't know. The insurance money won't give me enough to build what I need. I have to decide if any way exists to put something else in this spot. Now it just sits here and takes up space."

"What about an indoor riding arena?" She glanced up with her bottom lip sandwiched between her teeth.

He put his hands in his pockets and whistled through his teeth. "Didn't you want an arena at the inn?"

"I've tried to talk my mom into it for a while now, and she's not budging. She doesn't understand how much it could benefit us. She can't look past her nursery and her guests at the inn. I wish she could see we have the ability to do so much more. The inn has the potential to be a destination, not just a place for a weary traveler to stop on their way out of town."

He tilted his head to the side and glanced at her. "How?"

"People love horses. They love looking at horses, and they love riding horses. Right now, I offer riding lessons year-round. Locals who are serious about their riding continue their lessons in the cold months, but guests at the inn hardly ever want to ride when they're freezing their butts off. With access to an arena, they could ride all year." She bounced on the balls of her feet and moved her hands along with every word, excitement mounting in her chest.

Dylan leaned back on his heels. "Makes sense, but if I had the arena here, how would that affect the inn? Wouldn't that hurt your business?"

"Not necessarily. We always get calls from people who need to board their horses. We could send them here if you had the space. With inn guests, I could provide the lessons here and still get paid."

A beat passed, and Meg fought not to bite into her thumbnail. Dylan knew her too well, and the nerves running rampant in her stomach would be on full display if she caved to the temptation.

Dylan turned back to the destroyed barn. "Why would they come here just for lessons? Especially in the warmer months when they can stay at the inn?"

"Then we make them want to come here for other reasons." Enthusiasm rippled through her. Her idea could work here. If her mom didn't want to give her dreams the time of day, then she could make them work for Dylan.

"I'm not following you."

She raised a hand and gestured toward the rubble. "So, this space is just waiting to be used for something. What about the large patch of barren land on the left?"

Dylan studied the land. "We've never used this land. We couldn't get a tractor into the spot for planting, and it's on the edge of the property."

"What about growing some pumpkins? You could plant them by hand, so the tractor wouldn't be an issue."

"Pumpkins?" Dylan raised his brows.

Meg placed her fists on her hips. "Did you know no place in town sells pumpkins?"

"Why is that important?"

"Remember what I said about making the inn a destination? Well, maybe we can make your farm a destination instead."

"With horses and pumpkins?"

Meg laughed. "Just the tip of the iceberg, my friend."

"I need to sit to hear this." He grabbed Meg by the hand again and led her back into the kitchen. "How about I prepare some food, and you tell me what you've got up your sleeve."

Meg talked while Dylan cooked. The more she talked, the more excited she became. Numbers and ideas spilled out as they ate, and she continued discussing her ideas while he drove her into town and took her home. "Do you think it could work?" She held her breath and tapped a foot on the floor of his truck.

Dylan rested a forearm on the steering wheel. "I really do. Your ideas would take the farm in a different direction, but your plans sound amazing. I don't understand why your mom doesn't want to implement your suggestions."

Meg glanced out the window and watched the snow-covered fields pass by. "She thinks my ideas are silly."

He put his hand on her knee and gave it a gentle squeeze. "I don't think your ideas are silly at all. In fact, I think you're brilliant."

As she quickly wiped away the moisture from her eyes, Meg was glad he wasn't watching her. Dylan had no idea what his confidence in her meant. "Thank you."

Dylan turned onto her street and slowed. "Did you tell Jonah to bring Nora home this morning?"

"No. Why do you ask?" Meg glanced out the windshield and groaned. Jonah sat in his truck parked in her driveway with her dog. "I wonder how long he's been here."

"He didn't call you?" Dylan asked.

"I don't have my phone." Grabbing her phone after her fight with Blake had been the last thing on her mind yesterday. If she had it now, at least she might have gotten a message from Jonah about why he wanted to talk.

Dylan pulled in behind Jonah.

In an instant, Jonah was out of his truck.

Meg faced Dylan and smiled. "Let the fun begin." She climbed out of the truck.

Dylan stepped out into the snow and followed her.

"What happened to your lip?" Jonah demanded. "And where were you? Did you stay the night with Dylan?"

"Well, good morning to you, too." Meg huffed out

a humorless laugh.

"This isn't funny, Meg. I've been worried sick about you, and this friend of mine wouldn't tell me anything." He aimed narrowed eyes at Dylan.

"It wasn't up to Dylan to tell you anything," Meg shot back. "Instead of acting like a jerk, maybe you should thank your friend for taking care of me."

Jonah raised his brow. "Are you wearing Dylan's clothes?"

"Um, I'm taking off now," Dylan said. "I'll call you later, Meg."

She shot out her hand to touch his arm, ignoring Jonah's question.

He glanced back and their gazes connected. Without sparing Jonah another glance, he grabbed her and pulled her into his arms. "Good luck." His lips caressed hers before he left.

Jonah huffed and ground the tip of his boot against the frozen ground.

Meg stood for a minute and watched Dylan drive away. Her heart fluttered. When he was out of view, she pushed past her brother and made a beeline for her house. "Let my dog out of your truck before she has a stroke, will you? I can see her shaking from here."

Jonah grunted and opened the truck door for Nora, and then followed her to her front door. He held out a set of keys. "You'll need these to get in. Conner called me yesterday and told me about his call from Dylan. I told him to give me the keys. All the locks are changed."

"Thank you." She grabbed the keys.

"Will you tell me what happened?"

The softness of Jonah's voice squeezed her gut.

Sighing, Meg opened the door, and exhaustion tugged at her muscles. "Do I really have to? One glance at my lip tells you more than you want to know."

Jonah followed Meg inside. He stomped off the snow from his boots on the mat. "Can you tell me why you called Dylan for help and not me?"

"I didn't call Dylan. He showed up after Blake hit me. And luckily he did, or I'm not really sure what would've happened." Meg sat on the couch.

Nora jumped up beside her and sprawled across her lap.

Jonah stood in front of her with his hands in his jean's pockets. His gaze stayed glued to the wide-planked floor. "So, you stayed the night with him?"

"Where I spent the night is none of your business." Meg ran a hand over Nora's head and refused to give Jonah the satisfaction of raising her voice.

"How can where you stayed last night not be my business when it involves my little sister and my best friend? My best friend who has known you his entire life and is like a brother."

Meg held up a hand. "Stop right there. I will not discuss me and Dylan."

"Meg." He crouched in front of her. "Do you even know what you're doing? You and Blake just broke up. Dylan is pretty much a part of the family. You can't use him as a rebound. It's not right."

"Are you kidding me?" Meg leapt from the couch, the motion knocking Jonah to the floor. "You think I'm using Dylan to get over Blake? How dare you."

"I'm sorry. You don't know what you're jumping into. He's in love with you."

A burst of joy warmed her heart, then faded. "And

he was a fool to tell you, wasn't he?" She glared. Irritation ripped through her. "Don't you think Dylan should be the one to tell me, not you? You're his best friend in the world. How could you betray his confidence?"

Jonah rubbed a hand over his face and stood. "You're right. My place wasn't to tell you. But as much as I need to watch out for you, I need to keep an eye on him, too. He might be a big, tough guy, but he's a softie. If it's true, if he's really in love with you, you could crush him."

Pangs of resentment penetrated her heart. "I know Dylan just as well as you do, but the fact you need to say these things shows how little you know me."

"Of course I know you. You're my baby sister." He stared with round, wide eyes.

She fisted her hands on her hips. "How many times do you have to say I'm your baby sister? I'm not a kid anymore, Jonah. The fact is, you haven't really known me since I was a child, and I don't appreciate you stepping into my house and treating me like the horrible person you assume I am. Like I'm a person who would use someone who means the world to me—someone who has been around to support me when I really needed him. We both know he's been here more than you have."

Jonah placed a hand on her arm. "Listen, I know I haven't been around much the last few years, but I want to make up for lost time. I want to be here for you and get to know you as an adult. I'm struggling with looking at you and not seeing the little girl I remember."

Meg crossed her arms over her chest and lifted her

chin. "Well, you better try harder. I haven't been a little girl for a very long time. I'm an adult who has made my own decisions and lived my own life for quite a while. And as an adult, I'm asking you to respect the choices I make now and in the future. You need to let Dylan and I figure out what's best for us."

Jonah ran his hands through his hair. "I won't lie. I don't know how I feel about you and Dylan together. You two being a couple is weird. I'm not sure if I'm comfortable with it."

Meg narrowed her eyes. "Then it's a good thing I didn't ask for your permission to date him. Either figure out how to be okay with Dylan and I as a couple, or stay out of our way. We haven't decided the best path to take yet, but you need to let us choose our own direction. Now, if you'll excuse me. I need to get changed and head to Mom's. I have some horses to take care of."

She stormed into her bedroom, slammed the door behind her, and leaned against it with her eyes closed. She would not let Jonah ruin her excitement over a possible relationship with Dylan—wouldn't let him get inside her head and turn this around. The front door opened and closed. Good riddance, she didn't want to deal with him right now. If he wouldn't be supportive, he could stay away.

Chapter Ten

Dylan tightened his hands around the steering wheel. While he was in town, he might as well head over to see his parents. He wanted to talk to his mom. Lisa might be right. As much as he hated to admit it, his mom's constant care for Dad wore on her. She couldn't keep it up forever.

Dylan entered the apartment unannounced.

Mom bustled around the room, packing away the Christmas decorations.

A smile touched his lips. With all of the upheaval in his family over the last year, some things stayed the same. For as long as he could remember, his mom insisted on putting away all the decorations on January second. Without saying a word, he plucked off the star from the top of the tree and settled it in its box.

"Happy New Year. I didn't know you were stopping by today." Mary stopped tucking away ornaments, kissed his cheek, then returned to work. "Your dad's napping right now, so don't get too rowdy."

"I didn't plan a visit, but I found myself in town this morning and figured I'd come by to chat. I'll try my best not to get too crazy." Dylan couldn't hide the amusement in his voice.

"What were you doing in town so early?"

Dylan hesitated, concentrating on the ornaments he

nestled in their boxes. "I took Meg Sheffield home. She stayed at the house last night and needed a ride this morning."

Mary dipped her head and wrapped an ornament in an old paper towel. "You finally told her how you feel, huh?"

He dropped his hands from the tree, and his mouth fell open. "What do you know about my feelings toward Meg?"

"Oh please." Mary laughed. "You've been in love with her for years. You might hide your emotions from everyone else but not from your mama. So, what happened?"

Dylan told his mom the story of what transpired over the last couple of days, leaving out any details Meg might not want shared. He could trust his mom not to gossip, but Meg didn't like her business discussed. By the time he finished his story, the decorations were put away.

Mary stood at the stove flipping grilled cheese sandwiches. "You two talked all night. What did you decide?"

Dylan took a seat at the kitchen table and leaned back on the old wooden chair his parents owned since he was a kid. "We really didn't say one way or another. Our decision is more complicated than figuring out to date or not. Feelings are there, on both sides, and I don't think either of us could forget about what happened and go back to the way things were. But at the same time, other things need to be considered."

"Like what?" Mary fisted her hands on her hips.

"Like Jonah. He made it very clear he didn't like the idea of Meg and me together. Plus, Meg's engagement just ended. Now might be too soon to start a new relationship."

Mary waved the spatula in her hand. "Don't be silly. There's no perfect time to start anything. If you find someone who makes you happy, you move hell and high water to make the relationship work. The rest will work itself out."

"I hope you're right. The last couple of days showed me how much I want to be with Meg."

"You'll figure out everything." Mary set a platter of grilled cheese sandwiches on the table. She sat across from him and placed a sandwich on her plate.

"Speaking of figuring things out, Meg might have helped me with a plan to create more income at the farm." Dylan grabbed two sandwiches for his plate but waited for his mom's response before taking a bite. The salty smell of melted cheese made his mouth water.

"Oh, really?"

"She has this idea to make the farm a destination spot for families in the area. She thinks we could turn the ruined barn into a stable with an indoor arena for horseback riding. She also talked about planting pumpkins, and then creating an atmosphere for picking pumpkins and taking hayrides in the fall. She suggested getting more animals and making a petting zoo for kids to enjoy, and possibly making a small orchard for apple picking. She had a whole list of ideas. I think the space could be kind of great."

"And she came up with all of these ideas over the last two days?" Mary knitted together her brows.

Dylan shook his head and swallowed the crispy bread. "She's put a lot of time and research into her plans. She's talked to Annie about implementing some of her ideas at the inn, but Annie refuses to take her seriously."

"I'm surprised Annie wouldn't listen. For someone who used her creativity and innovation to make a living, I would think Annie would welcome new ideas for her businesses."

"Meg hasn't gone into detail, but it sounds like Annie wants to focus on what she has going on now and not expanding. When I brought up the subject, I could tell Annie's lack of interest hurt Meg. She'll tell me about it when she's ready. No need to push."

A smile touched Mary's lips. "You've always been good at that."

"At what?" He took another bite of his sandwich, and the melty cheese stretched across his tongue.

"At not pushing and letting people come to you in their own time. A special person is one who bides his time and lets people figure out things on their own."

"Not pushing isn't always a good thing." He fell silent. Had he been doing the same thing with his parents? Biding his time until his mom was forced to make the tough decisions? "How's Dad been this week? I'm sorry I haven't been around much since Christmas. I hate to admit it, but I was pretty shaken up about what happened the last time I was here."

"Admitting what happened with your father scared you isn't shameful." Mary patted Dylan's arm. "I'm scared every day. Each day, the man I've loved for so long disappears a little bit more. How quickly he's deteriorating is mind blowing."

"Has he ever hit you?" His mom rounded her eyes like a wounded animal and dropped her gaze to the table. Guilt punched him in the gut, but he had to ask.

"No, honey, he has never hit me." She paused, then lifted her gaze to meet his. "I won't lie. A few times he's gotten heated, and I wasn't sure if I could calm him. But I did, and the moment passed as quickly as it began."

"Do you still feel like you're capable of taking care of him?"

A frown tugged at Mary's lips. "What do you mean?"

"Caring for him is a lot of responsibility for one person. You have no time to do anything for yourself, and you never leave the house. You never complain, and I know you feel like it's your duty, but I don't want taking care of Dad to come at the cost of not caring for yourself." Dylan placed his mom's hand in his own. "I love you, Mom, and if we need to get help, we'll find a way."

"Thank you." Mary wiped the tears glittering in her eyes. "Every day gets a little harder, but I'm his wife. I vowed to love him and be there through sickness and in health." She shrugged and lifted her lips in a half smile. "Besides, we have enough to worry about with making sure the farm is taken care of. Financially, hiring someone else to care for your dad is too much."

He inhaled a deep breath. "Would you want me to sell the farm to afford extra help?"

Mary's mouth gaped open, and she flew from her seat, hands planted on her hips. "Dylan Michael, you can't be serious. The farm has been in our family for generations—it's in our blood! I will not hear of you selling it to help us."

"Okay, okay. Calm down." He lifted his palms then gestured toward her chair. "Trust me, I don't want to sell the farm either. What Meg is talking about could work. I just need to make sure you're on board with making some changes, and you wouldn't rather sell and use the money for other things."

Mary tilted her head to the side and narrowed her eyes to slits. "I'm surprised you would even consider selling. When you were younger, the farm was more of a nuisance. But now, I know what the land means to you. If we sold the land, your heart would break as much as mine."

"Well, the idea wasn't mine. I'm busting my butt and racking my brain to figure out how to give everyone everything they need." He glanced at his hands and fidgeted with the tablecloth. Should he tell her about Lisa? Screw it, why the hell not? She didn't deserve to be protected. "When Lisa was here, she mentioned selling the farm might be the only option."

Mary sank into her chair. She shook her head and firmed her lips. "I don't know what to do with your sister. I'd hoped she'd grow up by now, figured out what she wants out of life, and start working hard to get it. Instead, she's still searching for the easy way."

"If it helps, I do think she came from a good place when she suggested selling the farm. Mostly." He pinched together his lips.

"I'm glad you talked to me. I'll have a word with her about what needs to be done in order to keep this family heading in the right direction. And if she's really concerned, she can move back home and help a little more."

As his mom's words crashed into him, Dylan rocked back in his chair. Lisa was the favorite child. She'd always been allowed to come and go as she pleased and never pulled her weight. He didn't expect to hear disappointment from his mom when she spoke about Lisa. Relief washed over him. He wasn't the only one who wanted more from his sister.

He left his parents', and ten pounds of worry and burden dissipated. Even though thoughts of Meg plagued him. As he drove home, guilt tugged at his conscience. He didn't want to leave Meg alone to deal with Jonah, but Jonah was a stubborn pain in the butt who'd want to deal with them one on one. He'd made it clear he wasn't ready to think about them as a couple yet.

Hell, he and Meg hadn't decided if they were a couple yet. He wanted Meg to be his more than anything, but he didn't want to rush her. He yearned to pick up his phone and call her, but she had a lot of work to catch up on. He'd wait until later in the evening when she was home. Most of all, he didn't want to look needy. Three hours later, Dylan shed his thick coat by the door and trudged into the living room. He pulled his phone from his back pocket and called Meg.

"Hey, stranger." Meg greeted.

"Hi, how was your day?" He took a seat in his favorite chair and propped up his feet.

Betsy padded into the room and took her normal spot at his side.

"My day was interesting."

"Interesting is your theme lately." Dylan leaned back into the soft cushion.

"Ha! Ain't that the truth."

"So, what was interesting? Your talk with Jonah?"

"Talking with Jonah was part of it. He's got a pretty big stick up his butt when it comes to me and you, and I made it very clear he either removes the stick or pretend like it's not there."

Dylan laughed. "Please tell me you said those exact words. I can only imagine his reaction."

"I didn't use those exact words, but I think I got my point across. Either way, he wasn't happy. After he left, I headed to the barn to deal with the horses. I hid as much as I could, but word got to my mom something happened."

"Did you tell her what happened?" His heart pounded in his chest. Who all knew about Meg staying at his house?

"I didn't have to. Jonah must have called her as soon as he left and let her know. Which, of course, meant she fretted over me like I was a child, and then asked me what I planned to do about you."

"And what do you plan to do about me?" Even as every muscle in his body tensed, he kept his voice light.

"Whatever I want." Meg laughed. "I don't think I should tell my mom those plans before you and I make them. I evaded her questions as much as I possibly could, finished my work quickly, and ran home to hide until tomorrow. I'm surprised I haven't gotten a phone call from Emma yet, but I'm sure she's waiting for my call. She's usually pretty good about letting me reach out on this stuff. But I'm sure it's killing her."

"I have no doubt." He dropped a hand over the side of the chair and ran his fingers through Betsy's soft fur.

"What about you? How was the rest of your day?"

"Really good, actually. After I left your place, I visited my parents. I wanted to talk to my mom about a few things, and I talked to my dad some, as well. He had a good day, and seeing him more like himself was just what I needed."

"I'm glad. You needed to get back over there."

"Yeah, I did. I also talked a little about your ideas for the farm."

"You did? What did they say?"

Hearing her intake of breath, Dylan smiled. "Mom likes the idea. Even Dad seemed excited."

"Really?"

The doubt in her voice squeezed his chest. "When I told you that your ideas were brilliant, I wasn't just saying it to make you happy. I really meant it. I would love to talk a little more in depth and get a better understanding of how things would work. I also need to figure out the costs of getting something like this off the ground, and if I could swing it on top of hiring help when planting begins."

"Okay. Do you want to get together for dinner soon? I have a ton of notes on this stuff. You can look at everything I have. I know I don't have all the research you need, but it would be a good start."

"Any night this week works for me." The sooner the better, but he didn't want to pressure her.

"What are you doing right now?"

He relaxed against the chair and grinned. "Not a dang thing." Even if he had something else planned, he would cancel to meet Meg for dinner. Her eagerness to see him hammered his heart in his chest. They would make this work. They had to.

Chapter Eleven

A week passed, and a million questions zipped around Meg's brain. She stood in the middle of her kitchen and twirled a long strand of hair between her fingers. Each question increased the pounding in her head, and she pressed fingers into her closed eyes to alleviate the pain. She needed to talk to someone about Dylan. He had been so distant all week. Oh, he stopped by her house, and they saw each other every free second they had, but he wouldn't even touch her. She ached with desire every time he has near, and he never so much as brushed a finger over her skin.

She needed answers.

She punched in Emma's number.

"Why are men so confusing?" Meg paced from the kitchen to the living room, then back again. The path was short as she weaved between her worn furniture and into the small kitchen with only enough space to boast a two-person table.

"Sometimes I'm reminded how much I enjoy being an old, married woman." Emma chuckled.

Meg stuck her tongue at the screen, then placed it back against her ear. "Stop bragging. Not everyone's as lucky to have landed a Luke right out of the gate. Now focus."

"Okay, sorry. What's going on? After what happened last weekend, I figured Dylan had the hots for you. What's changed? Did he say something to make you feel differently?"

"He hasn't said anything." She stopped pacing and ran a hand through her hair, bunching it in her fist. A few strands slipped from the long braid she always wore when she worked.

"You're confused because a man isn't talking to you about his feelings? Oh, honey. Come on."

"I'm confused about everything. We're together every night, and all he talks about is the farm. Don't get me wrong, I'm happy he likes what I have to say and is interested in going forward with things, but I'd like to talk about more." A ping of insecurity pierced her gut. "After the first night we spent together, I thought we were on the same page. Now, I'm not so sure. He won't even touch me. He treats me the same as he did before."

"Have you talked about your feelings or what you want?"

"No, but I think I've been pretty clear about what I want."

"If there's one thing I've learned in my life, it's guys can't read your mind. Even nice, sweet, sensitive ones like Dylan. He's always been a slow mover, and I'm sure he thinks he's being respectful. If you want to pick up the pace a little bit, you need to tell him."

Meg licked her dry lips. "What if he changed his mind? What if he decided his friendship with Jonah is too important to risk, and he doesn't want to complicate his life?"

"Well, wouldn't it be nice to know for sure?"

Emma's voice got louder to compete with the wails of small children in the background. "I guess so." Meg sank onto the couch. "But instead of me asking him if he's changed his mind, I think you should come home and have dinner with us. Then he won't only talk about the farm, and you can watch how he acts."

"You can't be serious." Emma snorted. "You'd rather I drive me and my two small children all the way across the state to spy on you and Dylan than simply ask him a question?"

"Absolutely." She smiled at her outrageous request.

"You're ridiculous. However, I love you and want to help. I'll do it, but with one condition."

Meg winced. Emma had to have something up her sleeve to agree to her harebrained plan so easily. "What?"

"You bring him to Mom's, and we all have dinner. Jonah included. You two are driving me crazy. Both of you are mad about the other, and you both need to get over it."

Meg groaned. She should have known Emma would insist on getting everyone together and smoothing all the ruffled feathers. She hadn't talked to her brother since their discussion concerning Dylan at her house, and Dylan hadn't spoken to him either. Getting everyone together, sitting at one table, was probably a good idea...or a disaster waiting to happen.

She patted the couch, encouraging Nora to settle in beside her. "Fine. Dylan wants to talk to Mom anyway. He wants to make sure she won't be upset if he incorporates my ideas at his place. He wants to make sure she doesn't feel slighted. Why would she? She didn't want anything to do with them."

"That's not exactly true. I think she's just skeptical about change, and she already has a good thing going.

She doesn't want to hurt what she's worked so hard to build."

"Because my ideas would ruin her business? Thanks, Emma. Why does everyone talk about how hard she works for her business? What about everything I've done? I've worked my butt off to help her make the inn and nursery a success over the last few years, but no one remembers my contributions." She fisted her hand in Nora's fur.

"I think," Emma began slowly, "it's just a different way of looking at things. Mom took a risk when she made our home an inn, and another one when she opened the nursery. She's worked hard, with you at her side, to make them into a success. She's at the age now where she doesn't know if she wants to take any more chances. She's comfortable with where things are, and if she tried something new and it didn't work, the failure could be really scary for her future. You're young and an age where you should be taking risks and be willing to maybe make a mistake. You can't look at this like Mom doesn't believe in you."

Meg sighed, releasing the anger building inside her, and leaned back against the couch. She didn't want to fight with Emma. "Not taking it personally is hard, but I'm not concerned with Mom right now. I'm concerned with you coming here and offering me your infinite wisdom."

Emma laughed. "We have some things going on the next couple of nights. I'll talk to Luke and plan on driving home on Wednesday. We could have dinner Thursday night, and then maybe you and I can do some wedding stuff with Jillian."

Emma couldn't see her roll her eyes, but Meg did it

anyway. "I didn't know we were doing wedding stuff with Jillian."

"She hasn't talked to you about it, but we've discussed some things. I think helping her pick a dress would be fun. She doesn't have any sisters. We need to do this for her, so suck it up and deal."

"You said you only had one condition."

"Helping Jillian isn't a condition, more like a strong recommendation."

"You always have a way of getting what you want." Meg laughed and shook her head. "Dinner Thursday, and wedding stuff whenever you force me to go."

"Deal. I have to go. Sophie's giving her dad a hard time about taking a bath."

"Okay, go save your husband. Text me later when you know your plan. I love you."

"Love you, too"

"And, Emma, thank you."

"No problem. Bye."

Emma would help dissect her problem with Dylan, but now she had something else to dread. A family dinner filled with tension followed by wedding dress shopping.

****

Two days later, Dylan showed up at Meg's house to take her to her mom's, and her heart almost beat out of her chest. He looked so good with jeans that showcased his long legs and a moss green sweater. A lazy smile spread across his wide mouth when she stepped onto her front stoop. She gave him a little wave then locked her door.

From behind, Dylan wrapped his arms around her

and leaned down to nuzzle her neck.

She bit her lip to strangle the groan in her throat.

"I've missed you."

His breath was hot on her neck. She wiggled around to face him and offered him a weak smile. "I missed you, too." She lifted on her tiptoes to brush her lips against his, expecting the same friendly greetings she received all week. Instead, Dylan swept her up into the warmth of his body and hungrily devoured her. Desire roared in her head, and lust churned in the pit of her stomach. "Wow, you really did miss me," she teased.

"You have no idea." He placed his hand on the small of her back and led her to his truck, opening her door.

She hopped up and put on her seatbelt. Maybe she didn't need her sister's input, after all. Snow rose in rounded mounds on both sides of the street.

"Where's Nora?" He stared out the windshield, his gaze never wavering from the road. "Is she staying home tonight?"

"She's already at the inn. Sophie never wants Nora to leave her side when they're home, so I left her there when I was done working."

"I'm surprised to hear Emma and the kids are back already. A month hasn't passed since she was here for Christmas."

"Close to a month. She mentioned something about wedding dress shopping with Jillian on Saturday."

"I know you were a little upset when they got engaged. Are you still having a hard time?" He spared her a quick glance before looking back at the road. Then he tightened his grip on the steering wheel.

She bit the inside of her cheek to keep from smiling. "No, not at all. My being upset had nothing to do with not wanting Jonah and Jillian to be happy. I was upset that right when I gave up my happily ever after, they found theirs. Now I realize I didn't lose anything, I was just looking in the wrong place for happiness."

"And what about now?"

"I didn't have to look very far. Happiness snuck up on me."

Dylan squeezed her hand.

She laced her fingers through his, and her nerve endings tingled.

He pulled into the driveway at the inn.

Meg sneaked a peek at Dylan. "Are you nervous about having dinner with everyone?"

"Not at all. Should I be?" He tented his eyebrows.

"I don't think so. My family probably loves you more than they do me." She laughed, even if the truth of her words stung.

"No way. You're a lot easier on the eyes." He winked and then rounded the truck to help her down.

The front door burst open, and Sophie ran out faster than a streak of lightning. She hurled herself into Meg's arms.

"Sophia Marie, do not go outside. It's freezing!" Emma stood on the porch with her arms wrapped around herself.

Meg laughed and hugged Sophie tight. "You little booger. You'll get us both in trouble. Let's get inside."

"Hey, little lady." Dylan followed them inside. "How's my favorite girl?"

"Good. How's Big D?"

Hearing Dylan's long-time nickname coming from such a tiny person was too much for Meg to handle. Laughter bubbled from her mouth so hard she had to put down Sophie. "When did you start calling Dylan Big D?"

Sophie grinned. "Today. Mommy wants to see Big D's new side."

Meg was glad her face had been bitten by the harsh coldness outside so no one could see the heat flooding her face. Sophie was way too smart for her age.

Dylan raised one brow and smirked. "Do you know what she's talking about?"

"Not a clue." Meg hurried by Dylan, pulling along Sophie, and found the rest of her family sitting in the living room. She gave both her sister and mom a kiss on the cheek, smiled warmly at Jillian and Sam, and then nodded at Jonah with her lips pressed in a thin line.

"Hi, everyone." Dylan took Anderson from Emma. "I just saw this little guy, but he's bigger already."

Emma grinned. "He looks much smaller when you hold him."

Annie stood and hugged Dylan hard. "Dinner will be ready in ten minutes. Jonah, Emma, Meg, go ahead and get the table set."

When the food was ready, Meg found a seat and waited for Annie to say grace before digging into the homemade spaghetti and meatballs.

"Annie, I wanted to discuss something with you," Dylan said.

Annie placed a napkin on her lap and stared Dylan in the eye. "Something tells me it's not your intentions with my daughter you want to talk about."

Heat consumed Meg's face, and she wanted to

crawl under the table. "Mom!"

Annie laughed and waved a hand in the air. "I'm just teasing. What's going on, Dylan?"

Dylan glanced at Meg. "I'm not sure if Meg told you about what she and I have been discussing regarding my farm."

"No, she's hasn't said anything about your farm. Our Meg is pretty tight-lipped about those kinds of things."

"Well, as you are aware, my dad's Alzheimer's has gotten progressively worse over the past year. I've racked my brain to figure out how to secure our finances. Without Dad at the farm, I'll need to hire help in the spring. I also don't think my mom can be his only source of care pretty soon."

"I'm so sorry." Annie frowned.

He leaned forward, resting his forearms on the table. "Thank you. When Meg became aware of how bad things were, she volunteered to think of ways to help. She said you weren't really interested in expanding here, but I wanted to make sure you were okay with me trying some of her ideas at my place."

Annie glanced at Meg with raised brows before returning her focus to Dylan. "Of course. They're her ideas, and it's your land. You two can do whatever you want. You don't need my blessing."

"I know, but I just wanted to double check. I don't want any hard feelings."

Meg's entire body tensed. No hard feelings? What about her feelings? She bit into her lip, and the tinny taste of blood filled her mouth. Now wasn't the time to discuss her issues.

Dylan squeezed her leg under the table.

She clung to his hand like a lifeline.

"Sweet of you to check, but unnecessary. I really am sorry for all the hardships, and it's nice you'd want to try Meg's little ideas." Annie leaned across the table and patted Dylan's hand. "You're a thoughtful boy for wanting to help her. I just hope it helps you, as well. You wouldn't want to wind up in a worse position than when you started."

Blood pounded in her ears Meg pushed up from the table, knocking her plate to the floor as she stood. She was a grown woman. She didn't need to sit here and listen to her mom talk as if she were a child. "Excuse me. I'm not hungry anymore." She stormed into the kitchen and didn't bother to glance over her shoulder. Based on the silence she left behind, no one followed.

She wouldn't be so lucky for long.

Chapter Twelve

Dylan suffered through Jonah's glare from across the table. Silence hung in the air as thick as smoke, cut through only by the rising voices of mother and daughter from the kitchen. Dylan yearned to go to Meg and offer his support. But Meg needed to have this conversation with her mom, even if she didn't want to.

Sophie latched onto Emma's hand, and Anderson's loud cries pierced the stillness of the room.

"Jillian, would you mind taking the kids into the living room?" Emma rose to her feet. "I need to step in there and see what's going on."

"Good idea." Jillian picked up the baby, nuzzling him close, then grabbed Sophie's hand to take her into the next room. "Are you coming, Sam?"

Sam sat with a bite of pasta halfway to his mouth. "I've hardly eaten anything, and I'm starving. Can't I sit with the guys and finish my dinner?"

Jillian shot Jonah a warning look.

Dylan shifted in his seat.

"Fine, but if Jonah and Dylan ask you to leave, come and find me." She glanced from Jonah to Dylan and mouthed, *be nice*.

Once all the women, and most of the children, left, Dylan glanced at Jonah and forced a smile. "Jillian looks good with a baby in her arms."

Jonah locked his gaze on Jillian's retreating form.

"Jilly always looks good, but yes, she does."

Silence settled around them once more. Dylan rubbed his clammy hands up and down the thighs of his jeans and eyed the doorway. He wanted to get out of here. Being in an argument with Jonah was uncharted territory, and he had no clue how to make things better.

A cabinet door slammed, echoing through the room.

Dylan winced. "Doesn't sound good."

"That's nothing." Jonah chuckled. "You should have heard the way they used to fight when we were younger."

"I was here, remember?"

"Yeah, you've always been here. You spent as much time here as you did your place."

Memories flooded him, and Dylan smiled. "I hate fighting. I want to fix our problems, but I don't know how."

Jonah snorted. "You can turn back time and not hook up with my little sister." He winced and glanced at Sam.

Tightening his jaw, he balled his hands into fists and clenched them on top of the table. "I told you how I feel. I would think you, more than anyone, would know me well enough to understand I didn't say those things lightly. If Meg and I decide to be together, you'll never find another man who will treat her as good as I will."

Jonah sighed. "You two as a couple is still weird. I know if you two were together, Meg would be treated like a queen. I'm bothered by what could happen if it doesn't work. You're my best friend, my brother, and I don't want anything to ruin our friendship."

"Don't you think you're already hurting our

friendship?" Dylan asked quietly.

"Wait a minute." Sam set his fork on his plate. "You and Meg are boyfriend and girlfriend?"

Dylan chuckled. "Not quite. We're talking about being a couple and deciding if it's a good idea."

"And you don't like that?" Sam turned toward Jonah.

Johan shifted and cleared his throat. "I'm not sure, bud. Dylan dating Meg is a little hard. Dylan has been my best friend my whole life, and Meg's my sister. Seeing the two of them together is a big change."

"I understand." Sam nodded. "I had a hard time when you started dating my mom and wasn't very nice. But I made everyone sad, and then I did some stupid things. I should have just given you a chance. Then I would have known how cool you are a lot sooner."

Jonah rubbed a hand over his mouth and leaned back in his chair. "You're absolutely right, Sam." He glanced at Dylan. "And so are you. I'm already making this situation hard, without knowing how it will end. I need not to let your relationship affect us, or me and Meg, and just see what happens."

Dylan let out a long breath, releasing all the tension from his body. "Sounds like a good plan." After all the arguing, a nine-year-old was the voice of reason.

"See, it's a good thing I stayed." Sam beamed, and then continued eating his dinner.

Meg stomped into the dining room. "Can we go, please?"

"Yeah, sure." Dylan glanced at Jonah. "We'll talk more later. See ya, Sam."

Meg kept her head down and her mouth closed. She threaded her arms through her coat and slipped on her boots.

Sophie ran to her side. "Where are you going, Meg-Meg?"

"I'm sorry, baby girl, but I have to leave. I'll be back in the morning. Do you want to help me brush the horses?" She stroked Sophie's hair and steeled her resolve against her big, blue eyes.

"Yes! Can Nora stay?"

"Sure." She kissed her on the top of the head then scooted her back into the living room. She tied her boots, then turned to Dylan. "Are you ready?"

"Yep, let's go." Dylan trudged through the snow piled high on the lawn, cutting a direct path to his truck. "Are you all right?" he asked once they settled in.

"I'm fine."

Her tight words said otherwise. "Did you and your mom work out things?"

"My mom isn't interested in fixing our issues. She's interested in me not damaging your reputation."

"What?" The last thing he wanted was to be another problem between Meg and her mom.

"I really don't want to talk right now." Meg leaned back her head and closed her eyes. "I'm sorry tonight sucked so badly. I really didn't expect her condescending reaction."

Dylan maneuvered his way through town. Snow-covered trees lined the empty road, and Christmas lights still hung on most of the houses. "Neither did I, or I never would have brought up your ideas. The entire night wasn't a bust though. Jonah and I talked, and things are good there. He might still be awkward for a little bit, but he won't be a jerk about things anymore."

He pulled into Meg's driveway, and his phone

vibrated in his pocket. He grabbed the device and read a new text message, swearing under his breath.

"What's wrong?"

"My sister. Apparently, she came home and is at the house waiting. She wants to talk about the farm."

Meg furrowed her brow. "You didn't know she was coming?"

"No idea." Leave it to Lisa to ruin his plans. "I'm sorry, but I have to get home."

"You have no reason to be sorry, Dylan."

"I hate to leave you after what happened tonight. I know you don't want to talk about your mom. But I at least wanted to be around in case you change your mind."

"If I need you, I know where to find you." She leaned toward him and placed a quick peck on his cheek before opening her door. "Good night, and good luck with Lisa."

He drove toward home while his mind spun, blocking out the town as it whirled by. This night definitely wasn't turning out the way he wanted. He wanted to have a nice family dinner, resolve his differences with Jonah, and then have a real conversation about the future with Meg. Instead, dinner was strained, and Meg left upset with her mom. Now, he had to face his annoying sister and have an unpleasant conversation.

At least things were better with Jonah.

He stepped through the front door and groaned.

Lisa lay sprawled on his couch.

She had grabbed a bag of chips and tracked crumbs from the kitchen into the living room and all around the couch. Betsy sat in front of her, her tail thumping wildly, waiting for whatever scraps she could get. Dylan kicked off his boots and hung his coat on the hook beside the door. "How can you still be such a slob?" He grabbed the half-empty bag and took a seat beside her.

"Hello to you, too. You don't look happy to see me." She shifted her legs just enough so she wasn't touching his leg.

"It's been a long night, and spending the rest with you is not what I had in mind."

She rolled her eyes. "Sorry to be such an inconvenience."

"Stop being so dramatic, and tell me why you're here."

She sat and crossed her arms across her chest. "You give me a hard time about not being around to help, and then you're cranky about me coming home for a weekend? Maybe you need to figure out what you want."

He held up the bag of chips. "This is you helping? Coming here and watching television while you eat my chips?"

"No, I came home so we can talk. I had to wait for you before we could have a conversation, so I'm relaxing. Or is that not allowed?"

He sucked in a deep breath, letting it slowly exhale through his nose. "Okay, what would you like to talk about?"

"Mom called me this week about what you two talked about in regards to the farm. Don't you think my opinion should be considered when making these decisions?" Wrapping her arms around her middle, she widened her eyes.

"Not really." He shrugged, clenching his jaw. Any words he said would go in one ear and out the other. No need to waste his breath.

"Gee, thanks. But I disagree. This farm belongs to all of us, and I should get a say in what we do."

"Lisa, you made your opinion very clear the last time you were home. And frankly, neither Mom nor I agreed. Why would we talk to you about anything else we planned?"

She shifted to face him, tucking her feet beneath her. "Maybe because it's my farm just as much as yours."

He choked out a laugh. She had some nerve. "How do you figure? You've never worked here a day in your life. Even when we were kids, you did everything you could to get out of pulling your weight."

"I still have a stake here." She dipped her chin and red invaded her cheeks.

Hooking an arm over the back of the couch, he turned to face her. "Why? Your name isn't on any papers. You don't have a love for the land. Absolutely nothing ties you to this farm. Even if we sold it, you wouldn't get any money. Mom and Dad would get most of it, and I would end up with a share."

"How is that fair?" She jutted forward her chin and rounded her eyes.

He let out a humorless laugh. A million memories played in his head of mucking stalls while Lisa slept in and him working in the fields until all hours of the night while Lisa was out with friends. Life on the farm had never been fair—he'd worked himself to death, and Lisa never lifted a finger. "It's fair because I've worked my butt off for years to keep the farm going. I've also put a lot of my own money into this place. So yes, you getting nothing is very fair."

Lisa worked her jaw back and forth. "Does Mom think the same way? Did the two of you get together to conspire against me or something? I'm not saying I want money. You and Mom are too attached to this land and are not thinking clearly about what is the best option. Selling is the best option, and the best way to assure we have the needed money to see Dad taken care of."

"We need money, but another way will be found. Selling the farm is not an option." His ears rang, muffling the sound of her complaining, but not enough. He wished it would. Especially when her words twisted the guilt in his stomach and made a little bit of sense. Maybe she was right. Maybe he was too attached, but being close wasn't a bad thing. Lisa wasn't attached enough and wasn't willing to exhaust every possible option to save their farm. "Did Mom tell you my ideas?"

"She told me Meg's idea." Lisa crossed her arms over her chest and lifted her brow.

"Same thing." Dylan gritted his teeth.

"How? I don't even know how this would work, or how it would make us money. Meg will earn money, but not you."

"What are you talking about?" He straightened, her words striking a chord he didn't want to acknowledge.

"These are her ideas, and she's the one who needs to be around to make them work. Besides giving her the space, what else does she need you for?" She pressed her lips together, a tiny smirk lifting one corner. "Or will you put up the cost to create this magical place

Meg has dreamed up? It sounds like she's getting a damn good deal, and you're getting screwed. Who gets the profits? Meg will generously hand them over? Doesn't seem likely."

"We don't have everything figured out yet. We've analyzed the logistics to see if her idea is even possible. Besides, Meg can always pay rent for using our land, which would add to our income." Sweat formed at the base of his neck. He pinched the fabric of his jeans to keep from wiping it off. Lisa couldn't see the effect of her words. Whether he liked to admit or not, she made a point.

"You told Mom you can save the farm, plus earn enough money for help with Dad, and you haven't even considered how this would work financially?" She rested her temple on her fingertips and shook her head. "You're pretty naïve to think things will go the way you want because you're dealing with Meg. Or maybe Meg is being smart and using your connection to get you to turn a blind eye to this stuff."

He shook his head, even as the sweat poured down his back. "Meg wouldn't use me. We needed to make sure we could do everything she's proposing before we talked about how we'd handle the money."

"You think we have plenty of land to use her suggestions and plant what we always do?" She tilted her head to the side and narrowed her eyes.

He sat straight. This conversation was ridiculous. He couldn't let her get in his head. "I really do. The farm has a lot of wasted space."

"And you think Meg will be content to work for you?"

He weaved his fingers through his beard. "She

wouldn't be working for me."

"She'd be your employee like she is with her mom. How long will it be before she's searching for more again? Especially if her ideas prove lucrative." Lisa settled back against the couch cushion. "Do you really think she'll sit back while you get the recognition, and she's the hired help?"

He ground together his teeth and counted to five to keep his temper in check. Meg was so much more than hired help. "I'm sure Meg will be happy with whatever we come up with. What I'm not sure about is why you came all the way home to tell me this. You could have picked up the phone and called me." He narrowed his gaze.

"I'm concerned and wanted to check out what you have planned. I also want to talk to Mom about everything and spend some time with Dad."

"Just don't cause any trouble. I'm more than capable of figuring out what's best for the family. I'm the one who's done it for years. Now, if you'll excuse me, I'm heading to bed." He rubbed a hand over Betsy's soft fur, then made his way upstairs.

He lay in his bed, waiting for sleep to consume him. His mind drifted back to what Lisa said. Was he being naive about this whole idea? Was he letting his feelings for Meg cloud his judgment? He didn't want to think so, but the little voice of doubt from earlier grew bigger by the minute.

****

A quiet house greeted him in the morning. No surprise there. No way would Lisa be awake yet. He shed his bitterness like a second skin and started his daily chores. No use wasting time. He threw hay in the stalls for the cows, and his stomach rumbled. He needed to eat. Thirty minutes later, the chores were almost finished, and he could take a small break to grab some breakfast. Maybe he could sneak away for lunch later and meet Meg.

He sent her a quick text. His phone vibrated in his hand.

—*how about a pizza?*—

A smile touched his mouth, and anticipation fluttered around him. He hated being away from her. His stomach rumbled again, and he ignored it. If he pushed through the rest of his work, he could get into town a little early.

Three hours later, he'd finished his chores, showered, and spent some time cleaning the house. He parked on the square and hurried to pick up groceries at the market. After depositing the bags in his truck, he wandered over to grab a cup of coffee at Average Joe's. He'd take a cup over to Jillian at Kiddy Korner. He was curious to see if Jonah said anything about their conversation. He could bribe it out of her with a hot cup of coffee and a blueberry muffin. He opened the door to the coffee shop, and he stepped inside with leaden feet. His pulse thumped hard against his veins.

Meg and Lisa sat tucked away in the corner, their heads bent low together, and papers spread across the table. His heart beat wildly, and saliva filled his mouth. What the hell was going on?

Chapter Thirteen

Meg glanced up, locked gazes with Dylan, and butterflies danced in her stomach. She didn't plan to see him for a couple more hours.

He approached her table.

The butterflies morphed into shivers of apprehension. His lips pressed together in a thin line, and a thick vein bulged against the side of his neck.

He stepped in front of their table and narrowed his eyes on the papers spread in front of her. "Don't you two look cozy?"

Meg blinked at his harsh tone. "Hey, there." She shifted her gaze toward Lisa. Was he upset with Lisa? She hadn't mentioned arguing with Dylan.

Lisa smiled up at Dylan. "Do you want to join us? Meg mentioned you two were getting together soon for lunch. You could sit with a cup of coffee beforehand."

He shoved his hands in his front pockets and frowned. "Funny, Meg never mentioned she was seeing you today."

A flash of pain turned his emerald eyes hazel. "I didn't plan on it." She spoke carefully. What had she stepped into? "I ran into Lisa when I grabbed a cup of coffee, and she asked me to join her."

"You just happened to run into her?" He shifted his gaze from Meg to Lisa. "And you just happened to have my research on the farm with you?" Dylan flailed his hand in front of him.

"Yes, actually." Meg leaned back in her chair and folded her arms. She hadn't done anything wrong. Irritation flared in her chest. She hated being spoken to like a child.

"What's your problem, Dylan? I was with Mom earlier, and she lent me the paperwork." She picked up a piece of paper and shook it. "I ran into Meg, and I already had the papers. Why not pick her brain a little bit?"

"We already discussed you have nothing in this decision." He tightened his jaw.

"No, you said I have no stake in the farm. After I talked to Mom, she thought my new-found interest was wonderful. Then when I started talking to Meg, I understood why you wanted to shut me out." She glanced at Meg with a smile, then focused on Dylan.

Meg perked up on the edge of her seat. They weren't shutting anyone out of anything.

"What are you talking about?" He spat the words out of his mouth. His outstretched hand trembled.

"I have to admit; her ideas are fascinating." Lisa propped elbows on the table. "I asked her why she hadn't put her plans into motion sooner. She explained she didn't have the land and how she'd love to own enough land to build an arena. Isn't that interesting, Dylan?"

Dylan dropped his hand back to his side, and he swiped his tongue over his lips. "Very interesting."

"I asked if it would easier if she owned the land she used for her project, and she said absolutely. It really sounds like the best thing for Meg, and for us, would be selling her the farm. I'm sure Emma would lend her the money if she needed help." Lisa leaned against her chair and stared at Dylan.

Meg dropped her jaw and shot up her eyebrows. Lisa took everything she'd said out of context. She clasped together her hands on her stomach as nausea swam inside her. She opened her mouth to set the record straight, but the wounded look in Dylan's eyes stole her words. How could he believe Lisa?

Dylan turned on his heel and stormed out. He slammed the door hard behind him.

Meg tracked him through the front window as he stormed down the sidewalk. He stopped outside of The Village Idiot, paused, and then stepped inside. She snapped around her head and focused on Lisa. Irritation boiled in her gut. "What the hell are you doing?"

"I don't know what you mean." Lisa folded her hands on the table and tilted her head.

"You know exactly what I'm talking about. You basically told Dylan I wanted to buy his farm, his house, and his livelihood." She snapped her words. How dare Lisa use her in whatever game she played.

"I did no such thing. I simply told him what you said. You did say it would be nice to own your own land." Lisa lifted her coffee to her mouth and took a sip. A small smile poked above the mug.

Meg gripped the side of the table. She fought to calm the tightening of nerves, and her hands shook. Memories of the last time Lisa twisted her words flew into Meg's mind. Meg's date for homecoming dumped her junior year of high school because Lisa told him Meg preferred spending time with another boy. The boy Meg told Lisa about was her favorite horse, but her crush hadn't believed her. Now, the stakes were so much higher, and she wouldn't let Lisa get away with manipulating her. "I acknowledged owning land would be easier, but that was before I spoke with Dylan— before he was interested in using my ideas, and we developed a plan. I don't want to buy Dylan's home. Are you crazy?"

Lisa curled her hands around the mug and lowered it. "I didn't mean to upset either of you. I explained to Dylan what we discussed." She shrugged. "It's not my fault he misunderstood."

Meg stood, her chair tipping hard behind her. She pointed at Lisa, her nails biting into the flesh of her skin. Anger made her limb shake. "You know exactly what you did. You made him second-guess everything, and for what? So you can talk him into selling?" She spread out her hands, taking one step closer and hovering over Lisa. "What's your big plan? To swoop in with your own ideas and be the hero instead of the screw-up who continues to be a source of disappointment to her family?" Her pulse thundered in her ears. "Please, tell me. Because you'd never sabotage the only plan that could save your home without something up your sleeve."

Lisa's face reddened, and she ground together her teeth. "How dare you say those things!"

Meg dropped her hands and stepped back. "It's about time someone did. Now, here's a little piece of advice. Do what you will. Grow up and think about someone other than yourself for a change. You'd be surprised how much better off you'll be."

Meg stalked through the door, not wasting any more time on Lisa. She ran to The Village Idiot. The winter wind slammed against her, but she didn't care.

She had to clear up everything. Lisa was crazy and just trying to hurt Dylan with her sick plan. Meg pushed through the front door. She blinked to adjust to the dim light. The hair on the back of her neck stood up, and a stab of betrayal pierced her gut.

Dylan sat at the bar, one hand held his head on the bar while the other was stroked by Sally.

Taking a deep breath, she strode to Dylan and stood beside him. A few patrons dotted along the bar. The smell of their greasy meals hung heavy in the air. She placed a hand on his shoulder.

He flinched.

Raw, hot pain shot down to her toes. She withdrew her hand and put it in her pocket. "Can we talk?"

"We don't have anything to talk about." Dylan's gaze remained on the bar, his hand under Sally's.

Spit burned in the back of her mouth, and she swallowed hard, fighting the urge to hurl it at her. "Come on, Dylan. Let me explain."

"Explain what? That you used me to get what you want? That you knew your mom would never agree to do what you wanted, so why not flirt with the poor slob who's always given you everything he could?"

His voice was hard and cold. Meg gasped, and her heart dropped to the floor.

Dylan turned his head, and tears glimmered in his eyes.

"You know me better than that." She buried her hands deeper into her jeans pockets to keep from reaching to comfort him.

"Do I? You've always kept everyone at arm's length." Shaking his head, a laugh puffed through his mouth. "Why would I be stupid enough to think I would be any different? You treated me like a brother until you could get something from me. Never completely opened up about your life, until you could use old wounds to make me feel sorry for you. Lisa was right. I was blinded by my attachment. But not my attachment to the farm, my attachment to you made me see past what was really going on." He turned back to Sally. "I need another beer."

Meg took a deep breath and fought the pressure squeezing her insides. Dylan couldn't really think so little of her. "I understand what your sister said upset you, and you need to wrap your mind around the conversation. But please don't think the worst of me because she planted those seeds. She twisted my words. This situation isn't fair. I don't really want to talk in here, so I'll sit outside and wait. I'll wait until you're ready, so we can hash this out and put it behind us."

"I don't want to talk anymore, Meg. Not about the farm, not about us. I thought you were my future, but I was wrong. Just go home and forget it all." He locked his gaze forward and hunched over his beer bottle.

His words were like a punch in the gut. She left, and tears fell unhindered down her cheeks. Wind whipped around the corner and stung her face. She would wait, no matter how long it took. He didn't mean what he said. He was upset. She could make him understand. All he had to do was listen.

She sat on a bench outside the bar. The cold wood stung her bottom, and the moisture soaked through her jeans. But the discomfort didn't matter. Nothing mattered but getting Dylan to listen to her.

Celeste appeared by her side. "Meg? Is everything okay?"

Meg didn't spare a glance at her mother's best friend. She stared into the sunny day, not flinching at the bright sun reflecting off the snow and shining into her unblinking eyes. "It will be."

"What happened?" Celeste asked. "You've been sitting here for close to forty minutes like you're in shock. Can I help with anything?"

She glanced at Celeste, her dark hair blowing around her slender face, and the muscles in Meg's neck screamed. Time passed in a blur. Her face was numb. Everything inside her was numb. "I need to talk to Dylan."

"Okay. Do you know where he is?"

"He's in there." Meg pointed behind her at the bar. "He doesn't want to talk, but I have to wait until he's ready. When he's ready, I'll explain everything."

"Is there a reason why you have to wait outside? It's freezing." Celeste brushed her fingers across Meg's cheek. "You're ice cold, honey. Why don't you come over and sit in the store? Watch for Dylan, and when he leaves, you can talk."

Goose bumps tickled her flesh from the cold. Warming up a little bit won't hurt. "Okay. But as soon as I see him leave, I have to come back outside."

"I know." Celeste grabbed Meg's arm and helped her to her feet. She guided her to Florals and More. Celeste hurried into the back room then returned carrying two steaming mugs. She sat next to Meg on the sofa by the bay window and handed her a mug. "Here, drink this. The hot tea will warm you up."

Meg lifted the mug to her mouth and wrinkled her nose. She wasn't much of a tea drinker, but she'd lose any fight against Celeste. "Thank you. I didn't realize I was outside for so long. I guess I was a little preoccupied."

"Just a little?" Celeste tucked a long wisp of black hair behind her ear. "I've been glued to the window, watching the entire time you were outside. Do you want to tell me why talking to Dylan is so important?"

Groaning, Meg placed her cup on the table beside her. "Not really, but I know you'll drag it out of me eventually."

"You know me well." Celeste laughed, and the deep wrinkles across her brow rippled.

"I'm sure my mom kept you informed about everything going on the last few weeks." A pinch of resentment squeezed her insides.

"You mean about you and Dylan?"

Meg nodded. "We've spent a lot of time together. Everything's been good, at least I thought so."

Celeste took a sip of tea, and then cradled the mug in her lap. "You're not sure if things are good?"

Meg screwed her lips to the side. "Our relationship is confusing. The situation is different because of our history, as well as Jonah being a jerk about us being together. The relationship's been moving somewhat slowly. I'm not sure if the pace decreased because Dylan doesn't want to rush in to anything, or if he's lost interest."

"I have a hard time believing he's lost interest." Celeste frowned.

Meg couldn't help but smile. "Well, you're biased."

Celeste shrugged and leaned forward to set her mug on the coffee table. "I might be, but I know Dylan. If he pursued you, even just a little bit, he wouldn't do it without being committed. If he wasn't certain of his feelings, he wouldn't risk hurting you."

Cocking her head to the side, she glanced at Celeste. "I guess I never thought about it like that."

"Is that what you need to talk to him about?"

"No. Yes, but not right now. I talked with Lisa earlier in the coffee shop, and Dylan came in. He stopped by our table, and Lisa rattled on about how I wanted to own land for the ideas I shared with him." Meg stopped and took a sip of tea. The bitter liquid moistened her dry mouth. "I assume you know about the plan Dylan and I discussed for his farm, as well."

Celeste nodded, and a wild wisp of raven black hair fell from the bun secured at the nape of her long neck.

"Okay, well, Lisa told him I want to own land, and they should sell me theirs. She implied I intended to purchase their farm this whole time, and I used Dylan to get what I wanted. I just sat there, unable to even speak because I was so angry and confused, and Dylan just left. I followed him, after giving Lisa a piece of my mind, and tried to talk." Meg went silent, lost in the memory of Dylan's reaction. Frustration heated her blood. If he'd just talk to her, they could get this whole mess straightened out.

Celeste laid a hand on Meg's arm. "I guess Dylan didn't listen."

"Not at all. He didn't want to hear what I had to say, and he thinks I manipulated him." She bit the inside of her mouth to keep more tears from falling. "I can't believe he'd believe Lisa's lies."

"He's upset." Celeste wrapped her arms around Meg. "People say things they don't mean when they're upset. Once he calms down, he'll listen to what you have to say, and everything will be fine."

Meg buried her face in Celeste's neck like she used to do as a kid, and the woman's floral perfume wafted up her nose. "Do you really think so?"

"I really do."

Sniffling back a sob, Meg wiped her nose. "Thank you. Maybe I need to go home and give him a little more time."

"Space might be a good idea. Why don't you head to your mom's and spend some time with Sophie? Nothing in this world can take your mind off your problems the way that little princess can."

She didn't really want to see her mom but couldn't avoid her much longer. Especially when Emma was there with the kids. She pulled away from Celeste's comforting embrace and nodded. "I'll head there and try to keep my mind off Dylan. I'll call him later."

Celeste skimmed her knuckles over Meg's cheek and gave her a smile. "Sounds like your best option. He'll listen to you eventually. I know it."

Meg glanced out the large picture window at the town square. She let her gaze wander once more toward the bar. She sucked in a breath, and her heart lodged in her throat.

Dylan was finally leaving, his head bent and his shoulders slumped forward.

Sally led him by the hand to her car.

Dylan's head was down, but a triumphant grin lit Sally's face as Dylan opened her door and she climbed inside. A lump formed in her throat, and she gulped back a sob.

She stared in the direction of the car that drove off

toward Dylan's house with the man she had no doubt she was falling in love with. With a sigh of defeat, she turned to Celeste. "Even if he'll listen, I don't think it matters anymore."

Chapter Fourteen

Dylan sat in Sally's car and stared out the window, watching the snow-covered fields pass by. Aside from an occasional grunt in response to Sally's endless prattling, he remained silent the whole way home. Her constant chatter meant he didn't have to contribute to the conversation. He remained focused on the pain radiating through his entire being.

Meg betrayed him. How could he be so stupid? His heart wrenched.

Sally parked her car in his driveway.

He opened his door and peered back into the car. "Thanks for the ride home." He made his way toward the front door, and gravel crunched behind him. He wanted to tell Sally to get back in her car and leave, but he couldn't be rude. Not after she'd given him a ride home.

"No problem. I don't like to see one of my best customers drive after drinking too much. Bad for business." Her voice bounced along with every step she took.

"I bet." He snorted. He opened the door and turned to say goodbye.

She lifted a hand and shoved his chest, forcing him inside. Her foot shot back and closed the door. She circled her arms around his neck and forced her mouth on his.

He firmed his lips, denying her access. He grabbed her shoulders and pushed her away. "What are you doing?" Disgust swirled in his stomach. He itched to wipe the taste of her from his lips.

"Seriously?" Sally purred. "I think it's pretty obvious, don't you?"

"Apparently not." He fisted his hands at his sides.

"I am being nice, and now I want you to be nice in return." She shimmied against him.

"Wait, what?"

A husky laugh rumbled from her throat. "You really are clueless, aren't you? Listen, I know you had a thing for me, and I was stupid for not taking you up on it earlier. I'm sorry. But now, I want to show you just how I sorry I am." She widened her eyes and twisted her lips into a pout.

"Uh, I wish I'd known your intentions." He took two steps in retreat and rubbed the back of his neck. "I might have had a crush a few months ago, but my feelings have changed. I don't want to start anything, Sally."

She rounded her eyes. "Why not? Because of Meg Sheffield? I saw what happened earlier. You don't want anything to do with her anymore. Who could blame you? The girl's got issues."

Anger flared hot in his gut. Regardless of where things stood between him and Meg, Sally had no right to speak poorly about Meg. He snaked a hand through his beard. "I'm sorry, Sally, but right now's not a good time. I really appreciate the ride, but that's all I expected." The urge to tug her lower lip when she stuck it out even farther gripped him. She looked ridiculous.

She folded her arms under her breasts and glanced

through long, black lashes. "Are you sure?"

He nodded, keeping his gaze off her breasts she'd propped up until they almost spilled out of her top and squarely on her heavily made-up face. "I'm sure."

"All right." She shrugged and scanned her gaze up and down his body. "But if you change your mind, you know where to find me. Just don't make me wait too long." She leaned against him once more, placed a kiss on the bottom of his chin, and walked out the door.

A sigh of relief escaped his lips. He sank in his chair in the living room and bent forward with his head in his hands, wrapping his mind around how things went so wrong so quickly.

Bang-bang-bang.

His front door swung open, and Jonah stormed into the living room. "Where the hell is she?"

Dylan knit together his brows. Just what he needed. Another round of arguing with Jonah about Meg. He opened his mouth, and then closed it, his gaze fixed on Jonah.

"Answer me. Where's Sally? I know you brought her home." Jonah scanned the room with his fists balled at his sides.

The only female in the room was Betsy, and she wasn't concerned enough to even open her eyes. Dylan shook his head, and déjà vu clouded his brain. Ignoring Jonah, he made his way into the kitchen and grabbed two beers. He sat at the table and waited for Jonah to come after him.

The steady thump of Jonah's boots preceded him into the kitchen. "Are you kidding me right now? You take a woman home from the bar who isn't Meg, then you walk away when I come here to confront you and kick your butt?"

"Sally isn't here, you idiot." Dylan extended an arm and waved it with his palm up. "Look around. Do you see her? Did you see her car when you tore up my driveway?"

Pausing, he tilted his head to the side. "I know she was here. Jillian saw you two leaving together, holding hands."

Dylan gritted his teeth. The last thing he wanted to do was explain himself. "I had too much to drink, and she drove me home, moron."

Taking a seat, Jonah grabbed the bottle in front of him. "Well, you might need to explain that to a couple people."

"I don't need to explain anything to anyone." He took a long sip of his beer. The cool liquid quickly mixed with the alcohol already swimming in his system. Warmth spread from his toes to his cheeks, but his heart remained cold.

"Meg might feel differently. I would like to know why she's so upset, and why you had too much to drink so early in the day." Jonah glared with the beer bottle pressed to his lips.

Snorting, Dylan peeled the corner of the label from his bottle. "When did you get so nosy?"

Jonah tilted his bottle toward Dylan. "When what you do makes my sister a mess."

"My leaving with Sally wouldn't have much of an effect on your sister." Dylan muttered under his breath.

"Excuse me?" He reared back his head, and his mouth hung open.

Dylan sighed. "Listen, I don't really want to get into what happened earlier. Let's just say I've had my eyes opened a little bit today."

"What do you mean?"

"Your sister's using me. I mean, think about it. How does her just starting to have feelings for me make any sense?" Dylan slumped his shoulders forward and shook his head. "Nah, we both know better. Someone like her doesn't want to be with someone like me."

"Are you kidding me? You know Meg. She never does anything for her own self-interest. She's the one who stayed behind to help our mom, she's the one who would give her right hand to help anyone in this town, and she's the woman you love." Jonah stared at the table. "You might know Meg better than I do, but I know you better than anyone else in this world. You wouldn't have told me you were in love with Meg if you weren't, and you wouldn't have fallen in love if she wasn't the one. I'm not sure what happened between you two today, but I'm sure it's a misunderstanding."

Dylan met Jonah's gaze, and a small kernel of hope sprang to life. "How do you know? How can you be so sure?"

"Because I've never seen Meg so defeated." Jonah met his stare head-on.

His heart slammed against his chest. The words he said at the bar crashed into him. He'd told her they had no future. "You saw her? What did she say?"

Jonah chuckled. "If you know her as well as I think you do, you know she didn't say anything. She didn't have to. I know what heartache looks like. Witnessing Meg upset should be enough of a reason to punch that handsome face of yours."

Dylan tried to grin, but his lips wouldn't cooperate. "I'd like to see you try."

Jonah tilted his beer to his lips then set the empty bottle on the table. "Call her, Dylan. You guys need to straighten out this misunderstanding, because it's obvious neither one of you are happy." He stood and glanced down. "And one last thing. If you're at fault— if you did something to hurt her—I will come back here to kick your butt." He gave a nod, then walked out the door.

Jonah was right. He'd let his own insecurities over Meg's feelings cloud his judgment. Worse, he'd allowed Lisa to manipulate him. He should have known better. His pulse pounded, and bile slid up the back of his throat. He had to make things right.

He picked up his cell phone and called Meg before he lost his nerve. The more times the phone rang in his ear, the harder his heart beat in his chest. He almost disconnected, resigning himself to the fact she wouldn't pick up.

"What do you want?" Meg asked.

Meg's voice was as cold as the icy blasts of wind slamming against his house. He swallowed hard at her tone. "Can we talk?" Jonah said she was defeated, not angry.

"I don't really think we have anything to talk about. You made sure of that."

He ran a hand through his hair. "Because I wouldn't talk to you in the bar earlier? You said you would wait until I was ready. I'm ready now. I was out of line, and I completely overreacted."

"Out of line? That's all you think about what you did?"

Meg's voice cracked. Her emotion squeezed his chest. "I'm sorry, Meg. I never should have let Lisa get in my head. Different emotions have stewed in my mind the last few weeks, and what she said confirmed all my stupid doubts."

"You've doubted us already, huh?" Meg snorted.

"No...yes...I don't know. I've doubted how you could be attracted to me. I've doubted how, after so long, you would see me in a different light and want the same thing I did. I've doubted I'm good enough for a woman like you. I just haven't gotten a chance to talk about how I've felt. I didn't want to scare you off." He rose from his chair and paced across the kitchen.

"So instead of scaring me off with your doubts and concerns, you decide to end things before they really began by sleeping with Sally. Good choice, Dylan."

He stopped in his tracks. Her accusation was like a sucker punch in the pit of his stomach. "What are you talking about? I never slept with Sally." He dropped his hand to the table.

"You two left the bar together. I was at Florals and More waiting. She looked mighty satisfied with herself when she was holding your hand and leading you to her car."

"Yes, Sally drove me home because I had too much to drink. Nothing happened. Okay, she kissed me, and I pushed her away, but that's it. Ask Jonah, he'll tell you." Panic filled his voice.

"Jonah? How would he know?"

"Apparently, you weren't the only one who saw me and Sally together. Jillian did, too, and called Jonah. He stormed the gates. He'll tell you no one was here." Alarm beat an unsteady rhyme in his heart. He couldn't have Meg thinking he'd fallen into bed with Sally.

Silence filled the line, and Dylan held his breath.

She had to believe him.

"So what, you talked to your sister, and she told you she's the liar and not me?"

"I haven't talked to Lisa yet. I plan to, but I wanted to talk to you first. Listen, I think we have a lot to discuss, and I don't want to do it over the phone. Will you please have dinner with me tonight? Give me a chance to explain."

"Okay."

Dylan sighed, and the bile in his throat disappeared. "Thank you. I know you're at your mom's. I'll pick you up there so you can visit with your sister and the kids."

"I'm not dressed to go out. I'll go home first."

"How about we just stay in town? Get the pizza we planned earlier? It doesn't matter what you wear. You'll be the most beautiful woman in the room. Stay where you are, and I'll be by around six."

The tension in his neck disappeared, and his heart lifted. He and Meg might not have solved all of their problems, but they started. Now, only one more issue needed to be seen to. He couldn't let Lisa get away with what she did. He needed to figure out her end game. She insisted money wasn't her motivation, and maybe he needed to believe her. He called and asked her to pick him up so he could get a ride into town for his truck. He would wait until they were back at his parent's house to talk. He needed to speak with her and their mom, all three together. This vital discussion was long overdue.

****

Ten minutes later, Dylan, Lisa, and Mary all sat around Mary's kitchen table.

144

His dad's soft snoring drifted in from the living room and competed with the ticking of the clock. Dylan glanced at Lisa. A million comments and accusations burned the tip of his tongue, but he kept them inside. None of the comments and accusations would be helpful. "First off, I want to say I don't appreciate you using Meg to get what you want. She has done nothing but help me, and to put her in a bad position was plain wrong. From here on out, you leave her out of your games."

"I have no idea what you mean." Lisa crossed her arms over her chest and leaned back against her chair, the top of her nose lifted in the air.

Dylan gritted his teeth. So much for being nice. "You know exactly what I mean. While you're at it, stop this innocent act you're playing. You're smarter than you pretend and not fooling anyone."

"So now I act stupid?" She threw her hands in the air.

"You act like you haven't a clue what's going on or what your actions do to other people. You've always been good at games, but it won't work this time." Dylan narrowed his eyes.

She leaned her forearms on the table. "I'm not playing a game, Dylan. This is me, genuinely concerned about the future of this family. I'm opening your eyes a little to what could happen."

"You manipulated me into seeing things your way," Dylan shot back. "And in the process almost ruined a very good thing."

Lisa rolled her eyes. "How else was I supposed to get your attention? According to you, everything I do is based solely on what's best for me, and I have no say in what goes on around here."

Dylan laughed, but the sound held no humor. "When have you made a decision in your life not based on what was best for you?"

Mary cleared her throat. "Enough. We need to come together as a family. No one can fault you for being skeptical of your sister's intentions, but she has to know we do value her opinions."

"You think he's right to be skeptical of me? Gee, thanks, Mom." Lisa shook her head and lifted her gaze to the ceiling.

Mary waved a hand in Lisa's direction. "You should be ashamed of the stunt you pulled earlier. Don't pretend this whole conversation wasn't a stunt. We all know better. You'd better hope Dylan can smooth over things with Meg. Now, if you are serious about wanting to help us with these decisions, great. Dylan has carried the burden for far too long, and it hasn't been fair."

Lisa sighed and rubbed her temple. "I know Dylan has helped out way more than I have. I don't know...I guess I wanted to feel included. I know I'm the one who's absent, and I didn't know how to prove to you guys I'm serious about wanting to be around more."

"Are you serious?" Mary rested a hand on Lisa's arm and dipped her eyebrows together.

"I want to help in whatever way I can. It might take some time for you both to believe me." She glanced at Dylan. "I'm sorry if I caused problems for you and Meg. I didn't know you guys were seeing each other until I talked to Mom afterward. If I can do anything to help fix things, just ask."

"I think you've done enough." He pressed his lips together. He wanted to believe the nonsense she spouted, but a lifetime of habits was hard to break.

Mary pursed her lips and sent him a hard stare. "What do you have to say about Lisa wanting to help more?"

He shrugged. "She's right. A while has to pass to prove she's serious. But she deserves to be in the loop. I'm sorry if you felt like I shut you out, but I honestly didn't think you cared what we decided."

She leaned forward and rested a hand on his. "I do care, and I'd love to know more about your plans."

Dylan relented, relaxing into his chair. For Lisa to show so much interest meant a lot to his mom, and he hoped she was sincere. For now, he'd keep her abreast on everything, but he'd also keep his eye on her. Trust was something she would have to earn, and she had a long way to go.

Chapter Fifteen

"Why are you so nervous?" Emma picked up toys from the living room floor and corralled them into a bin.

"What?" Meg snapped up her head and wiped sweaty palms on the thighs of her jeans. "Did you say something?"

"Yes, you dork. I asked why you're so nervous. You've had dinner with Dylan before."

Meg stood in the middle of the living room in her mother's house and bit into her stubby thumbnail. "I know, but tonight feels different. Like a real date. That sounds stupid, but this dinner is kind of a big deal."

"I've got news for you, honey, you and Dylan were a big deal from the start. Besides, I would hate to think you'd wear your ratty jeans and a Pink Floyd T-shirt on your first real date."

Meg tugged at the hem of her shirt. Her stomach rolled. "Does it look bad? I didn't know we'd get dinner tonight. Should I go home and change? Dylan told me not to, but should I?"

"No, you shouldn't." Emma laughed. "Dylan knows who you are and doesn't care about you getting all fancy for pizza. Besides, he would know if you ran home to change." She narrowed her eyes and tilted her head to the side. "You could let your hair loose. Don't get me wrong, I would kill for my hair to look as good as yours in a braid. But maybe to add a little punch."

"You're making me more nervous." She yanked the rubber band from the bottom of her braid and ran her fingers through the long strands. Loose waves fell around her face. "Does it look all right? My hair was wet when I braided it this morning."

Emma glared and shook her head. "Sometimes, I really hate you."

"Stop. I'm serious."

"So am I. I'd work for hours to get those waves. The texture is gorgeous. Do you want to borrow some makeup? We don't have the same skin tone, but maybe a little mascara?"

"Okay, thanks."

Emma ran up to her room and was back a minute later with her makeup bag.

Meg dabbed her lashes with mascara and swiped some gloss on her lips. The doorbell rang, and her heart hammered in her chest. "He's here."

"Yep, and you, my dear, look amazing." Emma fluffed a piece of hair from Meg's face. "Now listen, I know something happened earlier. Don't let him off the hook too easy. You should make him work for forgiveness a little, but listen to what he has to say."

"Thanks, Emma." Meg hugged her then headed toward the door. She slowed her gait.

Dylan bent low and hugged Mom.

She'd avoided Annie as much as possible today, not saying more than five words. She'd hash everything out soon, but not today. She gave her mom a tense smile then faced Dylan. "Hi."

Dylan straightened and grinned. "Hi. Are you ready?"

"Yep. I'm starving." Well, starving might be an overstatement. Acid churned in her stomach, and nerves buzzed around her body all day. Food was the last thing she wanted.

"Nice seeing you, Annie. I'm sure I'll see you soon." Dylan dipped his chin, then opened the front door.

Meg gave her mom a small wave, then followed Dylan outside.

He slowed his pace.

She brushed up beside him. She hated the nerves that ripped through her. She couldn't remember ever feeling like this around Dylan, and she wished the anxiety would go away. Discussing what happened earlier would never happen if she couldn't relax.

Dylan settled in the truck and glanced at her. "You look beautiful with your hair down. I never get to see it loose."

She shot him a half smile.

"What's wrong, Meg? You don't seem like yourself."

The setting sun glowed behind him, casting a warm glow over his skin. She settled her clasped hands in her lap. "I'm sorry. I'm just a little nervous."

"What? Why should you be nervous?"

She kept her gaze on her hands and refused to meet his gaze.

Dylan lifted her chin with a thumb and forced her gaze to his. "Please, tell me why you're nervous."

"I don't know." She shrugged and searched for the words to explain. "I told Emma, this dinner feels like our first real date—like tonight is kind of a make-it-or-break-it moment."

He lifted his hand from her chin and grabbed her fingers. "Let me ask you a question. Do you want us to make it, or do you want us to break it?"

"I want us to make it," she whispered the words, but they echoed back in the truck's stillness.

Dylan lifted their joined hands and kissed her knuckles. "Then we will. The rest is just figuring out how."

Meg took a deep breath. "Sounds simple enough."

"Our relationship is only as simple as we make it." Dylan put his truck in Reverse and backed out of the driveway. He drove to That's Amore Pizzeria, never taking his hand from hers after shifting into Drive.

She shouldn't be surprised by how quickly her nerves disappeared. He always calmed her. No matter what the situation, Dylan could always talk her off the ledge. She didn't know why she wasted weeks of second-guessing his intentions and worrying about where their relationship was headed, when all she had to do was ask. He was always the one she went to with her problems. Why should this one be different?

The scent of garlic and too many crammed bodies smacked into her once inside the restaurant. "Wow. It's packed in here." She scanned the room and gestured to a table for two in the far corner. "Should we grab a seat?" She made her way to the table.

"Sure." Dylan followed. He sat across from her and nodded toward the menu. "Do you want to get a pizza, or are you in the mood for something else?"

"Have you ever known me not to be in the mood for pizza?" Meg furrowed her forehead and held back a laugh.

Dylan grinned. "I don't think I have. Meat lovers?"

"Perfect, and I'll have a cola. I want to stay level-headed for this conversation. We've had enough misunderstandings lately. I don't want alcohol to add any more confusion." She tented her brows and pressed together her lips. "Sounds like you've already had enough to drink today."

Dylan groaned. "I deserve that."

Meg bit the inside of her cheek to keep from saying more.

The server grabbed their order, then hurried toward the kitchen.

Dylan grabbed Meg's hand from across the table. He sat for a moment, staring at their hands as he rubbed his thumb in circles.

Ripples of pleasure vibrated through her.

"I'm sorry for what happened earlier," Dylan said. "I have no excuse for reacting the way I did. Lisa was up to no good when she showed up, and I shouldn't have been surprised she used you to get to me. She's always had this innate sense of what to say to push my buttons."

Meg shrugged. "I understand. I mean, I get along with Emma and Jonah most of the time, but we know how to get a rise out of each other. What bothers me is you believed the absolute worst. You and I have always been close. For you to shut me out and assume I was so manipulative, that reaction really threw me for a loop." Knots formed in her stomach. Dylan was her safe space. Having him turn on her without listening to her side was an experience she never wanted to live through again.

Dylan stared into Meg's eyes and pressed his lips together.

His intense gaze bore into her, and she shifted in her seat.

"Like I said, I have no excuse. I've been so happy about what's between us, but I wondered if I was a fool for thinking what we had was real. I won't lie, Meg. I've had strong feelings for you for a long time. I respected your relationship with Blake enough to keep those feelings to myself. But you going from seeing me as a good friend, to something a lot more, in such a short amount of time is a little hard to understand."

Her stomach muscles knotted. She'd gotten so good at hiding how unhappy she'd been with Blake, not even Dylan had seen it. She pulled back her hand and fiddled with the edge of the table. "Do you think I lied?"

"That's not it." He leaned back in his chair, and his gaze scoured the crowded restaurant before landing on her again. "More like hoping you weren't caught up in all the emotions and kind of riding the wave. I don't doubt you are genuine. I honestly don't think you could be any other way. I'm afraid what I feel is more than you could ever feel for me."

His words sliced through her soul. "I wish you opened about this sooner. We could have avoided a lot of confusion on both sides."

"You've had questions about me?" He tilted his head to the side and narrowed his eyes.

She fought not to chuckle at their horrible communication. "Yes."

"Why?" Dipping his chin low, he leaned forward. "I thought my feelings were clear."

Meg snorted out a laugh. "Are you serious? You kiss me silly on New Year's Eve, you rescue me from

Blake, and we have one amazing night together. Then things cooled off drastically. Yes, we spent a lot more time together, and I'd get a little kiss goodnight, but nothing more. I thought maybe you changed your mind, because I didn't live up to your expectations."

"How did you know I had any expectations?" Dylan whispered.

Meg lowered her gaze and twirled a piece of hair around her finger. Maybe she shouldn't tell him, but they'd agreed to get out everything on the table. "I heard you tell Jonah you were in love with me." She longed to hear the words again, but this time from Dylan.

Dylan rubbed his chin before running his hand back through his hair. "Well, I'm not sure what to say. Why question my feelings if you already knew what they were?"

"Like I said, you seemed to pull back after we spent the night together. I didn't know if I had done something wrong—"

"Being with you is better than I could have ever dreamed," he interrupted. "Don't you ever doubt how amazing you are and how incredible you make me feel. I'm sorry if you felt like I pulled back. I wanted to respect you. I didn't want to rush you—didn't want you to think I just wanted to take advantage after what happened with Blake."

Warmth hugged her body. "We make quite the pair, don't we? You're a gentleman, and I think respecting me means you lost interest. I'm helping you and starting a relationship, and you think it's too good to be true."

"Can I ask you a question?"

"Of course, you can ask me anything."

Dylan rested his elbows on the table and tented his index fingers under his chin. "Why didn't you tell me you overheard what I said to Jonah?"

How could she explain? She bit into her bottom lip. "At first, I pretended like I didn't hear you because I was afraid. I know you might think I developed all these feelings out of thin air, but I haven't." She sucked in a deep breath. Now wasn't the time to hold back anything. "If I'm really honest with myself, I've had these feelings for a while. I buried them down deep and made sure not to look at them too closely. After we kissed, everything changed. I was interested in seeing where our relationship would lead."

Shrugging, she widened her eyes. "But love? That's a big word. The idea of you being in love with me was a little overwhelming."

He reached for her hand and intertwined his fingers with hers. "Is it still overwhelming?"

A smile touched her lips. "No," she whispered. "The more time we spend together, the more I like the idea. I didn't say anything because so much time passed. Besides, you should tell me when the time was right and not because I heard something I wasn't supposed to."

Dinner arrived, and Dylan placed a slice of pizza on Meg's plate, and then his own.

The tangy smell of oregano and garlic wafted to her nose, and her stomach growled. Now that she wasn't tied in knots anymore, her appetite was back in full force. Her mouth closed around the warm cheese, and she moaned. She finished half her slice, then set it on the plate. "Are we good now?"

Dylan nodded. "I think so. As long as you know my feelings have only strengthened, and I intend to keep you in my life for as long as you let me."

Her blood hummed, and her heart raced. "Sounds wonderful. I hope you know my feelings are real. You've opened my eyes to what a real relationship can be, and I don't want to lose what we have. Don't get me wrong, I'm happy we can use my ideas to help your farm, but that's secondary." She connected her gaze to his, and all the doubts and fears from the past few weeks evaporated. "You're what I want. Everything else is extra. It's an amazing extra, but it wouldn't mean much if I didn't have you by my side."

"Even though I finally realized that, I still like hearing it." He nodded toward her plate. "How's the pizza?"

"It's good, but it always is." She smiled and dabbed a napkin against her mouth.

Dylan wiped sauce off the side of her lip. "Were you saving sauce for later?"

"Not anymore." Meg giggled. She wiggled her eyebrows and smiled. "I might be in the mood for something else later."

"I hope I can help with whatever you have in mind."

His irises darkened. Lust simmered hot in her belly. She swiped her tongue across her lips. "You look like you'd rather have me than the pizza."

"Obviously." Shouts erupted by the door and drew Dylan's attention. "You've got to be kidding me. Why is Blake not rotting in a jail cell?"

Blinking at the sudden change of his tone, she glanced behind her shoulder and groaned. "I don't know. Conner called the police. They should have arrested him for burning down your barn."

Dylan frowned. "I don't want to stick around to find out what's going on. Let's box up the pizza and take it back to my place."

"Sounds great." Meg signaled for the server.

She caught more than the server's attention.

"Well, look who's here." Blake sneered as he stopped at their table with two of his buddies following.

Hate filled his bloodshot eyes, and a haze of smoke clung to him. *Great, he's drunk.* The alcohol, as well as his friends, bolstered his courage. "What are you doing out of jail?" She couldn't keep the contempt from her words.

Blake shrugged. "My folks posted bail. I go back to court in a couple of weeks, but my lawyer thinks I can walk away with community service. Just wanted to stop over to see the happy couple." He turned his focus on Dylan. "How's she treating you, Dylan? I hope she's putting out for you more than she did with me. I tell you what, she's a real pain in the butt most of the time. You'd think she'd make up for that in other ways."

"You need to keep your mouth shut." Dylan clenched his teeth and tightened his fists into balls on top of the table. The vein under his jaw pulsed.

Heat engulfed her face, but she wouldn't take the bait and start an argument. She placed a hand on Dylan's arm. Blake wasn't worth their time. "Blake's always been a sore loser. Besides, I don't think he wants us to do much talking. He'd hate for his buddies to know what happened the last time we saw him."

"You mean when I confronted you about sleeping with someone else as soon as I left town? I should have known you wouldn't keep your legs closed," Blake snapped.

Dylan erupted from the table, grabbed Blake by the front of his shirt, and lifted him off his feet so they were face to face. "Don't ever talk about Meg. You and I both know what kind of man you are. Not only are you the type who hits women, but you're the type who lies on the floor and cries when she fights back. Stay away from her, stay away from me, or I will kill you." He threw Blake to the floor and glanced at Meg. "Screw the pizza. I'll fix you something to eat at home if you're still hungry. Let's go."

A shiver of anticipation ran from the top of her head to the tips of her toes. She stepped over Blake, grabbed Dylan's hand, and walked beside him out of the restaurant. She was hungry all right, but Dylan would have to fulfill her needs with something a lot more appetizing than food.

Chapter Sixteen

"I'm sorry." Dylan gripped the rough leather of the steering wheel, and his knuckles turned white.

"What in the world do you have to be sorry for? You were amazing," Meg said.

The breathlessness of her voice lifted his lips, but he shook his head. "I shouldn't have let him get to me. I should have kept my mouth shut and walked away. But I couldn't let him slander you." His focus remained fixed on the road—his hands on the wheel. Rage simmered under his skin. He'd lost his temper earlier. He had to get control of himself. "I can't believe they let him out."

"I can't believe he's free either." She placed a hand on his knee. "Thank you for standing up for me. I really do appreciate it."

The muscles in his thigh tensed. He itched to roll down his window and let the cool, night air wash away the heat pulsing through his body. A buzzing of air vibrated throughout his truck. An electrical current drew him to Meg. He roamed his gaze over her body. A dark flush stained her cheeks, and her chest heaved in and out. Her leg bounced up and down, jiggling along with the bumps in the road.

He gripped the wheel harder. If he touched his fingers to her skin, he'd never take his hands off her. He parked the truck and faced her.

Her tongue moistened her lips, and a soft moan escaped her throat.

"We need to get inside." He jumped down from the truck. He half walked-half jogged to the front of the house. He opened the door and urged her inside. Slamming the door closed, he caged her against the hard wood, fisted his hands in her hair, and molded his lips over hers. Every ounce of his being craved every part of her. She would have no more misunderstanding of his intentions. He wanted her, and he wanted her now.

Meg rose to her tiptoes, keeping their mouths together. Huffing a sigh, she looped her arms around his neck and wrapped her legs around his waist. She buried her face into his neck. "I need you now, Dylan." She lifted her head and their lips met again.

Dylan pulled away and skimmed his knuckles against her soft cheek. "I need you, too, but we should slow this down. I've wanted this moment for so long. I want to take my time and taste every inch of you. I can't when we're standing in my hallway with our clothes still on."

Meg laughed. "We can start working on the clothes part." She climbed down from his grasp and backed toward the stairs. She unzipped her coat and tossed it behind her.

He charged her, picked her up, and threw her over his shoulder, running full speed to his room. He laid her on his bed and inched over her, moving as stealthily as an animal stalking its prey.

He kissed her cheek and forced his voice low next to her ear. "I love you."

Meg leaned up and pressed her lips to his.

"Hearing those words is so much better. I'm falling hard, Dylan, and I'm almost there."

"You take all the time you need, honey. I'm not going anywhere." Lightness lifted his heart. He had all the patience in the world. When Meg finally said the words, he'd be the happiest man alive.

****

With the sliver of morning sun from his window the only light to guide him, Dylan slipped through his bedroom door. The floorboards squeaked under his weight, and he winced. He'd spent another night on the couch without Meg in his arms. He needed a cold shower to get her out of his system, but that would have to wait until after he completed his chores.

Meg shifted beneath his comforter and faced him with barely opened eyes. She stretched her arms high above her head and sat. "What are you doing?"

Sleep coated her voice, and Dylan smiled. "Getting dressed. I have stuff to get done."

Meg blinked fast and pushed the blanket off her lap. "Give me a minute, and I'll help you."

"Don't worry. Not much needs to be done this morning. Just keep the bed warm for me, and I'll be back before you know it."

"Don't be ridiculous. I don't mind helping. I need to see to the horses once we're done here, anyway." She swung her legs over the edge of the bed.

Grabbing a long-sleeved shirt from his drawer, he yanked it over his head. "No, you don't. I texted Emma last night and asked her to take care of the horses. She said she would, as long I promised you'd go dress shopping later with her, Jillian, and Catie."

"I'd rather do chores and feed horses." Groaning,

161

Meg fell back into the bed and hid under the blanket.

Dylan chuckled. "Shopping won't be bad. She mentioned Sophie wanted to try on flower girl dresses. I'm sure you don't want to miss her playing princess."

"Wait a minute." She narrowed her eyes. "If you made sure Emma would take care of the horses this morning, you were pretty sure I'd stay the night."

Grinning, he leaned down and kissed her forehead. "Let's just call it optimistic." Dylan rushed through his morning routine in record time. The second his foot stepped through the kitchen door, he put breakfast in Betsy's bowl to keep her happy and ran up the stairs. He stopped at the foot of the bed. He drank in Meg's sleeping form. Her head rested on the pillow with the blanket tucked around her. He was glad she fell back asleep. She didn't often get a chance to sleep in.

God, she was beautiful.

He snuck in beside her and wrapped her into his embrace. His hoodie scrunched up around his neck.

"You're so cold!" she shrieked, pulling away and laughing.

"Just my hands. And you're so warm. Come here and heat me up." He refused to let her go.

She finally relented and snuggled against him.

He circled his arms around her, kissed the back of her head, and buried his head in her hair. The silky strands tickled his face, and her coconut shampoo swarmed his senses as he drifted back to sleep with the woman he loved in his arms.

****

Cold air whipped through the split railing of the white-washed porch at Annie's inn. Dylan enjoyed a few more hours with Meg, but he couldn't keep her tucked away from her family forever. "I really don't want to leave your side today." He nuzzled her neck. He didn't have a choice. Emma would hunt them down if he wasn't on time.

"No one knows we're here yet. Let's just go back to your place. Jillian won't mind." Meg linked her fingers with his and pulled him toward the stairs.

"Jillian might not mind, but Emma would. She's always scared me a little. I don't want to make her mad." He rooted his feet to the porch, resisting her pull.

Meg lifted her brows. "A big guy like you is afraid of Emma?"

"Hell, yeah. Aren't you?" He tucked a stray piece of her hair behind her ear.

"Maybe a little bit, but I'll deny admitting my fear if you ever tell her," Meg said.

Dylan chuckled. "Fine. It will be our secret."

The door flew open, and Sophie squealed and jumped up and down. "We're going shopping, Meg-Meg. I get a pretty dress. I love pretty dresses! Come on." She grabbed Meg's hand and dragged her in the house.

Meg glanced over her shoulder with a smile. "Call me later."

Giving them a quick wave, he caught sight from the corner of his eye of Annie entering the nursery. He wanted to talk to her about what happened at dinner the other night. Now was the perfect time to catch her without anyone else around. Following her path, he found her shuffling through papers at her desk. He knocked on her doorframe, and then took a seat.

Annie glanced up and knit together her brows. "Please tell me I haven't lost my mind, and you just got here."

"If you've lost your mind, I'm positive I'm not the one to blame."

Annie tossed papers on her desk and braced her elbows on her armrests. "Ha! I'm not so sure. You've given me just as many gray hairs as the rest of my kids."

He leaned back and crossed an ankle over his knee. "I don't see any gray hairs from where I'm sitting."

"You've always been a very sweet and charming boy, haven't you? And you're right, I don't have gray hairs, just fake blonde ones." Annie gave him a wink. "What brings you here? I'm guessing you finally brought my daughter home."

Heat scorched his cheeks. "Yes, ma'am. Safe and sound."

"And is she happy?"

He shifted his gaze to the floor and kept the image of Meg's swollen lips and flushed cheeks from his mind. "Yes. Well, at least she was until Sophie fetched her and reminded her she had pretty dresses to try on."

Annie laughed. "Playing dress up would dampen her spirits. I'm glad you two worked out your problem. I don't want to know the details. I'm just glad you fixed your issues. I like you two together."

"Really?" He lifted his gaze. "I wasn't sure how you felt about Meg and I being in a relationship."

"I can't think of any other man I'd feel better about my Meg settling down with."

His heart swelled. "That means a lot to me."

"What I think shouldn't mean much to you, but I'm glad it concerns you. I have a feeling, however, seeking my approval for your relationship isn't why you're here."

He shifted in his seat. "You're right, it's not. I want to talk about what happened at dinner the other night. I don't feel right about you and Meg fighting over my reputation. I know you have your concerns about Meg and me using her ideas at my farm, but I want to reassure you I don't. I'm extremely confident in what Meg has planned, or I wouldn't go forward with them. I've studied her research, as well as doing my own, and I'm convinced this option is best for me and my family."

Annie heaved a large sigh and folded her hands in front of her. "I won't lie. I am worried about you. I love you like a son, and I would hate to see something Meg cooked up backfiring and you losing the farm. Trust me, I know what it's like to be backed into a corner and forced into making drastic changes to help your family." Frowning, she dipped her chin and locked her gaze to his. "Do you think I wanted to sell our farmland after my husband died? Do you think I wanted to turn my home into an inn, where my children would be forced to live with strangers always around? I would have given anything to make things different, but I didn't have a choice. I would hate to see you make changes forced on you and for those choices to blow up in your face."

He leaned forward and rested his forearms on his thighs. "I appreciate you looking out for me, but you shouldn't at Meg's expense. I don't feel forced into making these changes—at least not by Meg. She's been nothing but understanding and helpful, making sure I know no hard feelings will exist if I decide to go another way. But I've looked at a hundred different options, and Meg's plan is the only way."

She leaned back in her chair and drew together her brows. "Do you really think it will work? You can save your farm by building an indoor arena on your property? I don't see how you'd make money. Especially with what it will cost to rebuild your barn."

Confusion brewed in his mind. "You think all I'm building is an arena for Meg to give riding lessons?"

Annie frowned. "Well, yes. She's pestered me about it for years. I don't want buildings taking up all my land. I want my guests to have a nice view and a place to wander around."

Dylan shook his head. "She's never discussed everything else she wanted?" Annie had no idea the extent of Meg's dream, yet she'd shut it down. No wonder Meg was hesitant.

"She's mentioned a few other things here and there but nothing in detail. Something about buying a half dozen goats or planting some pumpkins in my garden."

Dylan sat back and rubbed a hand over his mouth. Either Annie didn't listen to Meg, or Meg didn't really talk to her mom. "You need to talk to Meg."

Annie threw her hands in the air. "I've tried, but she won't listen."

"Let me rephrase that, you need to listen to Meg. You have an amazing daughter with an amazing brain. She developed an entire idea not just to save my farm but put it on the map. She approached you about what she had in mind, and I'd hate to think you were so dismissive that you didn't even give her a chance."

Annie winced. "I'd hate to think that, too."

Dylan stood and covered her hand. "Talk to her, Annie. Let her know you're on her side, and you believe in her."

She widened her eyes. "Of course, I do!"

"She doesn't think so, and honestly, neither did I until now."

Chapter Seventeen

Meg waded through the taffeta and lace gowns fluttering from hangers on either side of her in the main room of Bridal Works. She lifted a finger and trailed it along the beaded bodice of a princess style gown and shuddered. "How did I end up here?"

"Would you be quiet? We're here for Jillian. You don't want to hurt her feelings." Emma darted her gaze up and down the aisle. "Thank God, she's busy fussing over Sophie with Catie so she can't hear your constant complaining."

Meg followed her gaze and chuckled. "How did Sophie steal the spotlight from the bride?"

"What can I say?" Emma shrugged and shook her head. "She has a gift. We might want to save them before Sophie talks them into letting her try on every dress here."

Sophie's shrieks of delight drifted across the store. Meg turned to the raised stand surrounded by mirrors, and moisture pooled at the corners of her eyes.

Sophie twirled in a cream teacup dress. Her giggles rolled out faster and faster as she spun around on her tiptoes and then fell into a heap of organza that engulfed her tiny little body as she sat on the floor.

"Where did my Sophie go?" Emma called, pretending to search for her. "She was right here. Where could she have gone?"

"Here, Mommy!"

Sophie's giggle morphed into an all-out belly laugh as she waved her arms wildly in the air. She hated to admit it, but Dylan was right. Seeing Sophie here was something she was glad to be a part of. She hoped most of the attention would stay on Sophie and Jillian, and she wouldn't be forced into trying on tons of dresses. She glanced over in Catie's direction, and dread punched into her gut. Jillian's best friend held at least ten different bridesmaid dresses. "Are you trying on all of those dresses?"

Catie beamed. "Whatever Jillian wants the maid of honor to try on."

"Don't worry, Meg." Jillian offered her a small smile. "I figured Emma could try whatever dresses she thinks both of you would like. I know shopping isn't exactly your thing, and you both will look good in anything. Just make sure to tell us if you don't like a particular one."

Meg smirked. "I can manage that."

Sophie ran over and grabbed Emma's hand. "Play dress up, Mommy?"

Emma chuckled and swung their joined hands back and forth, training her gaze on Jillian. "What do you want me to put on first, Jillian?"

Jillian grabbed several dresses from the selection on the rack Catie guarded. She gave some to Emma and some to Catie.

Both women, along with Sophie, found their dressing rooms.

Meg sat, waiting for the dresses to be revealed.

"Have you talked to your mom?" Jillian kept her gaze locked on the closed dressing room doors.

"Not really." Meg crossed her ankles and leaned back in the chair. Shopping wasn't too bad when she didn't have to try on anything. "I'm not exactly sure what to say."

"I understand. Her reaction surprised me the other night. Your family always sticks together. I assumed she would back you on anything."

Meg rolled her eyes and snorted. "She would back Emma or Jonah. Backing me is a different story."

Jillian shifted to face her and crinkled her eyes. "Do you really believe she'd give Jonah or Emma more support?"

Resentment gurgled in her stomach. "I do. I'll always be seen as the baby of the family. Never as the woman who worked by her side for years to help build her businesses, and not as the woman who could potentially make those businesses even more successful." She pinched the thighs of her jeans, hating the tears that burned behind her eyes. "I'm the one who stayed here to make sure Mom wasn't alone when everyone else left."

"You mean you didn't stay in Smithview because you wanted to?"

Meg shrugged. "Mom was heartbroken when Jonah left and joined the Marines. She was proud as hell, and even understood why he did it, but not having him here still broke her heart. When Emma left for college, her absence was almost as hard. She didn't have to constantly worry about her like she did for Jonah, but she hated Emma was so far away. She assumed Emma would return after college, and her not coming home was a hard pill to swallow. When it was my turn to graduate and move on with my life, I couldn't leave her."

"I always thought you liked working with your mom?" Jillian tilted her head to the side and furrowed her brow.

"I can't imagine not working with my horses every day, and I love managing the nursery. The land is in my blood, more than it ever was with Jonah or Emma. Mom and I share that passion, and we work well together." She shrugged, searching for the words to explain her feelings. "I just wish I could do more. I wish I would have experienced more. Mom thinks I don't have the knowledge, or the understanding, to contribute to what she's built."

"Have you ever told her how you feel?"

"No, what's the point? She's made her feelings perfectly clear." Her stomach clenched.

Jillian placed a hand on Meg's arm. "Well, for what it's worth, I think your idea is brilliant. I don't know all the ins and outs of your plan, but it sounds amazing."

Gratitude warmed her center. "That means a lot. Especially coming from you."

Jillian frowned. "Why from me?"

Meg lifted the side of her mouth and kept her gaze fixed on her jeans. "What you've created at Kiddy Korner inspired me to think outside the box."

"Really?" Jillian sat back in her chair and ran a hand through her hair.

Meg locked her gaze with Jillian and smiled. "Yes, really. You didn't just open a successful children's bookstore. You created a space where parents could bring their kids for fun and entertainment. You created a destination. I want the same thing for Dylan's farm."

"It will be amazing, Meg. That you would use Kiddy Korner as inspiration means a lot."

Meg lifted a shoulder. "Not just your store, but you. You did it all yourself. You built your business, and then you expanded it with Books Above. I'd like to think if you can do it, so can I."

Jillian grabbed her hand and gave it a squeeze. "I know you can. Don't let anyone ever make you doubt yourself. If I can do anything to help, all you have to do is ask. You need to talk to your mom, though. You never know. She might surprise you."

"What do you think?" Emma asked. "Sophie picked this one out."

Meg grimaced. "No, no, no." She stood, shaking her head as she grabbed the dresses waiting to go into the dressing rooms. "No way will you see me wearing anything even close to that thing. Too much pink, too many ruffles. Go ahead and put your clothes back on, Emma. I'll take care of finding the perfect dress."

After Meg picked out the bridesmaid dresses, Sophie chose her flower girl dress, and Jillian decided on a wedding gown, they treated themselves to lunch at Jillian's favorite Italian restaurant. Meg placed her order and snuggled close to Sophie on the vinyl seat of their booth.

Catie pursed her lips and wiggled her eyebrows. "Okay, Meg, now it's time to spill the beans about you and Dylan."

Flames of heat licked her face, and she hid behind her menu. Catie was Jillian's best friend and had also grown up in Smithview. She was an acquaintance, but not someone she knew well. Discussing her personal life with people she was close with was hard enough.

She had no desire to talk about her relationship with Catie. Peering over her menu, she glanced at Emma. Maybe she'd help her.

"I'm not sure Meg wants to talk about Dylan," Jillian chimed in.

"I think he's something I might want to talk about," Emma said.

She would kill Emma.

"Especially since I had to get out of my nice, comfortable bed before Anderson was even awake this morning to feed her horses." Emma cleared her throat and pursed her lips.

Catie and Jillian faced Meg, mouths open and eyebrows raised high.

Meg sighed and threw her menu on the table. She wasn't getting out of this. "I hate you sometimes," she said under her breath.

"But you love me all the time, so go ahead and spill the beans." Emma set her menu aside and focused on Meg.

"I second that," said Catie. "Dylan's so handsome and rugged. He's always so sweet, but something tells me more is going on. Like something down deep is dying to break out."

Jillian laughed. "Down, girl. I'm not sure Meg wants you talking about how sexy you think her man is, and I don't think your husband would appreciate it either."

"Oh, phooey. Emma would agree an active imagination is key to having a successful marriage. I can't help it if my imagination has once or twice wondered how good Mr. Gilbert is with those very large hands." Catie threw back her head and laughed.

Meg couldn't help but giggle along with the rest of the women. "Don't worry, he's very, very good with those hands."

Emma shot up her eyebrows and beamed. "Seriously? Was last night the first time you made this discovery?"

"Don't expect me to go into detail here, especially with your daughter present." Meg shifted her gaze toward Sophie.

Emma rolled her eyes. "Trust me, when Sophie's playing on my phone, she's oblivious to everything else. You don't have to go into detail, but did you guys work out whatever was going on yesterday?"

"Wait, what was going on yesterday?" Catie dipped together her brows. "You already had a fight?"

"More like a misunderstanding. Which, by the way, thanks for having my back. Dylan told me Jonah was upset." Meg aimed a smile at Jillian.

"What do Jonah and Jillian know that I don't?" Emma narrowed her eyes. "You were in such a bad mood yesterday you didn't tell me anything."

"Jillian saw Dylan leaving The Village Idiot with Sally, after he and I had our misunderstanding." A pang of hurt pulsed through her. Although she and Dylan worked out things, the image of Dylan with another woman was burned in her brain.

"What?" Emma and Catie shouted in unison.

Sophie glanced up. "Dylan left with Sally." After she spoke, she returned to her game.

"She isn't paying any attention, huh, Emma?" Meg asked. Choosing her words carefully, she gave a very short and condensed version of what happened the day before.

Jillian interrupted. "Make sure to remind me to give Dylan a hug. I'm glad someone gave that idiot a piece of their mind. I might end up doing more if I see him around town."

"Amen," agreed Catie.

"Everyone thinks you're too good for him," Emma said quietly.

Meg glanced around the table, and her mouth fell open. "Why didn't anyone ever tell me?"

"We didn't want to hurt your feelings. He was the man you chose to marry. We didn't want to make you mad." Emma rested a hand over Meg's.

"He wasn't always such a jerk. The first few years were great." She inhaled a deep breath and crumpled a napkin in her hands. "I can't believe I wasted so much time. I couldn't believe the person Blake became in the last couple years was the real him." Three sets of watery eyes stared with nothing but compassion etched on their faces. And for once, their concern did nothing but make Meg's heart double in size. Here were people who loved her—who she could share life's ups and downs with.

Something she should have done more of. "I'm sorry. I didn't mean to bring everyone down." Meg forced a chuckle.

"Don't you dare apologize for opening up. I hate you've gone through such a bad relationship and didn't talk to me." Emma grabbed a napkin and dabbed the corner of her eyes.

"I could have if I had wanted to. And honestly, Blake and I didn't spend much time together. He would rather drink with his friends, while I would rather be with my horses or spend time with Dylan." Meg stopped and smiled. "I was so oblivious to how I felt. I look back at the last couple of years, and it's so clear to me. How could I have not seen how Dylan felt about me? How could I not realize I had feelings for him?"

"Life's funny," Jillian said. "Sometimes we're so caught in our own stubborn ways, we don't stop and see what's smacking us in the face."

Catie grinned. "You would know, wouldn't you? If you'd opened your eyes sooner, this wedding would have taken place years ago."

"True." Jillian wiggled her eyebrows. "What about you, Meg? What does that mean for you and Dylan?"

Her lips curved into a slow smile. "I might have found the man I've always dreamed of."

****

Meg watched Emma carry a sleeping Sophie inside. She'd returned to the inn later than anticipated, and she was eager to get going. She'd told Dylan to call her, but she couldn't sit and wait. Taking out her phone, she called Dylan.

"Hi there. How'd it go?" Dylan asked.

"You were right. I'm glad I went." Meg climbed into her truck and brought the engine to life. She let the truck idle so she could concentrate on her conversation.

"I figured you would be. Did Sophie have a blast?"

Meg chuckled. "She was hilarious. She talked Emma into letting her try on every flower girl dress in the store. I took some pictures for you."

"I'd love to see them."

"Good. How about now?"

"You just can't stay away, huh?"

She could practically hear his grin. "Apparently not. But if it's too much to have me stay over again tonight, I can head back into my mom's and stay here with Emma. I'm sure she'd love to have a good, old-fashioned slumber party."

"Emma's had plenty of sleepovers with you. Besides, I think you'd have more fun with me."

Her pulse quickened, and she shifted the truck into Drive, letting the wheels roll toward the front of the driveway. "Oh really? Is this you being optimistic again?"

"You bet it is."

Meg erupted into laughter. "I guess we'll find out. I need to stop by my place first to pick up some stuff."

"Don't you dare. I have everything you'll need here."

"But what will I do without my pajamas?" Grinning, she turned the opposite direction of her house and headed toward Dylan's.

"Don't you worry. I'm sure we'll come up with something."

Oh, she had an idea of two. "If you insist. I'll see you soon."

Traffic was nonexistent on her way out of town. A dusting of snow covered the barren fields on either side of the road. She slid into Dylan's driveway, hopped out of her truck, and let herself into his house. The entryway was dark except for one, lone candle lit on the table by the door. She grabbed a note beside the candle, and her heart hammered in her chest.

Meg,
Come upstairs. I'll be waiting.
D

She ran up the stairs and burst into Dylan's bedroom. She tried to smother her giggles. He wasn't there. More candles illuminated the empty room, and another note rested on the bed.

Meg,

Go into the bathroom.

D

She entered the darkness and flipped on the light. A new, pink toothbrush sat on the sink. A hairbrush rested beside it, along with the face wash she always used.

"I thought you could use a few things when you stayed here."

Meg whirled around to see Dylan standing behind her, holding a beautiful silk robe in his hands. "You bought all of this for me?"

"I'm not a big fan of you wearing clothes when you're here. You might want a robe to cover up with. You'd look good in this one, but I put a warmer one on the hook behind the door. Something more substantial if you're walking around the house would be wiser."

Meg caressed the delicate robe he extended, and emotion constricted her airway. "This is the nicest thing anyone's ever done. Thank you."

"It's no big deal."

"Yes, it is," she whispered. Resting her hands on his hard chest, she inched him out of the bathroom. She grabbed the robe and draped it over the dresser. "I don't think we'll need this tonight." She took his hand and led him to the bed, planning to show him how grateful she truly was.

Chapter Eighteen

The next morning, Dylan scrambled some eggs and put on the coffee pot. Scents of breakfast filled the air and made his mouth water. He fixed a plate for Meg and set it in front of her. The fleece robe he'd bought hung heavy on her small frame.

Meg sat at the kitchen table and scooped a spoonful of eggs in her mouth. "I might have you do all my shopping."

Dylan handed her a cup of coffee, and then sat across from her. "Honey, I'll buy you anything you want."

Meg beamed. "You know, I never knew I could be this happy. I always thought at least one part of my life had to be incomplete."

"And now?" Her words warmed a piece of his soul, but he held his breath waiting for her response.

She cradled her mug in her hands. "I guess I'm not happy about where I'm at with my mom right now, but I know we'll be fine."

"Nothing's ever perfect, but I'm glad you're happy with us." He took a sip of his coffee. The caffeine buzzed inside his veins, and the bitter liquid slid down his throat. He put down his mug, grabbed a piece of bacon, and tossed it to Betsy before snagging a piece for himself.

"How could I not be?"

"What do you have planned for the rest of the day? Spending time with Emma and the kids?"

"No, they're going home today. After we finish eating, I'll head to the barn to deal with the horses. Then I need to pop into the nursery. I played hooky on Friday, so I need to make sure everything's in order for the upcoming week." She sipped her coffee, then peered over the rim. "What about you?"

"Not too much. I need to look into hiring help around here for planting once spring hits, and I'm heading to my parents for dinner later. Lisa's still in town, and Mom insists we have a nice meal together before she leaves. Want to come?" His family had known Meg for years, but not as the woman he was in a relationship with. Meg agreeing to have dinner with them would mean a lot.

She widened her eyes. "I'd love to. Well, maybe not seeing Lisa, but I'd love to spend some time with your parents. I don't know them well."

"I should warn you, I'm not sure what kind of mood Dad will be in. You'd love the man he used to be, but now, he's more of a wild card."

Meg set her mug on the table. "I'm sure I'll love him, no matter what. Deep down, he'll always be the father you love. No disease can destroy the memories you have."

His chest tightened. Grief, fresh and raw, beat through him. Watching someone you loved slip away little by little was the hardest thing he'd ever done. "I know, but that doesn't make dealing with Dad's failing health any easier."

"I'm sure it doesn't."

He sat in comfortable silence while they finished

their breakfast.

Meg grabbed their empty plates and placed them in the sink. "Where's the dish soap?"

"You don't have to wash those. I can clean up after you leave." He extended a hand toward the dishes filling the sink.

"I don't mind. Besides, you somehow convinced me not to help you again this morning. I need to keep a change of clothes in my truck so I have work clothes to throw on in the mornings." Ducking, she checked the cabinet under the sink and retrieved the soap.

Dylan walked behind her and wrapped his arms around her as she washed the dirty dishes. "Why would you keep them in your truck? Just keep some stuff in a drawer upstairs."

She glanced over her shoulder. "Are you sure?"

"Of course, why wouldn't I be?" The idea of sharing a piece of his home with her warmed his heart.

"I don't want you to feel like I'm taking over your space, or like things are moving too quickly." Meg twirled the ends of her hair between her fingers.

He chuckled. "You can't be serious. As far as I'm concerned, this relationship is years in the making. I'm willing to go as fast, or as slow, as you are. All you have to do is say the word, and I'll move around things so you have all the space you need. Besides, it'll be lonely around here without you."

"I did want to ask you one thing." Meg turned into him and rested her palms on his chest. "Can I stay here tonight, and can I bring Nora? I've been okay with leaving her at my mom's all weekend because of Sophie, but I want her with me now since Emma's going home."

He lowered his mouth to her neck, placing small kisses up the side. He nibbled at the lobe of her ear. "Nora is always welcome here."

She shivered. "I've had her here when I've come out to visit, but never all night. I wanted to make sure you and Betsy are good with it."

Dylan lifted his head and glanced at Betsy. "What do you think, girl? Are you up for having a playmate around the house?"

Betsy gave one bark in response.

Dylan laughed. "Then the situation is all settled. How about I pick up you and Nora tonight around five, and then we'll drop her off here before heading to my parents?"

"It's a date." Meg grinned. "Now let me wash these dishes so I can complete my work for the day. The sooner I finish, the sooner I'll be with you again."

He had no doubt Nora and Betsy would have a great time together, but he wasn't so sure about how dinner would go. The meal would depend on his dad and if he'd be the man Dylan loved and respected, or if his disease would sweep in and steal the spotlight.

****

The sun slid closer to the horizon and cast an orangish glow around the old century home Meg lived in. Dylan was halfway to the porch, the snow crunching under his boots, when the front door squeaked open.

Nora ran to him.

He knelt to scratch behind her ears. A brown boot stopped below his nose. He scanned his gaze upward, taking in the shapely calf hugged behind the supple leather. He stood slowly. The rest of her body came into view, and a shiver of desire raced down his spine. "You look beautiful, Meg."

A flush crept across her cheeks, and she dragged the hem of her dress farther over her knees. "Thanks. I thought I'd leave the T-shirts at home and look somewhat decent for your family." She lifted a hand, hoisting a duffel bag in the air. "I brought some stuff for your place. I hope I don't scare you off by the size." She lifted her mouth and widened her eyes.

Dylan grabbed the bag, and then gave her a kiss on the cheek. "Lucky for you, I don't scare easy." Ushering her to his truck with a light touch to the small of her back, he helped her inside then climbed in and drove to meet his family after dropping off Nora. He rested his hand on her knee as she told him about her day, then turned into his parents' parking lot and slid into a spot close to the apartment. He shut off the truck and pulled the keys out of the ignition. "Are you ready?"

Meg took a deep, shaky breath. "I think so. I'm a little nervous."

"But you hide it so well." Dylan coughed to hide a laugh.

Meg slapped his arm. "I can't help my nerves. I want to make a good first impression."

"Tonight isn't the first time you've met my family. They already know and like you. You have nothing to be nervous about."

"This is my first time being around them as your…"

"Girlfriend?"

"Is that what you told them?" Her body was still and her eyes wide.

"They know we're seeing each other, but I don't

think I've used that exact word. Would I be out of line if I did?" His heart hammered in his chest, and he studied her, waiting for her response.

Meg grinned and melted back into her seat. "Not at all."

He released a pent-up breath. "Good. Now let's get in there. I'm starving, and my mom made her homemade noodles to impress you." Dylan led Meg into the apartment.

Mom strode toward them with a red-and-white-checked dishcloth in her hands. She wrapped Dylan in a quick hug before squeezing Meg's shoulders. "We're so happy to have you here, dear. I hope you're hungry. Everything's ready. You come on in with me and take a seat."

"Thank you, Mrs. Gilbert. Everything smells amazing."

Mary waved a hand in the air. "Don't act all formal around me. I've never wanted you to call me Mrs. Gilbert in the past, and I most certainly don't want you to do so now."

Dylan chuckled and followed them to the table. "Don't scare her off with your bossiness, Mom."

"Oh, stop it. I want her to be comfortable. You can have a seat right over here beside Dylan." She grabbed the back of an empty chair and pulled it out.

"Sounds perfect, thank you." Meg glanced across the table and nodded a hello to Lisa, then focused on Walter. "Am I to assume I'm not supposed to call you Mr. Gilbert?" She widened her grin.

Dylan held his breath. He could never tell how his dad would react.

Walter burst into a fit of laughter.

Tension seeped from Dylan's shoulders. Dad was in a good mood tonight.

"Girl, you can call me whatever the heck you want. Now let's sit down and eat before the food gets cold." Walter grabbed the bowl of mashed potatoes and heaped a spoonful onto his plate.

Dylan scooted in Meg's seat and sat next to her. Bowls and platters littered the table. The homemade noodles passed under his nose, and his mouth watered. His mom only made them on special occasions. Scents of garlic and butter and home took over the room. His stomach rumbled. He scooped a large mound on his plate, and then passed the bowl to his dad.

Walter placed noodles on his plate, then glanced at Meg. "So, I hear you're the mastermind behind all these changes we're considering at the farm. I'd like to know where you got your ideas and maybe get a better picture of what you and my son have in mind."

Meg's gaze flickered to Dylan.

He nodded his encouragement.

She cleared her throat and straightened in her seat. "I wanted my mother to agree to build an indoor arena at the inn. I take care of the stables at her place, and we've built quite the reputation for riding lessons. I have a lot of students who take regular lessons, and we also offer lessons to guests at the inn. That revenue takes a huge hit in the winter months, and I'm convinced we'd see a lot more revenue if we offered students an indoor arena." She filled her plate with filled while she spoke.

"Makes sense." Walter nodded along with his words.

"I think so." Meg grabbed a biscuit. "I've studied

the numbers to see how much we've made over the years just from guests of the inn taking spontaneous lessons. When I realized how much we really made, I was floored. Now, most people who stay at the inn are not coming to take riding lessons. They're staying because they have events in the area, or they're passing through and don't have many options for a place to stay. I'm sure these people find themselves hanging around with nothing to occupy their time. They think, what the heck? Might as well ride a horse. People wanting to pass their time taking riding lesions got me thinking. What else would people pay for if they found themselves with time to kill and a little extra money to spend?"

"And you think people would pay to come out to a farm?" Lisa's eyes narrowed on Meg.

"I do." Meg nodded and forked a bite of chicken. "Think about it. What do families like to do in the fall?"

"Go trick or treating? Carve pumpkins?" Lisa splayed her hands in front of her and shrugged.

Meg pointed her fork toward Lisa. "Exactly. They like to spend time together doing fun, fall-themed activities. From Smithview, the drive to a small farm where you can buy pumpkins and get a cup of apple cider is fifty minutes. Anything more is a good ninety minutes away."

"What else is there?" Walter spread butter on a roll then took a bite.

"A family can have an entire experience they'll remember forever. You can provide hayrides, corn mazes, pumpkin carving, and scarecrows. Mums, caramel apples, and kettle corn are available to sell. You give people an incredible experience, and they come back every single year."

Dylan's chest swelled. She was so damn confident about her plan. How could it not work? Grinning, he shoveled his mom's mouth-watering home cooking into his mouth. An explosion of salt and crispy skin from the fried chicken hit his taste buds.

"That does sound nice." Mary nodded and took a sip from her water glass. "It sounds like fall would be very busy and riding lessons in the winter. But what about the rest of the year? Would we make enough off those two seasons to give us the profit we need?"

Meg dabbed the corner of her mouth with a napkin then placed it back on her lap. "This part is up to you. The arena will give you a place for lessons, as well as stalls to lease out for boarding horses. Trust me, boarding horses brings in good money by itself. You can stop there and see how things take off before deciding to do more, or you can plan more now so you're prepared when doing your initial remodel and expansion."

"What are the other possibilities?" Lisa leaned forward in her chair.

"Well, you already have a half dozen animals. By adding a few more barn animals, you could open a small petting zoo for children. If you already have horses and a trainer, you could think about offering children's birthday parties." She set down her fork and settled her clasped hands on the table. "If you wanted to go bigger, you could create a venue for weddings and other events. Right now, the inn is the only place in town consistently booking these events. My mom does a great job, but the only issue she runs into is a lack of indoor space when the weather turns bad. You could fill that need and offer a year-round space."

Mary wrung her hands and tilted her head to the side. "You don't think us opening an event space would hurt your mom's business, do you? I would hate for any hard feelings to develop."

Meg sighed. "I've talked to my mom, and she has no interest. Her priorities are the inn and nursery. Having another option in town won't hurt her chances of functions being booked at the inn. They would be two very different venues with opposite atmospheres."

Dylan tilted back his chair on two legs and studied his family. He'd made up his mind, but they needed to figure out their thoughts. His gaze narrowed on the slight trembling of his dad's hands, and anxiety danced in the pit of his stomach.

"True, and the majority of what we'd do wouldn't affect her at all." Mary's shoulders relaxed.

Walter darted his gaze between Meg and Dylan with his now-clasped hands on the table. "I think everything you said sounds well thought out, well researched, and like a damn good idea. My concern is we'd have a lot of work at the farm to build this little destination. Where are we getting the money? Have you two figured out how much the renovations will cost?"

"We ran a lot of numbers." Dylan glanced at Meg, then focused on Dad. "We looked at all the different scenarios and broke down costs based on each specific project. The only one that could vary significantly from our projected cost is the barn renovation. If we do just an arena and build stalls, the cost is high but not alarming. If we go ahead and add to the barn to make an event space, the cost gets a little scary."

Lisa rested her chin on a hand. "Can't we do the

initial renovation with the insurance money from the fire and wait to do more? Then we make sure we have money coming in before we overextend ourselves."

Dylan nodded. "We could. Waiting would be a lot less scary, but it might cost us more money in the end. If we have students taking lessons and boarding their horses, we'd lose their business while we undertake another remodel. Completing all the renovations at once might make more sense."

"If we're doing this, we might as well do it right." Walter cleared his throat and darted his gaze around the table. "To make money all year round, we'll need the full renovation. I agree with Dylan—waiting would cost more in the long run. The insurance money won't go far, but we'll get the rest of the money."

The trepidation in his gut grew. Dad's words made sense, but his eyes glazed over with a confusion Dylan was too used to witnessing. He glanced at his mom, wanting to keep the conversation on the right track. His dad didn't fully understand the state of their finances. He nodded. "Okay then, we'll figure it out."

Walter's hand stopped halfway to his mouth, and he fixed his narrowed gaze at the mashed potatoes. He threw the fork on his plate, and his lips moved with unspoken words.

Oh no. While his mom and sister discussed the farm, Dylan shoveled food into his mouth as fast as possible. Apprehension stole any taste from registering on his tongue. Dread took over his stomach, and he pushed away his plate, unable to eat another bite. He needed to get Meg out of here. "The hour is getting a little late. Time for Meg and me to take off. Thanks for everything, Mom."

"Would you like me to help you clean before we go?" Meg picked up her plate.

She hadn't even eaten half of her food. He didn't want to rush off, but he had no choice. Thank God, Meg wasn't asking any questions.

Walter banged his fists on the table. "You put down those dishes, girl. Who do you think you are? Coming into my house and stealing my plates. You have some nerve."

Mary took Walter's hand and murmured in his ear.

Meg froze, eyes wide and lips parted.

Dylan crouched beside his dad. "Hey, Dad, I have to talk about planting season. I need some advice. How about we take a seat in the living room, and we let Mom and Lisa deal with this mess?"

Walter shifted his gaze to Dylan. "No problem, boy. It's almost time to get back out in those fields again. Pretty soon, you'll be old enough to sit in the tractor with me. Of course, I'd have had you in there sooner if your mom wasn't so over protective."

Dylan helped his dad stand and led him to his chair. He knelt in front of him, easing him back and propping up his feet. His heart thundered, and he mentally counted to ten to calm his bouncing nerves. Tears threatened to fill his eyes, and he cleared his throat to push them back. His dad droned on about the farm, but no sounds registered in Dylan's brain. He glanced toward Meg, and their gazes met. His racing heart stilled, and his father's words rang in his ears.

Meg was his rock—his anchor. She would keep him from drifting away during the nightmare.

Chapter Nineteen

The door shut behind them, and Meg gave Dylan's hand a reassuring squeeze.

Sighing, he pressed his lips flat. "I won't ever get used to seeing him change in the blink of an eye from my dad to a stranger I barely recognize."

Meg walked beside him toward his truck, and her head spun. Cool blasts of winter air splashed against her warm cheeks. "I didn't really know what to expect. I was alarmed by how fast his demeanor changed."

"I could tell he was slipping. I've spent so much time with him, I'm pretty good at reading the signs. That's why I wanted to leave. I didn't want you to see him when he gets confused. I'm sorry if he scared you." He stopped beside the passenger door of the truck and faced her.

Emotion made his voice thick, and she hugged his arm close to her side. "Dylan, don't ever think I don't want to see who your dad is. The man he used to be, or the one he's slowly becoming. No matter what, he's your father, and I'm honored to spend time with him."

"Thank you. That's sweet."

"I'm not being sweet. I'm being honest. I can see how hard watching him deteriorate is, and I hate you have to go through this. But I was amazed watching you with him. You knew what to say and how to react." She blinked back tears. He didn't need her getting emotional right now.

Dylan shrugged. "Not always. My mom needs help. He's getting worse, and he's too much for her to deal with."

"You guys will figure out what's best." Gratitude squeezed her heart that her parent was well. She was young when she'd lost her father, and the idea her mother wouldn't always be around was too much to imagine—even if her mom drove her crazy sometimes.

Dylan opened her door.

She climbed in.

He slapped her bottom.

Laughing, she swatted him away. All right, he was done talking about his dad.

Climbing into the cab, he grinned. "Ready to head back and see how the dogs fared?"

"Sure. Why don't we stop by my place first and grab my truck? Me not having it is silly. Then you don't have to worry about driving me to work in the morning."

"I don't mind driving you." He shifted the engine into first gear and slid onto the street.

"I know you don't, but there's really no need. Drop me off at my house, and I'll follow you to yours."

Dylan weaved through the quiet streets.

Lamp posts dotted the empty sidewalks, and specks of snow fell through their beams of light as he drove to her house. Meg straightened and stared out the window. "Is that my mom's car?"

"Were you expecting to see your mom tonight?" Dylan parked his truck.

"Not at all. She didn't call me to ask to stop over. Why would she just show up here and wait for me to get home?" Her blood warmed in her veins. This stunt was so like her mom to drop in without caring about her plans. She could have at least sent her a text.

"Maybe she was afraid you'd tell her not to come if she asked."

Meg snorted. "She's a smart woman."

"Why don't you head inside and talk? Take your time, see what she wants, and then head out to my place when you're done." Facing her, he gave her a small smile.

She rested her head on the back of her seat. "Do I have to? Maybe we can slowly back out of the driveway, and she'll never know we were here."

He leaned forward and tucked a strand of hair behind her ear. "If you really want me to, I will. But do you think you can relax tonight if you're wondering what she wanted? You might as well talk to her now and get it over with."

She blew a hard breath out of her nose. "Fine. I can't promise I'll be in a good mood after I'm done."

Dylan leaned over and nibbled her ear. "I can help."

Meg scowled. His tongue touched her earlobe, and heat shot through her veins. She pushed him away and laughed. "I'll see you in a few." Her brain told her to move at a snail's pace, but the harsh coldness snaked up her dress. Instead, she jogged, and her breath floated in wisps in front of her. She didn't bother to find her keys. If her mom was in the house, she wouldn't have locked the door again. She stepped inside.

Annie flickered her gaze to the door before she lifted the remote and shut off the TV. She clasped her hands in her lap and watched Meg with steady eyes.

Meg sighed and slipped her feet out of her boots. An awkward stillness pulsed between them.

"Hi," Annie said.

Meg crossed her arms over her chest. She stayed by the door, because she wasn't planning on being here long. "Hi. What are you doing here?"

"I wanted to talk, and discussing things here would be better than talking at work tomorrow."

Irritation itched her skin. "How long have you been here? You could have called, and I would have let you know when I'd be home. Actually, you're lucky I showed up at all. Dylan dropped me off to get my truck, and then I'm heading to his place for the night."

Annie shrugged, a tight smile on her lips. "I haven't been here long. If you didn't show up, I'd try again tomorrow." She patted the empty seat beside her on the sofa. "Please, come sit for a second."

Meg crossed the room with her gaze fixed on the floor then sat on the sofa. She slumped deep into the cushions and pinched the bridge of her nose. Exhaustion settled in her bones. "What is it you think we need to talk about? You've made your feelings perfectly clear, and I don't want to hear any more of your opinions."

"I need to apologize for not allowing you to talk about everything you have going on in your wonderful brain. Someone told me I might not be the best listener. Give me a chance to listen to what you've tried to tell me. I never meant to make you feel like I don't believe in you, or I don't support you. I'm very sorry." She tucked her fingers under Meg's chin and lifted. "So please, let me in and show me what I've missed by closing off myself. Tell me what you're working on."

Tears stung Meg's eyes, and she quickly wiped them away. "Someone had the balls to tell you that you aren't a good listener? I'd love to know who."

"If you must know, it was Dylan."

"What?" She sat straight. "When did you talk to Dylan?"

A half smile lifted the side of Annie's mouth. "He stopped by the nursery the other day and put me in my place. He forced me to see how things look through your eyes."

Meg shook her head, and locks of hair spilled across her forehead. "He never told me."

Annie shifted, inching closer. "Dylan knows you well, my dear. He knows you can fight your own battles, and you take pride in doing so. I'm sure he didn't want to make you feel like he was intruding, but he needed to speak his piece. I'm glad he did."

"So am I." Meg wasn't used to people standing up for her, but Dylan's willingness to step in and help make things right warmed her heart. "I don't understand, though. I've told you for months about what I wanted to do at the inn. How did you not hear me?"

Annie sighed. "I don't have an answer. Every time you've talked about expanding at the inn, you always led with building the indoor arena. Once those words came out, I wasn't interested in hearing the rest."

Meg picked at an unraveling string by her wrist. "But why? Why are you so against the arena?"

Annie chuckled. "I'm not the only one who isn't a good listener. I don't want all our land being taken over by buildings, barns, and more animals. I think it's great you've provided a service to our guests, but I don't want things shoved down their throats. A lot of people choose to stay with us for relaxation and simplicity. I've worked hard to create a specific atmosphere, and along with it a certain reputation. I don't want to change either."

"Or do you just think what I want would be a waste of money and a big failure?" Resentment rang in her voice. Her mom said the right words, but did she really mean them?

Annie chuckled and dipped her chin. "I have no doubt you can do anything you put your mind to. I can only imagine the details you have swimming in your head, and I'm serious when I say I want to hear them. But risks might exist you're not aware of." She held up a hand. "Not because you haven't done your research, or because you don't know what you're doing, but because you've never had to live with the fear of taking those risks. I have. I remember the terror of not knowing if things would work out, or if I could provide a good life for my family. I don't want to take risks again."

Her mom's words slammed into her chest. "Do you really think I don't understand the risks involved in making renovations?"

"If you take a risk and it doesn't work out, you have the rest of your life ahead to find new ones to take. You don't understand that if I take a risk and things don't go as planned, I don't have anywhere else to go. I'd put everything I've worked so hard for on the line." Annie opened her mouth, snapping it close before anything came out. She shifted in her seat and placed a hand on Meg's arm. "My past experience can't help but shape my outlook. Losing your father and figuring out how to earn my own income were very similar to what Dylan's facing. You're risking your time and perhaps some money. For Dylan, he's risking his family's home. I know how he feels."

Taking a deep breath, Meg readjusted the hem of her dress to cover her knees. "So you don't think we should try because my plans might not work?"

"I'm scared at seeing you going forth with your plans. I've worked my butt off for years to have something to give my children. Do you think I opened the nursery because I was bored? I did it because you hated the inn and would never keep it when I'm gone. But a nursery was something you and I both would enjoy. It's something I could pass down, and maybe, one day you can pass on to your children." Frowning, she tucked a strand of hair behind Meg's ear. "Everything I did, every sacrifice I made, I did for you three. I never wanted any of you to struggle the way I did when your father died. I didn't want you to have to give up so much to survive. So, when I say I'm scared to see you take a risk, it's because no mother wants to see her child struggle. Even if she knows the struggle will be worth the sacrifice and growth in the end."

Absorbing everything her mom said, Meg bit into her thumbnail. How had she never known these details? Emotion swam thick in her throat. "You think I can do it? You think I can help turn Dylan's farm into a success?"

Annie smiled and pushed a piece of hair from Meg's forehead. "I know you can, honey."

"But you don't even know exactly what we're planning."

"I don't, not completely, but it doesn't matter. I

know you, and you have the heart and the mind to make anything a success. I also know Dylan, and he doesn't make decisions about his farm lightly. You two are quite the team."

"Thanks, Mom." A moment passed, and Meg bit into her bottom lip. For so long, she'd yearned for her mom's support and approval. "Do you want to hear our plans?"

Annie smiled. "I'm dying to know."

Meg spent the next hour sharing all of her research. Annie had a sharp mind and a great deal of experience. Her mom's opinion meant a lot. Meg went over every last detail, then held her breath in anticipation of what Annie would say. After getting past their issues, the last thing she wanted was for her mom not to approve of anything she'd shared. She glanced at Annie. "Well?"

Annie threw her arms around Meg and gathered her close. She pulled away and stared into her eyes. "You're brilliant."

"You really think so?" Tears burned behind her eyes, and a smile curved her lips.

"Your plan is amazing. And I don't think this idea will just do wonders for the Gilbert's farm, but for this town as well."

Meg snickered. "Are you wishing you had given it a chance after all?"

Annie laughed. "I meant what I said. I don't want to change what exists at the inn. Do I think your ideas might have worked there? Maybe. But I think they will have better results at a working farm. Have you spoken with Mary and Walter about all this?"

"We talked to them tonight. Dylan filled them in on some of our ideas beforehand, but we discussed every detail at dinner."

Annie raised her brows. "What are their thoughts?"

"They're excited. Even Lisa, which surprised me. Walter was in a good frame of mind for most of the evening, and he wants to do all the renovations now. He says they'll figure out how to get the money. Although I agree with his decision, he isn't aware of a lot of things. On top of everything else they have going on, Dylan and his mom are more concerned about how they'll pay for all they need."

"I might have a couple of suggestions."

"Really?" Meg widened her eyes, her mom's eagerness to help make her dream a reality in any way filling her with happiness.

"Who are you planning to hire?"

"We haven't decided."

Annie hooked up an eyebrow and grinned. "You and Dylan both know a contractor in the area who would give you one hell of a deal."

She slapped her forehead with the heel of her hand. "I didn't even think about talking to Jonah about doing the work."

"Well, you've had a few distractions. I know he would love to help Dylan. I also know someone else who would love to help."

Meg tilted her head to the side and narrowed her gaze. "Who?"

Annie shrugged. "Me."

Meg knitted together her brows. "I don't understand. How could you help?"

"Let me lend Dylan the money." Annie locked her gaze with Meg.

"How? Why?" Meg blinked and struggled to keep

up with the drastic change in her mom's attitude.

"I told you. I've been lucky, and my risks have paid off. Besides, I want to show you I'm behind you. Maybe not in the way you initially wanted, but behind you nonetheless."

Meg fell into Annie and hugged her tight. Tears fell down her face and onto her mom's shoulders. "I don't even know what to say, Mom. Your offer is so generous."

Annie leaned back and wiped the tears off Meg's face. She cupped her cheek. "Nonsense. You and Dylan are two of my favorite people, and if I can help you both, I want to. I want to be a part of this, Meg. In whatever way."

Warmth filled her to the tips of her toes. "Thank you, Mom. Now get out of my house so I can go see Dylan and tell him the good news."

Fifteen minutes later, Meg ran into Dylan's house and found him lying on the couch, both dogs cuddled on top of him. She hunched over in the doorway and gasped for air.

The dogs jumped off him and rushed to her, jumping in the air to greet her.

As she pushed off the dogs, Meg laughed and avoided their welcoming licks.

"You're not in a bad mood. I assume your talk went better than you expected?" Dylan sat and grinned.

"So much better, and I have you to thank." She shook her head, still not quite believing the drastic change in her mom.

Dylan tented his brows. "Me? What did I do?"

"My mom told me she had her eyes forced open by a certain visitor." Meg hooked up an eyebrow and pressed her lips together to hide her amusement.

Dylan shrugged. "All I did was tell her how I saw things."

She crossed the room and sat in his lap. "You did a little more than that. Thank you."

Dylan tightened his arms around her waist. "You guys worked out everything?"

"After we talked through our issues, she wanted to hear all of my ideas. I showed her everything—all my notes and research. She was really impressed. She even had a couple of ideas to help with the costs." Wanting him even closer, she looped her arms around his neck.

He grinned. "Doesn't surprise me. Your mom has a good mind for business. What were her ideas?"

"The first one was to ask Jonah to help with construction. He hasn't had his contractor's license very long, so he isn't super busy right now. You know he would give us a really good deal." She waited for his response, knowing what it would be. Hiring Jonah as their contractor was a no-brainer.

"I thought about talking to Jonah but hadn't mentioned it to you yet. He's the logical choice. What other suggestions did she have?" He leaned in, tucking his head in the crook of her shoulder.

She rested her chin on top of his head. "She wants to lend us the money to help with the renovations."

Dylan sat straight, his jaw hung open and wide. "How does she have the money?"

She kept her arms firmly in place. She hoped Dylan would see Mom's offer as a good opportunity. "She said the risks she's taken in the past have paid off. She wants to be a part of what we build in any way she can, and she wants to help with the financing. We didn't talk any details. I wanted to discuss it with you first. But do you see what this means? She's not just blowing smoke when she says she wants to be supportive. She really does believe in my dream—in our dream."

"Well, I'll be damned" A grin spread across Dylan's face. "I've always liked your mom. We'll think about the ins and outs of what this means later, right now I feel like celebrating."

"How do you do that?" Lust swirled in her belly. She had a few ideas.

"Do what?" He tilted his head and studied her.

"Read my mind so easily."

"It's not so difficult with a mind as dirty as yours."

A mischievous glint sparked in his eyes. Meg laughed so hard her stomach muscles quivered. "I guess it's true what they say then. Great minds think alike."

Their minds might be aligned, but she still hadn't laid out her heart. The words he longed to hear would come. He just had to be patient.

Chapter Twenty

Dylan opened the glass door to Average Joe's, and the bell above the door chimed. The gut-punching scent of coffee tickled his nostrils. He glanced around the crowded room.

Jonah waved from his seat with his breakfast spread in front of him.

Dylan nodded, hurried through the line, and grabbed a cup of coffee at the counter before joining him. "How did you get here so quick?" He sat across from him at the two-person table.

Jonah shoved a muffin in his mouth and lifted a shoulder. "I stayed at Jillian's last night, so I was only a couple blocks away when you called."

Dylan arched an eyebrow. "Have you decided to move in before the wedding?"

Jonah shook his head. "Sam is with his dad for the next couple days. I stay at the house with Jillian when he's gone. She doesn't want me there overnight when Sam is home until we get married—worried about the example she might set. I respect her decision." He shrugged. "Besides, I can move in soon."

"Did you guys set a date yet?" Dylan brought his cup to his lips to blow on the hot liquid, and then set it on the table.

"We're getting married in March. We just picked the date last night."

"Well, that's fast."

Jonah grinned "We didn't see any reason to wait. We'd get married sooner if we could, but I want to give Jillian the wedding she deserves. She says she doesn't need the whole big wedding thing, but I know she wants one."

"Doesn't every woman?" Dylan chuckled and took a sip of coffee. The bitter brew burned his tongue.

"I'm pretty sure they do. Besides, I want all our family and friends to be a part of the day and our celebration. We want Sam to be a part of the planning and understand our marriage will make us all a family."

Emotion tightened Dylan's chest. If anyone deserved a happy ending, it was Jonah. "I'm happy for you, man. You and Jillian were meant to be together."

"Thanks. I know you didn't ask to meet me here to talk about me and Jillian, but before we get to what's on your mind, I have something to ask." Jonah shifted in his seat.

"Sure, what's up?"

Jonah cradled his coffee in his hands and moved his thumb over the cardboard sleeve, his gaze fixed on the table. "Will you be my best man?"

"Seriously?" Dylan leaned his forearms on the table and focused his gaze on Jonah.

Jonah cleared his throat and met Dylan's gaze. "Yeah, man. Who else would I ask? You've been my best friend since we were boys. You fought by my side in Iraq. You're my brother."

"Of course I will. You wanting me by your side when you get married means a lot, Jonah." He fought to keep the emotion out of his voice. The last month had been hell being at odds with Jonah. Now, they could put it all behind them. "Does this mean I get to plan a wild bachelor party?"

Jonah snorted. "You'll have to ask Jillian and maybe Meg."

Amusement and a little fear laced through Jonah's words, and Dylan laughed. "Low key and simple it is."

"Probably a good choice. Now, what do you have on your mind?" Jonah leaned back in his chair and crossed his arms over his chest.

Dylan leaned back as well but kept his arms rested on the table. "Meg and I worked out most of the details regarding the farm, and we're ready to move forward with everything. The one crucial piece of the puzzle is finding someone to help with the renovations. I wish I could do everything myself, but I don't have the skills. I need someone I can trust and who'll let me work alongside them. The farm is the heart and soul of my family, and I want to have a hand in shaping it into what it will be."

"Are you asking me to help you?" Jonah dipped together his brows.

"I'm asking if you'll let me hire you. You have a business to build, and I would never want to take advantage of our friendship. I want us to help each other out and build something together we all can be proud of." He took a sip of strong, black coffee and waited for Jonah's answer. Jonah could be stubborn, but Dylan wouldn't budge. He would pay him for his time, whether he liked it or not.

"Dude, did you not hear what I said to you about being my brother? I would love to help you in any way I can. I'm not sure how much of your help I'll want." He scratched the stubble poking through on his chin. "I mean, I've seen you with a hammer before."

Dylan grinned. "How hard can building a barn be if you can do it?"

"Ouch, I see how it is." Jonah curled his lips in a grimace and rubbed his chest.

Dylan laughed at Jonah's wounded expression. "I don't want to step on your toes. I'll give you as much space as you need to do the job right, but I would like to help as much as possible."

"Don't worry. I bet we can get Meg to give you a few pointers."

Dylan snorted. "You're probably right. Does this mean you're on board?"

"Absolutely. We need to sit down and discuss your plans. I can't give you any idea right now of how long things will take or how much it will cost. I'll let you pay for materials, but you won't pay for labor, especially if I get to bust your chops a little."

Dylan shook his head. "You're providing a service, and I intend on paying you."

"Not happening. You can fight me on this all you want, but you won't change my mind. I don't have much happening right now anyway, and you and I can probably do most of it ourselves. Conner can pitch in, and if I know my sister, she'll insist on helping out as well. If I need to pull in someone else, I'll let you pay their wages. Sound fair?"

"Are you kidding? Your offer to help without charging me for your labor has to be the nicest thing you've ever done. I mean, you're a real pain in the butt most of the time, so I guess you haven't set the bar too high for yourself. But still."

"Aren't you just hilarious." Jonah lifted his gaze to

the ceiling.

"I think I'm pretty funny." Dylan shrugged. "How about we get together for dinner tomorrow night so we can draw up the plans?"

"How about tonight? Sam's still at Antonio's. Let's all go out for dinner."

"Are you sure?" Dylan cocked his head to the side. "You said it might be a while before you're comfortable with me and Meg being together."

"I know what I said." He squeezed the back of his neck. "Honestly, it's kind of weird how normal you two together are. I just needed to get past the initial shock."

"Good." Dylan grabbed his cup of coffee and took a drink. He stared down at the cup and wrinkled his nose. "Nothing is worse than cold coffee. I need to buy another cup, and then head out. I have some more details to see to. Text me and let me know where you want to go tonight. I'm sure Meg will be up for anything." He stepped out of the coffee shop and smiled at his good fortune.

Annie's little yellow car was parked in front of Florals and More.

He couldn't help the spring in his step as he strolled down the sidewalk, slowing only to sip at the piping hot cup he held in his hand. He stepped into the flower shop, and the ringing of the bell over the door announced his arrival. The scent of flowers wafted up his nose. He didn't stop in here often, and he let his gaze wander and stopped short when his eyes rested on Celeste.

She glared from the far corner of the room, and then strode toward him, coming to an abrupt halt with her hands on her hips. "Did you and Meg get everything worked out? Or do I have to ask you to leave?"

"Meg and I are good. We had a misunderstanding." He hated the quiver of fear in his gut, but Celeste always intimidated him with her hard stare and no-nononsense attitude.

"Good to hear."

Her voice was brisk and her face hard. He dipped his head. "Yes, ma'am." Celeste didn't relax her stance, and her hazel eyes issued a silent warning.

"Is there anything I can help you with?"

"I, uh, saw Annie's car outside. I hoped to speak with her."

Celeste tilted her head toward the rear of the store. "She's in the back, no doubt busy messing up my system. Go on and see her."

"Thanks." Dylan hurried away. Man, nothing sent him running like an angry woman.

Annie waited behind the counter, and she pressed together her lips until laughter bubbled from her throat. "Meg has more protectors in this town than she's aware of. She'll love that."

Dylan grunted. "We don't have to tell her how Celeste scared me."

"I won't if you won't. What can I do for you?"

He wrapped his arms around Annie and lifted her off her feet. Squeezing her tight, he kissed her cheek loudly. "Thank you."

"Put me down." Annie squealed and kicked her feet in the air.

Dylan placed her back down on her feet. "Meg told me about your talk last night. I'm glad you two understand each other. Neither of you liked where you were. Thank you for being so generous and offering to loan us the money for the renovations. I wanted to speak with you myself, though, just to make sure lending us the money is something you really want to do."

She waved a hand through the air. "Of course I do. Why wouldn't I want to help you? If I'd known how much this meant to Meg, I would have suggested loaning her the money a while ago. I guess it's a good thing I didn't, huh?" Annie shot him a wink.

"I guess so. Meg and I talked last night about the best way to deal with borrowing money. My family owns the farm, but it's Meg's idea. Both of us have a vested interest in this project, and we want to be vested financially as well so the stakes are equal. We'll be partners, so the best way to move forward is for both our names to be on any documents."

Annie furrowed her brow. "Do you really think I want to draw up documents for you two? Meg's my daughter, and I've known you most of your life. I don't need any fancy paperwork dictating how to handle things. We're adults, and we can figure it out ourselves. Heck, I'll just hand you the money, and you can pay me back whenever. It really isn't a big deal."

Dylan shook his head. Emotion clogged his throat. Annie had always treated him like family, but her offer to loan him money went above and beyond. "Nonsense. I appreciate your trust, but I insist we do this right. We'll have legal documents drawn up. I want all the t's crossed and the i's dotted. I don't want any misunderstanding about how and when this money is to be paid back."

Smiling, Annie held up her hands. "Whatever you

want. We'll get this taken care of right away."

****

Fatigue pulled at Dylan's muscles, and he mopped beads of sweat from his forehead with the back of his hand. The week produced a lot of progress on the farm, but much work still needed to be done. The sound of tires bouncing along gravel caught his attention, and he turned to watch his mother and Annie park beside his truck. What were they doing here? Who was with Dad?

They shuffled out of his mother's car, both dressed in old work shirts and well-worn pants.

"Why am I afraid to ask what you two are up to?" Dylan greeted his mom with a kiss on the cheek and nodded toward Annie. This conversation better be quick. Jonah waited. They had a lot of work to do today.

"We're here to help." Annie hoisted the paintbrush in her hand in the air.

"That's right." Mary gave a sharp nod. "Annie asked Celeste to sit with your father for a little while so I could chip in. All week I've been itchin' to come here. I can't let all this get done without getting my hands a little dirty. It wouldn't be right if you were the only Gilbert busting your butt to put this family on the right path."

"What do you plan to do?" Dylan prayed the scowl on his face hid his amusement. "Grab a hammer and let Jonah put you to work?"

"Who do you think taught him how to use his hammer?" Annie dipped down her chin and smirked. "I have a feeling your mom could do anything she wanted. However, we had something different in mind."

"Annie and I want to spruce up the rest of the

place. These buildings have been shabby for years. I can't tell you the last time we put on a new coat of paint. We'll start with the cow barn. Isn't that the one you're turning into the children's petting zoo?"

"Yes." He drew the word into three syllables. Arguing would be a waste of time, and the barn was the perfect place for them to test their painting abilities.

"Perfect. We have paint in the car. A brilliant red with white trim, just what children picture when they think of a barn." Mary beamed a bright smile.

"Are you ladies sure? The weather is warm for February, but it's still pretty cold."

"I think we can handle a little chilly air," Mary said. "You go back to whatever you were doing, and let us worry about us."

Dylan shook his head and left them to their own devices. They couldn't get into too much trouble, at least he hoped not.

At the end of the second week of work, Dylan stood in front of the big, red barn. Meg's dream was finally becoming a reality, and excitement shot up and down his spine at the possibilities. Two warm arms wrapped around him from behind, and Meg burrowed her face into his back. His excitement over the farm transformed into pure desire.

"How long have you stood here while Jonah does all the work?" Meg asked.

The sound of hammering from the other side of the barn echoed around them. Dylan chuckled and lifted his hands to place them over hers. "Oh, you know, pretty much all morning. I hope Jonah won't notice he's been alone for hours now."

"I bet," Meg said. "Really, though, what are you

doing out here?"

"I needed a minute to take in everything. I still have a hard time believing it's all really happening." Everything was coming together, but one thing would make his life perfect—Meg actually telling him that she loved him. The question of why she hadn't said the words sat on the tip of his tongue. He swallowed them, not wanting to ruin the moment.

She squeezed him. "I know what you mean. Everything's coming together a lot quicker than I thought it would."

Dylan pulled Meg into his embrace. "I'm not just talking about the farm. I'm talking about us. Sometimes, I feel like my heart might beat right out of my chest due to pure happiness. I don't think I've ever been this excited to see what the future holds."

Meg tucked her head below his chin. "I could never go back to the way things were before. I honestly don't know how I could ever move forward without you."

"You'll never have to find out." He kissed the top of her head. "Did you want to grab something to eat before you get to work?"

"No, thanks. I ate before I left the nursery. Unlike some people around here, I don't want to be a slacker."

"If I promise to pull my weight the rest of the day, will you reward me with a cold beer and good food when we're done?"

"Sounds perfect. Now come on, let's go see what my brother will torture us with today. I'm not sure how much more my muscles can handle." Meg winced and rubbed her right shoulder.

Dylan grabbed her hand and walked beside her. "I

can help you with your soreness later."

Meg groaned. "If you're teasing me, I might have to kill you. If you're not teasing me, I might have to steal you right now and take you up on your offer."

Jonah rounded the corner. "There you guys are. I need some help over this way, Dylan."

"I'm here for whatever you need." Although his words were directed at Jonah, he kept his gaze trained on Meg. He winked and slapped her bottom before he walked away. Only one beer waited at the end of the day. He couldn't get more in before taking Meg's mind far from the pain in her beautiful body.

Chapter Twenty-One

Exhaustion seeped into every ounce of Meg's body. The brisk cold air encased her, and her stomach growled in angry protest of her lack of lunch. Meg yearned to take a nice, hot shower and then melt into bed with Dylan. Why had she promised they could go into town for dinner? But Dylan was starving. Heck, she was starving.

After working all day on the renovations, the time was much too late to think about cooking something for dinner. Meg hopped into her truck with Dylan by her side and headed into town. Every space around the town square was filled, forcing Meg to park a block away. The brutal wind barreled against Meg, and she snuggled closer to Dylan until they reached The Village Idiot. She stared at the crowd of people gathered inside the bar's front entrance.

"Wow, it hasn't been this packed in here since New Year's Eve." Dylan leaned down and spoke against her cheek.

His breath tickled her ear. Memories churned through her mind of when Dylan's warm mouth kissed hers for the first time. She bit her lip to fight the smile threatening to take over her mouth.

"Two stools are empty at the bar. Would you want to sit there?"

Meg hadn't been at the bar since the day her and

Dylan fought. The thought of seeing Sally made her blood boil, but she wouldn't let her disdain for Sally keep her from getting a full stomach. "Sounds good." She led the way to the seats.

"What do you want to drink?" Dylan sat and waved toward the bartender.

"I'll take a beer." She sat beside him and leaned forward on the bar, scanning the room for Sally.

Al, the owner of the bar, hurried over. "Do you two know what you want? No need to get either of you a menu. You must have the whole thing memorized."

"I'm good. What about you, Meg?" He glanced at her.

She nodded. "A light beer and a dozen hot wings."

"I'll have the same and throw in some onion rings."

"Easy enough. It might take a little longer than usual. I think the warmer weather caused everyone to come out in full force tonight."

"No worries. As long as you bring those beers," Dylan said.

Meg's beer arrived, and she took a drink before setting down her glass in front of her. "I need to use the restroom before the food gets here. I'll be right back." Meg hopped off her stool and hurried to the bathroom. She huffed in frustration at the line and glanced around. Warmth spread through her as an image of Dylan leaning down to kiss her with the crazy New Year's hat on his head swam in her mind. Her smile stayed in place until she stepped out of the bathroom. Her stomach dropped.

Sally sat in her vacant seat with her arms wrapped around Dylan's neck.

He unfolded her arms and placed them on her lap .

How in the world could the woman keep a sultry smile plastered on her face as a man turned her down?

Dylan pressed his lips into a firm line, and the muscles in his back tightened.

Meg stopped behind Sally and fisted her hands at her sides. "Aren't you tired of him turning you down?"

"I don't know what you're talking about." Sally kept her back to Meg. "We're just sitting here chatting, aren't we, Dylan?"

"I'm sitting here drinking a beer and waiting for Meg. I don't know what you're doing." He narrowed his gaze and tightened his jaw.

"I think it's pretty obvious what she's trying." Meg's voice was tight as she reined in her temper.

Sally swiveled on her stool with pursed lips.

As she placed her hands on Dylan's shoulders, Meg stared her in the eye. They relaxed under her touch. "You've played the same game for years. Don't you think it's time to give it up? Your games obviously aren't working."

"I'm not playing a game, dear. I'm showing Dylan what he's missing by wasting his time on you." Sally sneered then turned toward Dylan. "Sooner or later, he'll realize you're not worth his time. If I were a betting woman, I'd say sooner. I mean, Blake's been in here night after night telling everyone how you're dying to get him back." Shifting, she refocused on Meg. "So, what game are you playing Meg? Are you keeping Dylan on the hook until Blake takes you back? That's not very nice of you. Poor Dylan. He's way too sweet to put up with you."

Meg dropped her jaw and disgust curdled in her

stomach like spoiled milk. "Whatever story Blake is spitting out of his mouth is total garbage."

"Of course you would say that." Sally rested a hand between Dylan's shoulder blades. "You don't want to get caught."

Dylan rolled back his shoulder to shake off Sally's hand.

"Caught doing what?" Meg laughed. "Caught staying with Dylan every night and spending most of every day with him? Dylan and I both know either you're lying, or Blake's lying. Either way, I don't need to defend myself."

Dylan stood and signaled for Al. "Can you do me a favor? Will you put our stuff in to-go boxes? I want to get out of here before I lose my appetite."

Al nodded and retreated toward the kitchen.

Dylan faced Sally. "As for you, enough, please. I've tried being nice, but I'm losing my patience. I don't want to feel like I can't come here anymore, with or without Meg. I also have a feeling if I tell my friend Al over there I won't come in because I don't want to be forced to be around you, he won't be too happy about losing one of his best customers. Are we clear?"

Sally stuck out her bottom lip and placed fisted hands on her hips. "I want to help you. We've known each other for a long time, and I don't want her to hurt you. I'm not trying to cause any problems."

"No one's buying your innocent act, Sally. Just leave." Dylan reached around her and grabbed Meg's arm, pulling her close to his side. "You good with leaving as soon as Al delivers our food?"

"You bet I am." Sally slinked away like a dog with its tail between its legs, and a grin twitched on Meg's mouth.

Dylan grabbed the white, plastic bag Al offered and tugged Meg toward the exit.

Meg kept her gaze on Dylan's broad back as he led her to the front of the crowded bar. Warmth flooded her entire body, and her heart beat an erratic rhythm. Her feelings for Dylan intensified by the minute, and she couldn't avoid telling him much longer. The question was, what was the right way to confess those three little words?

****

The next day at the nursery, Meg weaved between the leftover poinsettias and heaps of bagged dirt. February was always a slow month, and today was no exception. Making sure her mom was nowhere in sight, she snuck into the office to call Emma. She was dying to talk to her sister, and she paced as the phone rang in her ear.

"Hey, Meg."

Emma's voice was bright and cheerful when she finally answered. "Hi. What are you doing?" Meg bubbled with excitement, but she knew her sister well enough to let her get any conversation off her chest first.

"Nothing much. I just got the kids down for a nap about twenty minutes ago. Both of them sleeping at the same time is a small miracle. I toyed with the idea of getting stuff done around the house, but ended up talking to Mom instead."

"Oh yeah? I haven't seen her much today. She has some new guests, and they're keeping her pretty busy." Meg picked up a pen from the desk and clicked the end again and again.

"She said she's baking up a storm. Plus, there's the bridal shower she wants to throw for Jonah and Jillian. Their getting married so quickly doesn't give her much time to plan something. Her and Celeste will drive everyone crazy—Jillian most of all."

Meg stopped pacing and wrinkled her nose. "She hasn't mentioned anything about a shower. Neither has Jonah. When is she planning on throwing the party?"

"The end of the month. That gives her a few weeks to put everything together. Should be enough time. Honestly, I don't think she's said anything to Jonah. She planned to talk to Jillian about the date, but I bet Jonah will be kept out of the loop for the most part. Mom wants to do an untraditional shower with the men there, so I'm sure he'll love that."

Meg sank into the old ratty desk chair and listened to Emma prattle on for a few more minutes. She was used to giving her sister the time she needed to let everything spill before she made any real contributions to the conversation. After spending all day at home with the kids, Emma took every chance she could to speak to adults. That usually meant spewing out words rapid fire, as though she were afraid she'd be summoned at any moment—which happened often.

Once Emma slowed, Meg inhaled a deep breath. "I need to tell you something."

"Okay. What's up?"

"I'm in love with Dylan."

"And?" Emma asked.

"And what? I'm in love with Dylan, and I just realized it last night. I wasn't sure until this thing with Sally happened at the bar. Everything just clicked into place." Her voice pitched high as she spoke. Her heart beat as quickly as the words falling out of her mouth.

"Well, it's about time. I appreciate you calling to tell me this, but why do you sound a little panicked?"

"I'm not panicked. I'm just nervous about telling him." She tossed the pen on the desk.

"You're calling to tell me, but you haven't told him yet?"

She shoved a hand through her hair. "I don't want to just blurt out 'I love you.' I want the moment to be special. The moment was perfect when he told me. Pretty much everything he does is perfect. He's so thoughtful and sweet, and I'm this blunt tomboy who falls way short."

"Don't be silly. Dylan loves you for who you are. You don't need to be something you're not."

Meg waved away Emma's gentle tone even though her sister couldn't see. "I know, but I want to show him how much he means to me—go out of my way a little bit."

"Aw, my little sister's growing up," Emma said.

Sometimes she really wanted to strangle Emma. "Shut up. I need help. I don't know how to do this stuff." Her voice leaked with desperation.

Emma laughed. "I'm sorry. I'll be serious. So, you want to do something sweet and romantic?"

Meg sighed. "Yes."

"Something unexpected?"

Oh my God, her patience was dwindling. Wasn't that what she'd just said? She bit back a groan. "Yes."

"Okay, let's think. Do you guys have anything planned soon? A night out or an event to go to?"

"Not at all. We both work, and then help Jonah at the farm until dark. We're bone tired every night and usually fall right to sleep as soon as we finish eating dinner."

"Fall right asleep, huh? Sounds hot."

"I'm hanging up." Embarrassment and irritation burned her cheeks.

"Sorry. Totally serious now." A beat of silence passed. "Wow, we're pathetic. I'm married, but you have no excuse for not remembering Valentine's Day is in a few days."

She rolled her eyes. "I hate Valentine's Day. It's so cheesy."

"We all need a little cheesy in our lives. Now, should I assume you and Dylan haven't made any plans?

"Absolutely not. He hasn't mentioned anything, but he knows me well enough to know Valentine's Day is not my thing." She tapped her booted foot against the floor.

"Exactly."

"Exactly what? I don't understand." Her words came out clipped. She fought every impulse to slam her phone against the desk.

"Why don't you suggest Dylan come to your house on Valentine's Day? I'm sure Dylan won't plan anything because he, as well as the rest of us, knows you won't want to do anything. Knowing Dylan, he'll probably do something simple and sweet just to mark the occasion, but you let him know you want to hang out at your place for the night and relax. Then when he shows up, you completely floor him by going all out— home-cooked dinner, candlelight, the works."

Meg wrinkled her nose. "Really? Sounds so elaborate."

"Planning something extravagant is the point, isn't it? Something Dylan would never expect?"

"Yeah, I guess. Do you think he'd like something like that?"

"I think hearing you say you love him will be the happiest moment of his life, and it won't matter how you say those words. You could be covered in mud and smell like horses, and Dylan would think the moment was perfect. But I do think he will appreciate the effort."

"You're right." Meg sighed and stood, crossing the small office to stare out the lone window. "Do I really have to cook? Mom making something I take the credit for would be better."

"Sounds like a good idea, and I'm pretty sure Dylan would agree."

****

Valentine's Day arrived, and nerves jumped around Meg's body like Sophie with too much sugar. She had never put this much effort into a date before. She took the day off work so she could make sure her house was spotless and everything was in place before Dylan arrived. She poked around the house, anxiously rearranging everything for the hundredth time. The doorbell rang, and she ran to the door.

"Thank God you're here. I was afraid you'd be late." Rushing her mom into the house, she grabbed the bowls from her hands and headed toward the kitchen.

"Goodness, girl, slow down. It's not even six yet. What time did you tell him to come over?"

"Not until six thirty."

"So, why the craziness?" Annie followed her into the kitchen.

"I can't help it. I have this idea of how I want everything to go tonight, and I'm all anxious it won't happen." She rested the dishes on the counter and peeled back the coverings. The scent of fresh baked rolls made her mouth water.

"Meg, take a breath and come here."

She smoothed the foil back over the food to keep it warm. "I can't. Don't you have more stuff in your car?"

"Yes, I do, and we'll get to it in a minute. But first, please come here." Annie rested a hand on Meg's elbow.

Meg swallowed a groan and faced Annie. "What?"

"You look beautiful." Tears misted Annie's eyes. "I don't get to see you dolled up very often. Sometimes I forget how good you clean up. You must have taken hours to curl your hair."

Meg twirled a long curl around her finger and frowned. "It did, and I bought this stupid dress and heels." She lifted her foot, pointing her toes to show off the sky-high black stilettos. "Why do women wear heels? I want my sneakers."

Annie chuckled. "I hope you aren't planning on pouting when Dylan gets here."

Meg rolled her eyes. "I'm not. I plan on taking off these shoes as soon as he sees me in them though."

"I don't blame you. I agree with you on the heels thing." Annie pointed down at the shoes. "Your sister is the only one in this family who still buys them."

"Makes sense since she was the one who insisted I get them."

"She would." Annie snorted. "But high heels aside, Dylan will have his socks knocked off when he walks in here. Honey, everything looks amazing."

Meg glanced around at what she had created in her little house. "It really does, doesn't it? I want him to hurry and get here so I can relax. As soon as I see him, the nerves will disappear."

Annie clapped together her hands under her chin. "That's so sweet. I'm glad you two have found each other."

"Yeah, yeah, yeah. Everyone's happy we're together. Everything's good. But right now, I need to get this food out so Dylan thinks I slaved away all day cooking."

Annie cradled Meg's cheek in her hand. "Sweetheart, that boy knows you better than almost anyone on this earth. How you arrange the food doesn't matter. No way he'll ever believe you cooked this food."

Meg laughed and a bit of tension slipped from her shoulders. "You're probably right. Let's hope he's enough of a gentleman not mention it."

"Dylan's smart enough not to mention anything to put him in the doghouse. You two have fun. I'll take Nora home with me, and the two of us will cuddle on the couch and have our own little Valentine's celebration."

Once the food was all inside, Meg watched her mom walk out to her car, Nora leading the way. She closed the door and hurried to get the food ready. She fluttered around putting everything where she wanted it. When she was happy with her display, she took a seat and waited. He wouldn't be late. Maybe he'd even show up a little early and take her out of her misery.

Headlights poured through her front window, and she shot to her feet. She stumbled in her shoes on her way to the door. Stupid heels. Meg opened the door wide and stood in the doorway before Dylan could ring the bell.

Dylan gasped and widened his eyes. "What in the world did you do?"

Awe filled his voice and appreciation made the green of his eyes shine like fire. Her heart pounded, and she sucked in a large breath. "Nothing much. Just another night in." Meg winked, and then stepped into her house, leaving him to follow.

Chapter Twenty-Two

Dylan watched the shadows of the flames from the candles danced across Meg's pale skin. His beautiful Meg. Love poured through him. She was incredible, and she was his. He stepped into the house. From the far corner of his mind he registered music playing softly in the background. Without saying a word, he gathered her into his arms and swayed to the soft beat. He buried his face in her hair and inhaled the scent of coconut and lavender.

"What did you do?" he asked again in a hushed whisper. He pulled her closer and enjoyed the warmth of her body as they swayed along with the music.

"I wanted to do something special—something you would never expect." She lifted her face. "Did you have any idea?"

Worry danced in her eyes. "None at all. I feel like a fool for not doing anything for you. I know how much you hate Valentine's Day, so I arranged to have flowers delivered tomorrow instead. I'm a jerk." He ran a hand over the back of his neck.

Meg buried her face in his chest.

His heart pounded like a drum beneath her cheek.

"Your thoughtfulness reminds me again how well you know me."

He held her in his arms for a while longer, memorizing the curves of her back with his hands.

The song ended, and Meg grabbed his hand and led him to the table set for two.

Dylan pulled on her hand to stop her. "Can I look at you for a second?"

"You get one second and nothing more." Meg lifted her chin and flung her arms in the air. "Then the heels are coming off, and the hair might have to go up."

"I'm good with you taking off the heels, but leave the hair down." He lifted his hand and brushed a strand away from her face. "I like it down. I can run my fingers through it whenever I want."

She grinned. "I can't promise anything, but I'll try. At least for a little while longer."

Dylan trailed a hand from her face down over her dress, feeling the black, satiny fabric as it caressed the curves it hugged. "New dress?"

Meg ran her hands over her hips and caught her bottom lip between her teeth. "Sure is. Do you like it?"

He groaned. How could a simple black dress be so lethal on her body? "I do. I'll have a hard time keeping my hands off you."

"Well, you need to behave yourself. At least until after we eat."

Wanting just one taste of her before he ate, he tugged her hand and urged her toward him.

She squealed, wiggled out of his grasp, and rounded the edge of the table.

Dylan chuckled and stepped closer to the table. The savory smell of garlic and gravy smacked him in the face. He peered into the covered dishes, inhaling deeply. "Did you make Salisbury steak?"

"It's your mom's recipe. There're also homemade mashed potatoes, rolls, broccoli, and mac and cheese."

He widened his eyes at the casserole dishes of food. All his favorite foods stared up at him. Holy cow, enough to feed an army covered the table. His stomach growled, and saliva flooded his mouth. "You've got to be kidding me. Everything smells amazing. I can't believe you did all this."

With her gaze downcast, she nodded and sat. "Let's eat before the food gets cold."

Dylan sat across from her and piled food on his plate. He took a bite of steak and the savory juices filled his mouth. Closing his eyes, he moaned. The tender meat melted in his mouth. He opened his eyes and glanced at her. "You know, Meg, I never knew you could cook so well. Did your mom teach you?"

Meg cleared her throat and placed a napkin over her mouth. "Something like that."

"You must be a good student. Anytime you want to try more recipes, I'd be more than willing to be your taste tester."

She placed her napkin on her lap, and a smile touched her mouth. "I'll remember that."

He choked down a laugh. No way Meg cooked any of this food, but he didn't care. Whoever cooked the meal did a good job. He scooped the last bite of potatoes into his mouth. The smooth, buttery mounds slid down his throat, and he set down his fork.

"Do you want dessert now or later?" Meg stood and secured their empty plates in her hands.

He raised his eyebrows. "Depends. What do you have in mind?"

Meg disappeared into the kitchen and returned carrying a platter of chocolate-covered strawberries. "I figured if I did the whole cliché Valentine's date night,

I might as well pull out all the stops."

"Looks perfect." The strawberries were a nice touch, but he kept his gaze locked on hers.

"Good, I'm glad you think so. The only catch is we need to eat them somewhere else."

"Now I'm intrigued." Desire rippled through his veins. God, he hoped chocolate would be covering her soft skin soon.

"Follow me. You're a smart guy. I'm sure you'll figure it out." She curled her fingers into his and led him through the kitchen and toward her bedroom.

Her hips swayed from side to side, her legs long with the help of her heels. He was glad she kept them on. Her neatly made bed came into view, and his palms dampened. A large robe sat on top of her comforter, and he ran the tips of his fingers over the soft material. His gaze drifted to the red, lacy nightgown beside it. His heart pounded. He opened his mouth to speak, but Meg was gone. "Meg?"

Meg sauntered back in the room with a bottle of champagne in one hand and lotion in the other. She set the opened bottle of champagne by two glasses on the bedside table and hoisted the lotion in the air. "Get comfortable."

Dylan tented his eyebrows and slid his lips into a smirk. "How comfortable do you want me?"

Meg laughed. "Down, boy. I just want your socks off. I want to give you a foot massage."

Hesitation slowed his movements. "You want to touch my feet?"

Meg poured champagne into both of the glasses and handed him one. "If you're going to be shy, drink this. But trust me, I've seen your feet before." She took a sip from her glass then set it down and scooted back on the bed.

Dylan downed his glass, and bubbles danced in this throat. The sweet liquid sparked against his taste buds. He was more of a beer man, but the sweet wine would work. Leaning forward, he pulled off his socks then sat in front of Meg. The mattress dipped under his weight, and he fought the urge to lunge forward and press his lips to hers. She obviously had a plan, and he didn't want to do anything to ruin what was next on her agenda.

Meg squirted lotion in her hand and pulled his foot into her lap. "See, that wasn't so bad, was it?"

She wrapped her warm hands around the arch of his foot and the slick lotion slid against his tough skin. A moan rumbled from his throat. The tight muscles in his foot relaxed, and he leaned against the tufted backboard and glanced around the room. He ran his fingers over a soft pillow beside him and his gaze landed on a picture of Meg and Emma on the dresser. If he focused too much on Meg, he wouldn't keep his hands off her. "This is the first time I've been in your bedroom. It's nice."

"Thanks." Meg shrugged. "The space is okay. I don't spend enough time here to care much. I spend most of my time in the barn or at the inn."

"Having a nice place to come home to is always good, though. Comforts of home and all that." He'd only moved back to the farmhouse he'd grown up in during the previous year, but after spending four years in the military, any place with a solid roof over his head and a soft bed filled him with gratitude.

"I guess my house has always been just a house. To

me, home is at my mom's house. Going there, even though it's pretty much every day, is still going home. The sad part is the only home I know is an inn where I've never been completely comfortable. I've always hated the way strangers have free rein over the place." She fisted her hand and moved her knuckles over the arch of his foot.

His back arched in pleasure. "I can't imagine. My house now has always been my home. Don't get me wrong. The need to escape called after I graduated, and I was naive enough to think that the Marines offered me a better future. I'm proud I fought for this country, but being in Iraq showed me how much I really had back here. I will never again take it for granted. My home, my family...they're my everything." Meg's brilliant blue eyes softened and warmed his soul.

She smiled. "I love how strongly you feel for your family."

Dylan lifted her foot and placed it on his lap. Having Meg caress his foot felt amazing, but that didn't mean she couldn't get the same attention in return. He used one hand to rub the arch of her foot under her stockings, while the other hand caressed the side of her calf. "I'm glad you find my love for my family appealing, but can we talk about something else right now?"

"I think we can manage that." Meg closed her eyes and sighed. "I'm supposed to be spoiling you tonight."

"I can stop if you want." He stopped the motion of his hands.

"Nah, you should at least do the other foot first. You don't want it to feel left out."

Dylan chuckled. "Sounds logical." He placed her

right foot back on the bed and proceeded to rub her left one. "Not that I'm complaining, or anything, but what made you put together this special evening? I'm blown away. I mean, everything you've done tonight is so unexpected."

Meg shifted his foot to the side and cradled her hands around the other one, squirting more lotion in her hand before kneading the tips of her fingers into his skin. "I wanted to do something special. You're constantly doing things for me and always putting me and my needs first. For once, I wanted to show you how much you mean to me."

"Honey, you show me every day how much you care about me. This is amazing." Dylan waved an arm, indicating all the extravagance around them. "But don't ever think it's something you need to do. I would be impressed with takeout and a movie."

"You'd be more impressed with me in my pajamas, eating take-out on the couch, and watching a movie?" Meg dipped her brows low.

The tone of her voice showed her doubt, and he laughed. "Well, maybe not the take-out part. I really liked that home-cooked meal."

Meg pulled her foot from his hands and climbed out of bed. "We can still do that. I'll get the pj's, and you go pick a movie."

Dylan grabbed her around her waist and settled her on his lap. "Don't even think about leaving."

Laughing, she wiggled out of his grasp. "I do have one more surprise planned." She stood and swiped the red night gown from the bed.

His pulse quickened.

"I need to head into the restroom for a second, and

I want you to slip into the robe I laid out, and then we can watch that movie." She winked then strolled across the room into the en suite bathroom, closing the door behind her.

Dylan let out a long breath and ran a hand through his hair. Life with Meg was never boring, but the excitement brewing in the pit of his stomach told him tonight would be a night he would never forget.

Chapter Twenty-Three

The artificial light buzzed above her bathroom mirror. Meg braced her hands against the white pedestal sink and glanced at her reflection. Long strands of blonde hair frizzed around her face—the earlier tight curls now loose waves bouncing in every direction. She twirled her finger around the silky piece of material used to cinch her robe around her waist. She wore the red nightgown underneath, but she wanted Dylan's focus on her when she spoke about her feelings.

Now was the perfect time to tell him she loved him. She'd set the mood, taken him by surprise, and rubbed his feet, for Pete's sake. Now, she could go back into her room and tell Dylan the words that had danced on the tip of her tongue for days. Sucking in a deep breath, she stepped in her room, and her mouth went dry.

Dylan sat on the bed with the robe tucked around him and a chocolate-covered strawberry in his hand. "I found us a movie to watch." He tossed the strawberry in his mouth and licked chocolate from his fingers.

Disappointment pooled in her stomach. She hadn't been serious about watching a movie right now. "Really? What did you pick?" She crossed the room and sat beside him.

"Something super romantic, *Dumb and Dumber*." Dylan grinned and held up the DVD.

"Oh, good." A small sigh left her lips. They could watch the movie, and then she'd tell him how much she loved him. "I can't take too much more romance." She snuggled beside him and turned on the movie. She nibbled on strawberries and sipped champagne. By the time the movie was over, the light-hearted comedy and full stomach lulled her into a comfortable haze. Exhaustion tempted her to close her eyes and drift to sleep, but she would hate herself if the night didn't end the way she planned.

So far, everything had gone perfectly, but it wouldn't matter if she chickened out and kept her words to herself. She sneaked into the bathroom as the credits rolled to slip on her last surprise for the night and check her appearance one more time. When she finished, she closed the bathroom door behind her. She made her way back to the bed, her heart pounding wildly in her chest.

A low whistle rumbled from Dylan's throat. "I didn't think this night could get any better."

A sexy, seductive walk toward him would have been ideal, but she couldn't pull that off. She ran and jumped on the bed, landing on top of him and laughing as he tickled her sides. "Stop!" She squealed and slapped his hands. She gazed down into his eyes, and the playfulness stopped.

He skimmed his fingers up and down her back and sucked in a breath through his lips.

The moment she'd waited for had arrived. She leaned down and gently placed her lips on his. Breaking away, she rested a hand on his cheek and gave him a small smile. Her heart beat as fast as a freight train barreling down the tracks. "Dylan, you are the most wonderful man I've ever met." She spoke softly as she gazed into his mossy, green eyes. "You've been my friend for as long as I can remember, and I'm so lucky now you're my lover. I never imagined I would have this much joy and love and laughter in my life. I'm amazed daily by the feelings you continue to stir in me."

His lips curved. "I feel the same way."

She took a deep breath, the words she needed to say on the tip of her tongue.

Ring-ring-ring.

She glanced at his phone resting on her nightstand, and then back at him. "Do you need to answer your phone?"

"No, I don't want to talk to anyone else right now. Whoever it is, I'll call them back later." He rubbed his hands up and down her arms.

Goose bumps shivered on her skin. She inhaled a deep breath, ready to push forward. But the phone kept ringing. "I think you need to answer the phone. They're not giving up." Meg picked up his phone.

He took the device and glanced at the screen. "Weird. My mom's calling." Dylan sat up as he answered the phone. "Hi, Mom. What's going on?" He gripped the phone tighter, his knuckles turning white. His breath heaved out of his body, and Mary's frantic voice spilled out into the room.

Meg's blood turned cold. Whatever happened couldn't be good. She stood and scooped up her shirt, pulling it over her nightgown. Where were her pants? By the time Dylan was off the phone, Meg was dressed and extending his clothes.

"I have to get to my parents' house. My dad flipped

out and ran away. Mom has no idea where he is, and she couldn't go after him. She didn't tell me why. I need to see her to find out what happened, and I need to find my dad. I'm so sorry, Meg, but I have to leave."

"No, *we* have to leave. If your mom's upset and you need search for your dad, I can sit with her. She'll be a nervous wreck."

Dylan grabbed his pants and jammed a foot in the leg hole. He pulled them at the waist, but his foot caught in the fabric.

Meg grabbed his hand and squeezed hard.

He took a minute, his gaze focusing solely on her hand in his, and then he finished getting ready. "Are you sure? I have no idea how long finding him will take."

"Yes, I'm sure. It doesn't matter how long it takes. Your mom shouldn't be alone right now."

He gave her a quick kiss before heading for the door, his keys already in his hands. "Thank you. Why don't we drive separate? Then you can come back home if you need to, or if God forbid, I need you to drive my mom somewhere."

"Good idea." She grabbed her bag and followed him out of the house. The bitter cold smacked her in the face. She got in her truck, backed out of the driveway, and drove to Mary's apartment. She curled her hands tightly around the wheel, her mind empty of everything but Walter as she sped through the empty streets. *Please, God, let everything be okay.*

Dylan had already parked his truck and was running to the front door when she pulled into the parking lot. Parking, she jumped down from her truck and followed quickly.

Mary threw open the door and flung herself into Dylan's arms.

"What happened?" Dylan stroked the back of his mother's head.

"It all happened so fast. I didn't see it coming. I couldn't stop him." Tears fell down Mary's face as she clung to Dylan.

Mary's eyes were wild as her hands dug into his shoulders.

Meg's heart cracked in two. She placed a hand on Mary's arm and steered her toward the door. "Why don't we go inside so you can tell us what happened? It's too cold out here to talk." Meg entered the apartment and made a beeline for the kitchen. She opened cupboards and found coffee grounds to put in the coffee maker. She wasn't sure if Mary would want some, but Dylan would.

While the coffee brewed, she stepped into the living room. Dylan sat beside her on the couch. Meg tried not to grimace when the well-lit room exposed a glimmer of truth about what happened. Whatever had gone down, it hadn't been good.

Mary shook and rubbed her hands up and down her arms.

Meg wasn't sure if Mary shook from fear, or cold, but bruises appeared on Mary's forearms. She found a blanket in a basket by the sofa and placed it over Mary's shoulders then sat beside her. A large, red mark slashed across her cheek.

"Are you okay, Mom?" Dylan sat with his arm around her.

His body coiled, like a spring ready to snap. His jaw clenched tight, but his eyes remained soft and kind.

Mary held the blanket in place with shaking hands. "I'm fine. I'm worried about your dad. He dozed off in his chair after dinner, and he was in one of his moods when he woke up. I reassured him he was all right. He started screaming he needed to go home, and he didn't want to be stuck in this hellhole anymore. When I approached, he shoved me, and I stumbled backward. He yelled at me to leave him alone, and he came up on me so fast. I never in a million years thought he'd put his hands on me." Mary grazed her fingertips against the mark on her cheek and winced.

"I'm so sorry, Mom. Dad running away should have never happened. I should have done something sooner. We all saw he was declining. I should have known you needed more help. I let you down, Mom." Dylan hung his head. Tears fell onto his knees.

Meg bunched her hands in her lap to keep from comforting him. He'd hate that right now. Mary needed the comfort, not him.

"You look at me right now, young man." Mary cupped his chin. "You've done more for this family than should ever be required. You're not the keeper of your father, or of me, and it's not your fault this happened. You're right, we all saw how quickly he's declined. My own stubbornness is to blame for not asking for help. I thought I could handle him." Her voice cracked. She cleared her throat and straightened her spine. "But right now, we shouldn't sit here and argue about who's to blame. We need to find your father. It's late, and it's cold. Your dad didn't even stop to put on a coat, so we must find him before this situation gets any worse."

Dylan took a deep breath and lifted his head.

"You're right. I should go, and you should stay here with Meg in case he wanders home. Have you called the police?"

"Not yet."

"Before you call the police, maybe Dylan should head to the farm," Meg said.

"Why would I go to the farm? I don't need to stop home for anything." Dylan stood and headed for the door.

"You might find him there." Meg glanced at Mary. "Didn't you say when he woke up Walter mentioned wanting to go home?"

Mary bobbed her head. "Yes, yes, he did. Do you think he would have walked all the way there?"

Meg shrugged. "It's a good place to start, and the only place that would make sense to him, even if the idea of walking all the way there in this cold seems crazy to us."

"You might be right. I'll head there right away. Mom, go ahead and call the police just in case we're wrong."

"I'll call," Meg said. "Dylan, let me pour you some coffee before you leave. Mary, do you have a thermos in your cabinet?"

"I don't have time." He reached for the door knob.

Meg pursed her lips and steeled her eyes "Yes, you do. It will take thirty seconds." She left the room and found a thermos. She returned and handed it to Dylan. Stretching up on her toes, she kissed his cheek. "Good luck and be careful."

Dylan nodded, and then hurried out the door.

"Thank you for coming with him," Mary said from the couch. "I hate to admit it, but I really don't want to be alone right now."

Meg took a seat beside her. Nerves fluttered in her stomach. She wasn't the best with helping people navigate strong emotions. "Please try not to worry. Dylan will find him. If he gets to the farm and Walter isn't there, I'll call my mom to come sit with you while I search closer to the apartment." She studied Mary's face. The angry red on her cheek made Meg wince. "Would you like a cup of coffee? Or maybe a cold compress for your cheek?"

"No thank you, dear. My nerves are so shot I don't think my system could handle much of anything right now. I'm just so scared." Mary sniffed and tucked her top lip behind her teeth. Tears streamed down her face. "I'm sorry, you don't need to see me like this."

She clasped Mary's hands in hers. "Like what? A devoted wife who is worried about her husband?"

At her words of support, the floodgates opened and Mary cried harder. Meg didn't say a word. Nothing she said could soothe her anyway. She simply held her, rubbing her back and wiping away as many tears as she could. This woman truly loved her husband, and even though seeing her fall apart broke Meg's heart to watch her agonize over the safety of the man she loved, her emotions made Meg hopeful she'd love her husband this much after being married for so long. And hopefully, that man would be Dylan.

Ring-ring-ring.

Her palms grew moist when she answered the phone. *Please let it be good news.*

"He's here," Dylan said. "He's just standing in the driveway."

"Oh, thank God." The coiled tension in Meg's neck

loosened. "Mary, Dylan found him. He's at the farm."

"I'm getting him back in the truck and bringing him home. I'll probably stick around there until he's asleep for the night. If my mom's okay with being there alone, I'll take off for your place. In the morning, Mom and I can figure out what needs to be done. I don't think either of us can deal with these decisions tonight."

Something in his voice put her on alert. She wanted to be there to support him, even with just a quick hug before heading home. "I can wait here until you want to come back with me. Or I can sleep on the floor here if your mom wants us to stay."

"I appreciate the offer," Dylan said. "But I don't know how long I'll be, and honestly, it might be easier on my dad if you're not there."

"Okay, I understand." Her chest stung. He didn't want her here…but his attitude wasn't about her. "Good job finding him. I'll see you later."

She disconnected the call and sat with Mary for a few more minutes before she made her way home. She found the remains of the romantic evening she shared earlier with Dylan. Her heart sank to the floor. How had an evening that started with so much promise ended so badly?

She sighed. Tomorrow would come, and she'd tell Dylan everything. She'd tell him how much she loved him, and things would be perfect once again.

Chapter Twenty-Four

Dylan grabbed the jacket he brought for his dad, jumped down from the truck, and hurried toward him. The bitter wind whipped him in the face. His dad stood in the front of the newly constructed barn, his arms crossed tightly over his chest, and his feet planted firmly in the gravel. Dylan picked up his pace, the frigid night air spurring him on. If he stood outside much longer, his dad would get sick.

He lifted his legs carefully to silence the crunching under his boots and slipped the jacket over his dad's shoulders. He stood beside him, and a million questions bogged down his mind. "What are you doing here?"

Walter cut his hand through the air and gestured toward the barn. "I'm standing here looking at this bright and shiny new barn where my old one used to be. I'm looking beyond the barn and wondering why in the hell close to three acres of land have been cleared and are sitting there wasting space."

Dylan took a deep breath and let his father's words sink in. Walter had no idea what was happening here. He measured his words carefully, not wanting to upset his dad any more tonight. His best choice was to be as honest as possible. "I cleared the land so we can plant pumpkins soon. The old barn was turned into new stables with an indoor arena, and the building next to the barn will be used for different events people want to have here. The renovations aren't done yet, but it should be spectacular when it's finished."

Walter spun toward him, and a vein on his forehead bulged. Crimson flooded his face, and he clenched together his jaw. "Are you kidding me? You want to grow pumpkins and host events on my farm? Have you lost your mind?"

Dylan blinked. His dad's memory wasn't trustworthy, but how did he think all the new construction was built if he still lived on the farm? He laid a hand on Walter's shoulder. "Dad, we need to figure out a way to make a little more money. I've looked into every possible option, and creating a fun, family destination was the only way."

Walter shoved off Dylan's hand. "You need to make more money? For what? We've never needed more than what this land provided, and I'll be damned if I sit back and watch you exploit this family so you can make a few extra bucks."

Walter's words slammed into his gut like a wrecking ball. Dylan took a step back. "Exploit the family? You can't honestly believe I'd do that."

"I sure as hell do." Walter took a step toward him and pointed his finger in Dylan's face. "Why else would you insist on selling out the land that has been in this family for more generations than I can count?" Walter turned in a circle, sweeping his arm wide. "Look at this place. It's like you slutted it up with a new coat of lipstick. This isn't a working farm. It's a circus. What a stupid idea. You've made our family legacy into a laughing stock, and I've never been more ashamed to call you my son."

Walter stormed toward the house. He shot out his

hand to open the back door and struggled with the lock. He kicked the base of the door, and his voice rose in the stillness of the night with incoherent swearing.

The searing pain in Dylan's chest stole his breath, and his lungs burned. Lead pooled at his feet and rooted him to his spot. His dad's intense, negative reaction wasn't happening. He'd poured his blood, sweat, and tears into this renovation. He'd made these changes to help his family, not to destroy what they'd built. The burning in his chest spread throughout his body until fire filled his veins.

He'd made the wrong decision. Regret stirred in his stomach. He fisted a hand in his hair. He should never have changed the farm, the one place that would always be home to his dad. He needed to make things right—needed to figure out how.

The rattle of glass and a sharp cry brought his mind into focus. He breathed deeply, tried to steady his shaking soul, and stepped beside his dad. He gripped Walter's shoulders in his hands, and his dad's muscles tightened, then relaxed beneath his touch. All the fight slipped out of him. Dylan steered him to his truck and put him inside. He would take him home, and then he would figure out the rest. One way or another, he would find a way to make his dad proud of him again.

****

Dylan kept a firm hand on his dad's elbow and led him to the apartment. Exhaustion and disappointment weighed him down.

Mary flung open the door, gathered Walter into a fierce hug, and then led him inside.

The excitement of the night wore him out, and Dad fell asleep without putting up a fight.

Dylan sank into his dad's ratty old chair and stared into space. Numbness crept into his body and mind. He'd wait for his mom to come out of her bedroom, and then he needed to get out of here.

"Thank you for bringing him home."

Dylan shook his head and lifted his gaze. The haze buzzing around his brain wouldn't leave. "No need to thank me. I'm glad I found him quickly."

Mary narrowed her eyes. "Are you okay? You look upset."

"I'm fine. Just worried about Dad." He pushed up from the chair. "Are you all right by yourself for a while? I need to head over to Meg's for a minute. I can come right back."

She crossed the room to his side and rested a palm on his cheek. "Your dad won't wake until morning. You go, and don't worry about coming back. See Meg, and please tell her thank you again. She's a sweet girl."

"Yeah, sure." His voice was quiet. He kissed his mom on the top of the head, and then numbly walked out the door.

He didn't bother to call Meg. His emotions were raw, and his mind centered squarely on the cruel words his dad said. His drive was a blur—the streets passing by like a distant memory. He pulled into Meg's driveway and shut off the engine, resting his head on the wheel. Taking a deep breath, he gathered the strength to walk to her porch. He opened his door and half fell from the seat. He trudged to the house with his head hung and shoulders drooped.

Opening the door, Meg sagged against the frame and kept her hand gripped around the knob. "Come in. How's your dad? Do you need anything to drink or just want to head to bed?"

Dylan stared past her. The words he needed to say were hard to form. Finally, he focused his gaze. "I want to stop construction at the farm."

"Okay." Meg furrowed her brow. "You want to stop for a few days while you figure out what to do with your dad? I'm sure Jonah won't mind if you take off some time. He and I can keep working. You needing some time isn't a big deal."

"It is a big deal." His voice was loud and his words sharp. "I want to stop construction. Permanently. I'll eat the cost, and you can go back to working with your mom. Your idea was silly, anyway. I should have known all those crazy plans would never work. But I couldn't get past my constant need to help you." He shoved a hand through his hair. "Damnit, I put your needs above the needs of my family. I'm such an idiot."

Meg flinched, and then closed her eyes. "You can't be serious."

Dylan paced in front of her, the crunch of snow echoing through the night air. "Of course, I am, Meg." A hard knot of anger formed in the base of his throat. "I have to figure out how to make everything right. What am I go to do with those stupid changes? Such a waste of time."

She opened her eyes, and tears swam in the corners. She flexed her hand on the doorknob, causing it to turn with each movement. "I don't understand why you've changed your mind so suddenly."

Dylan stopped and glanced at her. She wouldn't move him with her tears this time. "My eyes were forced open. I have to go." Without another word, he stormed away and drove home. He parked in the exact same spot he was in not even an hour before. He found his way to the same place he stood with his dad and stared at all the work they'd done for nothing. Dropping to his knees, he screamed into the night and unleashed all the pain searing his chest. Once the screams were gone, he held his head in his hands and fought to get control over his emotions.

Gravel crunched behind him under heavy boots. "What the hell is your problem, man? Please tell me you have a good reason for crapping all over my sister, or I'll have no choice but to keep my promise and kick your pathetic butt."

Dylan glanced up at Jonah and didn't bother to wipe the moisture off his face. "Everything we've done out here, I did it wrong. I don't know how to fix my mistakes."

"Oh, hell." Jonah knelt next to him. "What's going on? Meg's at my mom's, and she's a mess. You're sitting in the freezing cold, and you look awful." Frowning, he scratched his jaw. "Is this about your dad? My mom called and mentioned something happened with him tonight."

"He's ashamed of me. Those words have never come from his mouth. He said I'm turning the farm into a circus, and I'm ruining everything our family has built." Dylan hung his head once more. His chest tightened. "How am I supposed to move forward knowing what he thinks?"

"That's bull, and you know it." Jonah shook his head.

Dylan stared at Jonah. "Excuse me?"

Jonah placed a hand on Dylan's shoulder. "Listen, I'm sorry about everything you're going through. I have no clue what it must be like to see him suffering, and I'm sure it's confusing as hell. But you and I know your dad has never been ashamed of you a day in your life, and he isn't ashamed of you now. Especially because you're changing the farm to bring more success."

"But, he said he was ashamed of me." Heat burned his cheeks.

"Oh, I heard you. I'm sure he said the words, but he didn't mean them. Besides, didn't he approve of all of this when you first presented the idea?" Jonah dipped his chin. "The real him, not the one who shows up and steals him away. The real Walter Gilbert was on board with this plan, and the real Walter Gilbert would never want you to doubt what you're doing for your family. He's proud of you, Dylan." Jonah squeezed his shoulder, and then stood. "Let's get inside. Nothing will get solved by sitting here in the cold."

Reality hit Dylan like a lightning bolt. "Good God, what did I do?"

Jonah lifted a shoulder. "You freaked out. That's understandable. You're under a ton of stress."

Dylan shut his eyes tight. "Meg."

Jonah whistled low. "Meg might be a different problem to solve. She's pretty upset. When my mom called me, she said she's never seen her like this. If you're feeling up to it, you might want to head there and clear up things."

Dylan scrambled to his feet and ran to his truck. "Thanks Jonah, I owe you one."

Fifteen minutes later, Dylan sprinted up the porch stairs at the inn, the moonlight lit his path. He pounded on the door. His breath heaved in and out of his chest.

Meg answered.

Tears streaks stained her cheeks, and her eyes were red and puffy. He'd done this to her. His stomach churned. He extended a hand to brush a piece of hair off her face.

She shook her head and stepped away.

Pain stabbed his heart. "Meg, I'm so sorry. Can we please talk?"

"We don't have anything left to say." She crossed her arms over her chest and firmed her lips.

Her voice was as chilly as the wind howling at his back. "Please let me explain. When I found my dad at the farm earlier, he was so angry. He was confused about what was going on, and he accused me of exploiting the family to make money. He told me he was ashamed of what I was doing. I panicked, Meg. I couldn't get his words out of my head. I lost it for a few minutes, and I'm so sorry I took it out on you."

Meg shifted her gaze to her feet. "I'm sorry you heard those things from your dad, but it doesn't give you the right to come after me."

"I know. I really do." He took a step forward. The need to comfort her made his insides itch. "I just—"

Meg held up her hand. "Stop. I don't want to hear any more. Tonight isn't the first time you've lashed out because of some sort of misunderstanding. It's not fair. I've been in a relationship before with someone who had excuse after excuse for the things he did, and I refuse to be in a toxic relationship again. Just because I'm in love with you doesn't mean I have to stand around and be your whipping post when things get hard."

Dylan widened his eyes, and his heart slammed wildly against his chest. "You're in love with me?"

A smile touched her mouth, even as tears glimmered in her eyes. "I guess I got a chance to tell you tonight after all. Yes, Dylan, I'm in love with you, but it doesn't matter now. I was stupid enough to think I needed to find the perfect moment to tell you." Meg shrugged. "I guess no such time exists, does it?"

He closed the distance between them and grabbed her hand so she couldn't walk away. "Wait, please. Meg, we can get past this. I promise this will never happen again. Just talk to me."

She shook off his touch. "We're done, Dylan. I don't want anything to do with the farm. Tear it down for all I care. And I don't want anything to do with you."

"You don't mean that." A lump formed in his throat.

"Go home. I don't want to see you anymore." Meg backed into the house and closed the door.

Dylan stared at the closed door, and the numbness from earlier returned to encase his body. The pain would come soon, and he wasn't looking forward to it. He wanted Meg for so long. How could he have messed up things so badly? She was his future. She had to realize they were meant to be together.

Slowly, he sank onto the porch steps. She would talk to him. They would work out everything, and things would go back to how they were before he'd ruined it. Back to when Meg was his.

Chapter Twenty-Five

Meg lifted away the curtains from the window. Dylan still sat on the porch steps.

"How long has he been out there?" Annie stood in the doorway between the living room and kitchen with a dish towel in her hands.

"A little over an hour." Meg shut the curtains and slumped back down on the couch in her mom's living room.

Annie frowned. "He's got to be cold."

"He's a grown man. He's smart enough to leave if he's cold. He should have left when I told him." The bitter taste of betrayal swam in her mouth. She savored it. Betrayal was better than pain. Right now, the pain in her heart was unbearable.

"You're right. But a man in love is seldom smart. Especially when he knows he's made a huge mistake." Annie tossed the towel on the back of a chair and took a seat next to Meg.

She leaned against her mom. Annie's long fingers soothed her tired head but didn't do anything for her heart. "Don't try to make me forgive him. I won't. Just because you love someone doesn't mean you can treat them like dirt over and over and expect them to get past the hurt."

"I couldn't agree more. But do you really think he treated you like dirt?"

Meg reared back and stared with wide eyes. "He's hurt me twice, more than any man ever has, and I don't feel like hanging around to see how bad it feels the third time."

Annie nodded and continued to stroke Meg's hair. "Makes sense. But don't close off yourself because you're afraid to get hurt. I agree, trusting someone after they've hurt you is tough, and I don't want you to think I'm on anyone else's side but yours, but Dylan is a good man with a lot going on. Sometimes chaos can cause lapses in judgment. You've known him all your life. Has he ever treated someone poorly or lashed out at those he loves?"

"No, but he can't continue to make the same mistakes. I don't have to continue to put up with being dumped on." She set her jaw and crossed her arms over her chest. "I refuse to."

Annie sighed. "You have to watch your heart, but sometimes when things get tough, we lash out at those we love the most because we think they'll always be there. Don't forget the wonderful qualities that not only made you fall in love with Dylan but led him to be your best friend for so long."

Meg leaned forward and peered at Annie through squinted eyes. "How did you know I was in love with him?"

Annie laughed. "Girl, we've all known."

Meg let her mom's words churn through her mind as Annie's fingers continued to run through her hair. Annie was right. Dylan didn't treat people cruelly or lash out. He was the most thoughtful, kind-hearted person in her life.

But she couldn't ignore the searing pain that

pierced through her heart. She couldn't push from her mind the way the air was forced from her lungs as he hurled insults at her and made her feel smaller than the dirt beneath his feet. "I need some time to think and some space. I'm not sure if giving him another chance is worth the risk. I don't think I've got it in me." If she had to deal with Dylan breaking her heart again, it might kill her. Or worse yet, keep her from ever opening up her heart to anyone again.

****

Exhaustion weighed down Meg after an afternoon spent shopping with Jillian. Her feet ached, and she yearned to kick off her shoes under the table of the casual restaurant Jillian chose for lunch. She set her menu on the table and waited for Jillian to place her order. Her stomach churned. She hadn't eaten much in weeks—not since the night she'd sent away Dylan. But Jillian suggested dinner after running errands for the bridal shower, and she didn't have anything better to do.

"Thanks for coming today." Jillian placed her menu on the table. "I could have made Sam come, but shopping was more enjoyable with you."

"Somehow I doubt that." She lifted one corner of her mouth and snorted. "I haven't been enjoyable for anyone over the last couple of weeks."

Jillian crinkled the corners of her eyes. "Have you talked to him at all?"

By him, she meant Dylan. Meg's stomach muscles clenched as his name ran through her mind. She shook her head. "He called last week, but I ignored him." She gave a small shrug and drifted her gaze to her clasped hands. "I guess he's stopped trying."

"Isn't that what you wanted? For him to stop trying?"

"I don't know what I want." She glanced at Jillian, and tears burned the back of her eyes. She pressed her tongue to the roof of her mouth, willing them to stop. She wouldn't cry again—not here. "I guess I want everything to go back to the way it was."

"You mean before you two started dating?" Jillian tented her brows.

She sighed. "No, back to when we were happy together. We were only together a couple of months, but they were the happiest I've ever been. That's what I want back."

Jillian frowned. "And you don't think that's possible?"

"I don't think so," Meg said, her voice cracking.

"Why not? I'm not saying anyone should be allowed to treat you badly or be disrespectful, but we all make mistakes. We all say things we don't mean when we're upset. I mean, have you met your brother?" Jillian snorted a laugh.

Meg lifted the corner of her mouth. "I know, and truthfully, the more time I've had to think, the more I realize the lashing out is not what I'm the most upset about. The night his dad ran off was rough, and I get he was upset." Sadness tightened her chest. "I'm crushed by the fact I found out he was blowing smoke up my butt about believing in me. He lied to me, and why? To make me happy, or to get me to see him in a different way? How can I trust him?"

"Do you really think he lied about believing in you? You think he'd put everything he has on the line to gain your attention?" Jillian shook her head, and then lifted her water glass to her lips.

"Has Jonah been working at Dylan's farm these last couple weeks?" Even though she already knew the answer, she held her breath for Jillian's response.

The server approached the table with their food and set it down in front of them.

Jillian picked up her fork and poked around her salad.

Her silence was all the answer Meg needed. "I thought so."

She shook her head. "I'm sorry, Meg."

She picked up her fork and forced a smile on her face. "Life goes on. Now, enough talk about Dylan. Are you ready for the shower?"

"I think so. Your mom needed me to pick up a few things today. Other than that, all I need to do is show up."

Meg pointed her fork at Jillian. "And to make sure Jonah shows up."

Jillian rolled her eyes. "Getting Jonah there will be the hardest part. He's annoyed your mom is making him go."

"Mom always gets her way," Meg said in a sing-song voice. "The party won't be too bad. At least cake will be there."

Dread gnawed its way through her stomach lining. Dylan was the best man. He'd be at the shower. She'd have to face him and would need something a lot stronger than cake to get her through.

****

A few days later, Meg sat on the front porch swing waiting for Emma to arrive. Her mom had been great the last few weeks, and she was happy she'd used the time to get closer with Jillian, but right now, she needed Emma. She wrapped her jacket tight around her shoulders and lazily swung back and forth. She relished the sun on her skin, but the breeze was quick to chase away the warmth.

Emma's black SUV pulled into the driveway.

A small cry of relief tumbled out of her mouth. She jumped up and ran down the stairs.

The car stopped, and Emma stepped out of the car and opened her arms to Meg.

Meg fell into her embrace.

"Tonight, my girl, we get drunk," Emma whispered in her ear.

In spite of herself, Meg smiled. She stood straight and locked her gaze with the sister she loved so much. "Sounds good to me."

"Get me out, Meg-Meg."

Sophie's shrill voice screeched from inside the car, and Meg grinned. "Yes, ma'am. How about we let your mama get Anderson, and I'll spring you loose?"

Meg spent the day playing with the kids. She couldn't believe how big Anderson was getting. His first birthday approached quickly, and he moved around the house with all the grace of a baby just learning to get around. He couldn't walk yet, but he could crawl fast enough to drive his sister crazy. Meg laughed every time he stole a toy from Sophie. Emma might roll her eyes with frustration every time Sophie protested, but it was music to her injured heart and Meg couldn't get enough.

After they ate dinner and the children settled into their beds, Emma held up a bottle of wine and motioned toward the back door. "Who's with me?"

"Count me in." Meg jumped to her feet and glanced at Annie. "Mom?"

Annie smiled. "I'll pass tonight. You two enjoy, and I'll listen for the little ones."

"Are you sure?" Emma opened the door to the deck. "I can hear them if we prop the door open."

"I'll settle for milk and cookies in front of the television. You girls have fun." Annie lifted the dome on the glass cake stand on the island and pulled out two chocolate chip cookies.

Meg hurried to her favorite spot on the deck. She leaned back on the white Adirondack chair and wrapped a soft blanket around her shoulders. She held out her empty wine glass to Emma.

Emma poured a generous amount of golden liquid. "Drink up."

Meg saluted her with the glass and took a sip. The smooth, fruity liquid warmed her to her toes. "Thanks. I'm glad you're home."

"Me too. I wish we could have come back sooner, but it didn't make sense when we already had this visit planned." Emma stared out toward the barren fields. "How are you doing?"

"I'm okay." The lie burned her tongue.

Emma tented her brows. "Really?"

"No." Sadness pinched her chest. She stared into her glass for a minute before she continued. "I miss him so much. It feels like he took a piece of me with him—a piece I'll never get back."

"I'm so sorry, Meg. I can't believe Dylan was such a jerk."

Meg faced Emma and looked her dead in the eyes. "I don't expect you to hate him. I don't hate him, even if it'd be easier if I did. I would never expect you to forget he's your friend because he and I didn't work out."

Emma patted Meg's hand. "I love Dylan like a brother, but I'm still mad. I'll get over what happened, and he'll continue to be a good friend, but for tonight I can hate him. We both can. We can, we will, and we do." Emma clinked her glass against Meg's, and then took a healthy drink of her wine.

Meg leaned back against her chair. "Thank you for cheering me up. Dealing with the breakup has been hard. I've been holed up here because I don't want to run into Dylan. I wake up, I work, and then I do whatever task Mom gives me to help her with the party. At this point, I know she's just making up stuff. I'm driving her a little crazy."

Emma sipped her wine. "I'm sure she appreciates the help."

Meg raised her eyebrows and stared at Emma. "Really?"

Emma laughed. "Okay, you're probably driving her crazy. But I'm sure Celeste is driving her just as crazy. The two of them throw one heck of a party, but the show they put on before their parties is almost more fun to watch."

Meg sat in silence, lost in her thoughts as she drank her wine. A light buzz hummed around her body.

"You'll see him at the shower in a few days. Are you nervous?"

The familiar dread sat heavy in Meg's stomach. "You have no idea. I have no idea how I'll control my emotions when he's here."

"You'll be fine. I'm here, and you can always use

Sophie as a distraction. She's your usual ploy when you want to avoid something." Emma smirked. "Seeing him for the first time with so many people around might make it a little less awkward."

"Yeah, maybe." She doubted it. Who was around when she and Dylan came face to face for the first time didn't matter. The encounter would be hard.

But seeing Dylan was a problem for another time. Tonight, she would sit outside with her sister and get drunk. She could worry about Dylan tomorrow. But when she fell asleep in her chair, Dylan's face dominated her mind.

Chapter Twenty-Six

Lying in bed, Dylan willed his mind to shut down and the muscles in his body to stop aching. It didn't work. Sleep was sparse lately, and all he wanted was the sweet escape from reality for a few hours. But escape seldom happened. Too many questions spun in his mind, and too many doubts ate at his conscience. Worse yet, the image of Meg's face was seared into his brain. Every time he closed his eyes, her tear-stained cheeks and sad eyes stared. He was in hell.

Meg wasn't the only one who haunted his nights. They had to put his dad in a nursing home, but he still had no clue how they'd pay for the long term. The meeting his mom set up for tomorrow morning should give them some answers. He gritted his teeth and closed his eyes once again. He tossed and turned as the image of Meg tormented him for another sleepless night.

****

"Good morning, Mom. How'd you sleep?" He stood in the parking lot beside his mom's open driver's side door and waited for her to stand.

"I'd say I slept a lot better than you did. Are you feeling all right?" She rested a hand to his forehead.

"I'm fine. Just a little restless last night." He nodded toward the nursing home. Light blue siding lined the house and white scalloped details decorated the pitched roof. "Let's get this meeting over with." He pushed open the front door and the scent of cinnamon and vanilla greeted him. He stepped into the lobby and sat on a floral upholstered love seat. Dylan grabbed a cookie, still warm, from a plate on the end table.

"It's so clean," Mary whispered and sat beside him. She clung to his hand.

"For what they charge, it better be immaculate." He took a bite of the cookie. "This tastes homemade."

A short man in a pin-striped suit stepped out of an office.

His welcoming smile made his eyes wrinkle at the corners. His jovial expression matched the fluffy pillows and homey pictures hanging in the waiting room.

He stretched out his hand. "Hello, Mr. Gilbert." He nodded to Mary. "Mrs. Gilbert. Thank you for coming in to see me today. Please, step into my office so we can chat."

Dylan stood and followed him into a spacious office. The sounds of laughter spilled in from behind him. Pictures of family members and smiling residents hung on the walls. People seemed happy here. This home would be a good fit for his dad. The only issue would be if they could afford a room.

"What did you think of the facility?"

"It's very nice, Mr. Adams," Dylan answered.

"Please, call me Ian. If you have any questions, feel free to ask."

"Okay." Dylan glanced at his mom, then shifted in his seat and refocused on Ian. "Our major question is, how are we supposed to pay for this? We've spoken to people in the admissions department, and we know how much to have my father here costs. What types of payment plans are available?"

Ian folded his hands on the desk. He glanced at Dylan, and then Mary. "I'm sorry. I was under the impression you were signing up your father for Medicaid."

"Why would you think we were getting Medicaid?" Dylan frowned. He never expected to qualify for the government program. The assistance it could provide was life changing.

"Well, I studied the financial records your mother supplied. Your father doesn't appear to have any substantial holdings in his name and hasn't for some time. There wouldn't be any reason why he wouldn't be approved for it, and Medicaid would pay for his stay here."

"That doesn't make any sense." Dylan stammered and glanced at his mom. Her wide eyes and opened mouth showed she was as surprised as him. "The farm, the house, everything should be in his name."

"No, they both are in your name, Mr. Gilbert."

Dylan leaned back in his chair and inhaled sharply through his nose. His heart pounded in his chest. What was he talking about? "Is this true, Mom? Is everything in my name?"

Mary shrugged. "We changed everything over to your name years ago, when your dad suffered his stroke. We weren't sure if he'd fully recover. Your dad worked on the farm once he was well, but you were the one in charge." She shook her head with a wide grin. "I had no idea putting the house in your name would have an impact on paying for your father's care."

Dylan covered his mouth with as hand and rubbed his face. Tension seeped from his neck. Laughter threatened to erupt from his mouth, but he choked it back. Unshed tears stung the back of his eyes, and he blinked furiously to keep them at bay. He dropped his hand and extended it to Ian. "Thank you so much. You've lifted the weight of the world from my shoulders."

Later that afternoon, cars filled the driveway of the inn, and Dylan sat for a full five minutes before gathering the courage to get out of his truck. He shoved his shaky hands into his pockets and strolled to the house. Birds chirped, announcing the arrival of spring. He stood in front of the door, took a large breath, and stepped inside. He hooked his coat on the crowded rack next to the door, pivoted, and slammed into a small body. His hands shot out and caught her shoulders. His brain registered her familiar scent and slight frame before his eyes did.

Meg.

She stopped, and then quickly turned and retreated into the kitchen.

Dylan's heart fell to the floor. She didn't even want to see him. She knew he would be here today. He hung his head and walked into the living room, dread filling every inch of his body. How was he supposed to spend two hours with a bunch of people celebrating love when his heart was broken in two?

"Hey, there." Emma crossed the room to his side. "I thought I saw you pull in. Have you seen Sophie yet? She's running around stealing cookies from everyone. She'll be a pain later with all the sugar she's eating."

"No, I haven't seen her, or the little guy." Dylan kept his gaze glued to the floor. He traced his toe over a worn crack on the hardwood.

"Anderson's sleeping. He went down about twenty minutes ago, and I hope he'll stay asleep throughout the party."

Dylan glanced up and offered her a small smile. He buried his hands in the pockets of his jeans. "Where's Jonah?"

She flicked her wrist toward the back of the house. "On the deck. You know how he gets with crowds. A couple other guys are with him, and I'm sure he'll stay outside until my mom makes him come inside. Why don't you join them?"

Going to the deck meant going through the kitchen. "I, uh, think I'll step outside for a minute. I need a little air."

Emma placed a hand on his arm. "You and I…we're good."

"Thanks, Emma, but I really can't be in here right now." The air grew thicker, and his lungs struggled for oxygen. He needed to get outside.

He stepped into the fresh air and took a deep breath. He glanced from side to side to make sure no one was around, and then headed to the barn. If he couldn't talk to Meg, at least he could go to the one place to bring him closer to her. He slid open the barn door and stepped into the aisle. The scent of hay filled the warm air. He patted the horses as they stuck their heads out in greeting then rounded the corner.

Meg stood beside Snowball with her head bent to the horse's nose.

Dylan turned to leave. The barn was her sanctuary—the place she went to escape. He didn't want to intrude on her privacy.

"Dylan?"

He whipped around his head. Her beautiful, pale face peeked out behind the shadows, and he couldn't keep his distance any longer. He strode to her and was at her side in a heartbeat. Wrapping his arms around her, he held her as she cried. Running his fingers though her hair, he wished to absorb her pain. He caused her heartache, and he should be the one to pay for his mistakes. Not Meg—never Meg.

"I didn't know you were in here." He pressed his mouth to her temple. "I would've never come inside if I'd known. I needed to get out of there—needed to come somewhere yours."

Meg took a step backward and wiped her eyes. "It's okay. I shouldn't have run away earlier. I panicked."

Dylan cupped her cheek in the palm of his hand. "I've missed you so much."

"I've missed you, too." Meg glanced at the ground. "But missing you doesn't mean we should get back together."

Dylan dropped his hand and nodded, disappointment sitting heavy in his gut. "I understand. I broke your trust. Can I at least try to earn back your trust? Even if just as a friend?"

"You'd do that?" She furrowed her brow.

"I'd do anything for you, Meg."

She lifted her gaze to his. "I don't know if I could ever go back to being friends. Honestly, I don't know what you could do to make things right."

"Will you go somewhere with me?" His heart pounded. This was the moment he'd worked so damn hard for.

Meg widened her eyes. "Now?"

"I planned to ask after the shower, but I can't wait. Do you think Jillian would be upset if we left for a minute?" He rubbed the back of his neck. "As soon as I show you, I'll bring you right back. I promise. But please, do this for me."

She bit her bottom lip, her gaze drifting around her.

She had to come with him. Showing her how he'd spent his time while they'd been apart was his only chance.

Tilting her head, she narrowed her gaze and hooked up the side of her mouth. "Okay."

Dylan released a small breath and triumph echoed in his head. He led her to his truck and buried his hands deep in his pockets to keep from reaching for her hand. He didn't want to scare her or make her think he was pressuring her to take him back. That was not what this was about. He could only hope by showing her he was a man of his word she would lower her guard enough to realize he was still the man of her dreams.

He drove out of town and fought to keep his gaze fixed on the road. His farm came into view, and her gaze burned a hole through the side of his head. He stared ahead and drove, saying nothing. He pulled into the driveway, under a new wooden sign that read *Gilbert Farms*. Near the house, he put the truck in park. From the corner of his eye, he stole a glance at her.

She cocked her head to the side and narrowed her eyes.

He hopped down and ran around to open her door. "Over here." He steered her in the direction of the barn. Leading her to the front of the new structure, he stood and studied her face. *Please let her love it.*

Meg dropped open her mouth. She waved a hand in

front of her. "I don't understand. Why show me the barn Jonah built?"

"Look up—above the door." Worry rested heavy on his shoulders. Showing her what he'd made was his hail Mary—his grand gesture to win back her trust.

Meg glanced up and tears filled her eyes.

Another new sign hung above the door; this one read *Sheffield Stables*.

"You named the stables after me?"

"Who else? You're the whole reason any of this amazing new creation is here." He puffed his chest, and pride filled his core. The awe and joy in her voice made all the sleepless nights and endless days worth it. All his anxiety melted away.

Meg shook her head. "I don't know what to say."

"Don't say anything yet. Come inside and see the rest." His heart pounded, and excitement surged through his body. He'd wanted to show Meg all his hard work for weeks, but he needed it to be finished first. He needed her to know how invested he was in her dream—in their dream.

He captured her hand, and the warmth of her skin on his caused bursts of anticipation to ripple through his body. He led her into the new stables. The scents of hay and polished leather hung heavy in the air.

Blinking back tears, Meg made a wide circle. "This is amazing."

"Does the barn have everything you wanted?" He held his breath. Everything had to be perfect. "Without you here to see to the details, I was afraid I'd miss something."

Meg strolled up and down the aisle and roamed her fingers over the wooden stalls. She peeked into the tack room, and her laughter spilled out.

The sound was music to his ears. Grinning, he stood at the other end of the aisle and drank in her reaction.

She turned, put both hands over her mouth, and shook her head.

Warmth invaded his heart. She loved it.

Dropping her hands to her sides, she glanced at him and smiled. She ran forward, launched herself into his arms, and pressed her lips to his.

Dylan wrapped his arms around her and pulled her closer. He travelled his hands up her back and once again found their way into her hair. "I love you, Meg. God, I love you so much. I'm sorry I was such a jerk."

Meg lifted her face and locked her gaze with his. "I love you, too, Dylan, but don't hurt me again."

"I promise. This last month without you almost killed me. When you refused to answer my calls, I knew I had to show you how much you mean in my life. Finishing the renovation was the only way I knew how. I was wrong to ever doubt you. I was wrong to ever think you aren't the smartest woman in the world and wrong to ever let you think I don't believe in you." He ran a finger along her cheek. "Because I do, Meg. I believe in everything you are, and I believe in us. Please tell me you believe in us, too."

Meg grinned. "You bet I do. Now shut up and kiss me."

Dylan happily obliged.

Epilogue

Music drifted in through the inn's open back door and into the kitchen. A collision of perfumes wafted from the collection of bridesmaids. Chatter and squeals of excitement competed for attention. Meg clapped her hands together twice and silenced the commotion. "All right, ladies, that's our cue. Mom, you're up."

Annie placed a quick kiss on Jillian's cheek. "You look beautiful, honey. Knock 'em dead."

Meg opened the door wider.

Annie smoothed the full, silk skirt on her blue dress before stepping out into the sunlight and down the deck stairs to the crowd below.

"You're next, Mrs. Adams." Meg smiled. Jillian looked so much like her mom, except for the gray hair now swept back into a classic chignon. Tears misted in Mrs. Adam's green eyes.

Jillian's mother stepped up to her daughter who had tears shining in her eyes. "I couldn't be happier for you. You're the most beautiful bride I've ever seen."

Jillian leaned forward and embraced her mom. "Thank you."

"Okay, this is a touching moment and all, but let's keep it moving." Meg glanced to where Jonah stood under the makeshift altar in Annie's garden. "Jonah's already fidgeting with his tie down there. We don't want to make him wait longer than he has to." Getting everyone down the aisle on time was her only job. She couldn't mess up the task, or she'd never hear the end of it.

Mrs. Adams touched Jillian's arm as she walked away and stepped out the door.

"All right, it's my turn. I'll see you down there." Meg winked at Jillian and blew a kiss toward Sophie. "Emma, make sure you step out when I reach the grass. Catie after that, and then Sophie."

"We can handle it." Emma waved her hands in a shooing gesture. "Get going."

Meg took a deep breath and stepped onto the deck. The tea-length lavender gown swished against her bare calves. She longed to run her fingers through the tight curls cascading down over her shoulders, but she clutched the bouquet of lilies to keep her hands from moving. Most of the town of Smithview littered the lawn. She hated having so many gazes on her. Heat crept up the back of her neck and settled on her cheeks. Her heart raced, and her palms grew damp against the bouquet of lilies she carried. She concentrated on putting one foot in front of the other.

God, please don't let me fall.

Her heel hit the grass, and she released a long breath. She drifted her gaze to Jonah, and she curved her lips into a smile. When she stepped onto the white runner, she shifted her attention to Dylan. Her heart lodged in her throat. Her nerves fled her body, and everyone around her disappeared.

His gaze locked with hers, never wavering, until she took her place.

Emma and Catie walked down next. Sophie followed.

At the sight of her prancing down the aisle, Meg giggled.

Sophie grabbed one petal at a time from her little basket and placed each petal on the ground beside her patent leather shoes as she took a step.

Emma's foot tapped the ground, silently urging her forward.

Meg bit her cheek to keep from laughing.

Sophie continued to take her time, lapping up the attention. She made it to the end of the aisle, turned toward the crowd, and curtsied.

"Oh, my God," Emma said under her breath. "I'll kill her."

"Oh, she's adorable. But I'll get her." Meg crouched to the ground, cleared her throat, and crooked a finger at Sophie.

She giggled and ran to her aunt.

Meg straightened and placed her arms around the girl's shoulders. Sophie wasn't going anywhere.

The music changed, and everyone stood. Jillian appeared with her father at her side. He beamed down at his daughter with the sun bouncing off his bald head.

Tears gathered in the corner of Meg's eyes. The simple lace dress Jillian wore was utter perfection. The delicate material swished as she walked down the aisle, her gaze never leaving Jonah's.

She stopped, and her father kissed her cheek and then sat. Jillian glanced down at Sam, who stood between her and Jonah, then back up at Jonah.

The ceremony started, and after facing the officiant, Meg couldn't help but glance around. The sun beat down warmly on her skin, and the flowers around them were in full bloom. Scents of lavender and lilac filled the air. They had lucked out. March wasn't always this warm.

She focused again on Jonah and Jillian and let the words of love and commitment the minister spoke float through her mind. She locked her gaze with Dylan's, and heat crept into her face as images of him in a tuxedo and her in a white dress popped into her mind.

"If the wedding party could take their seats, Jonah and Jillian would like this part of the ceremony to be for them and Sam only," the minister said.

Finally, she could sit. The seats for the wedding party were reserved in the front, and she claimed one between Dylan and Emma.

Dylan grabbed her hand, his fingers intertwined with hers, as the rest of the ceremony continued.

Jonah pulled out a small box. He placed a silver band on Jillian's finger, then he retrieved a dog tag on a silver chain from his pocket. He placed the necklace over Sam's head. "Sam, this necklace symbolizes my commitment to you. I will always be here for you—as a friend and a mentor. I will love you and aid you in whatever trials come your way. Today isn't just the day I marry your mom. Today is the day we become a family."

Sam beamed.

"I now pronounce you husband and wife. You may now kiss the bride."

Dylan lifted their joined hands and kissed her knuckles.

A peace settled over her, calming her soul and warming her heart. She had waited her whole life for this kind of happiness. Finally, with the love of her life by her side, Meg found her place in this world.

A word about the author...

Danielle M. Haas resides in Ohio with her husband and two children. She earned a BA in Political Science many moons ago from Bowling Green State University, but thought staying home with her two children and writing romance novels would be more fun than pursuing a career in politics.

She is a member of Romance Writers of America as well as her local North East Ohio chapter. She spends her days chasing her kids around, loving up her dog, and trying to find a spare minute to write about her favorite thing: love.

Danielle can be found blogging about her adventures in writing at:

www.daniellemhaas.com

~

via her Facebook page under:
Author Danielle Haas
or you can follow her twitter handle:
@authordhaas.

~

Another title by the author:
SECOND TIME AROUND